WITHDRAWN
P9-CRD-668
3 2487 00421

STACKS

The Gentle Hills

Far From the Dream
Whispers in the Valley
Keeper of the Harvest
Some Things Last Forever

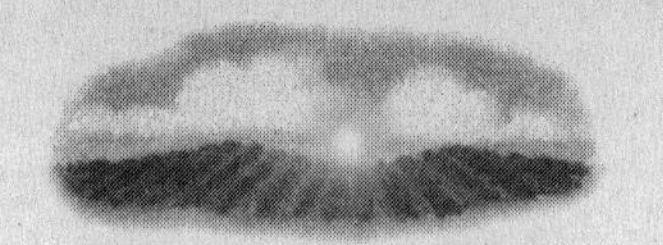

THE GENTLE HILLS / BOOK FOUR

LANCE WUBBELS

SOME THINGS LAST FOREVER

BETHANY HOUSE PUBLISHERS
MINNEAPOLIS, MINNESOTA 55438

Some Things Last Forever

Cover by Dan Thornberg,
Bethany House Publishers staff artist.

Published by Bethany House Publishers
A Ministry of Bethany Fellowship, Inc.
11300 Hampshire Avenue South
Minneapolis, Minnesota 55438

Printed in the United States of America.

Library of Congress Cataloging-in-Publication Data

Wubbels, Lance, 1952–
Some things last forever / Lance Wubbels.
p. m . —(The gentle hills; book 4)
I. Title. II. Series: Wubbels, Lance, 1952- Gentle hills ; bk. 4.
PS3573.U39S66 1996
813'.54—dc20 96–4504
ISBN 1–55661–421–7 (pbk.) CIP
ISBN 1–55661–824–7 (lg. print) AC

To My Dad

who filled so many pages
of these stories.

For a little guy,
a quiet and gentle man,
a loving man,
you were amazing.

By the same grace
that you held dear,
and that you extended to me,
I hope to live as well.

LANCE WUBBELS, the Managing Editor of Bethany House Publishers, taught biblical studies courses at Bethany College of Missions for many years. He is the award-winning writer of *One Small Miracle*, the heartwarming novel of the profound impact a teacher's gift of love makes on the life of one of her struggling students. He is also the compiler and editor of the Charles Spurgeon and F. B. Meyer Christian Living Classic books with Emerald Books. He and his family make their home in Bloomington, Minnesota.

Contents

Chapter One

Merry Christmas

"Marjie, you were crazy to try to pull that off."

Jerry Macmillan stretched an arm around his wife, who snuggled up against him on the davenport in their farmhouse living room. It was nearly midnight.

"What if I'd have fainted when you passed me that note?" he added. "Wouldn't that have been a nice touch for Ruth and Billy's wedding—the best man out cold on the floor while they said their vows?"

"You did look just a bit surprised." Marjie began to laugh again, remembering the shocked look that had come over her husband's face when he read the note she had passed him right in the middle of their best friends' wedding.

"I guess it was a little risky, standing up

there in front of the whole church," Marjie admitted and laughed some more. "We were lucky that the only ones who caught it were Chester and Margaret. If you hadn't been such a fumble fingers, even they wouldn't have noticed."

"They were right on our heels coming up the platform with the wedding party," Jerry replied. "How was I supposed to know you'd do a thing like that? Here I am all nervous, trying to figure out where we're supposed to stand, and you're passing out notes about Christmas presents being in the oven. The least you could have done was to simply say, *We're going to have a baby.*"

"Shoot, that wouldn't have been half as much fun," said Marjie, wrapping her arm around Jerry and giving him a big squeeze. "But I really didn't expect you to take so long to figure it out." She maneuvered around so she was looking straight into his eyes. "Are you excited about it?"

Jerry nodded and leaned his blond head back against the top of the davenport with a deep sigh. "Sure I'm excited, but you didn't give me much chance to think about it. How long have you known you were pregnant?"

"Since Thanksgiving."

"What?" exclaimed Jerry, snapping his head back up straight. "How could you not tell me?"

"I didn't have much else to give you for Christmas, so I thought I'd wait," Marjie answered. "Besides, I was hoping to hold the news until I was a couple months along . . . in case something went wrong."

"You been to the doc?"

"Yep," Marjie answered. "And he says there's no doubt about it. You remember when I went into town to get the candles for the wedding?"

Jerry nodded. "I thought you acted a little strange that day."

"That was the day," Marjie said. "I'd been feeling just like I felt when I got pregnant with Martha, so I was pretty sure we had another little one on the way. But this time you're not running off to war and leaving me to fend for myself." She made a mock-menacing face. "You just wait till it's ninety degrees in mid-June and I weigh four hundred pounds and feel like I'm a giant bowling ball and—"

"Maybe I can talk the navy into taking me back for a short stint," Jerry teased, leaning his head back again and yawning. "Maybe those Jap subs aren't so bad after all."

"It ain't a pretty sight," Marjie agreed, her face softening into a wistful smile. "But I have to tell you, it's worth the struggle when you get to see that little newborn for the first time and hold her in your arms. Or him. Oh, Jerry, I just wish you could have been there when Martha was born. I was such a mess—crying for joy and laughing all at the same time."

"And you forgot about all the pain and misery—"

"Who are you kidding?" Marjie broke in and laughed. "That's a bogus line if I ever heard one. I didn't forget a thing; that hurt like crazy. Which is one of the reasons why this time you're going to be there with me in the delivery room—"

"Whoa! Hold on there!" countered Jerry, shaking his head and blowing out some air. "That's one place you're gonna have to count me out. Besides, the doc wouldn't ever allow a man in the delivery room."

"Wanta bet? Maybe you'd like to call him tomorrow and check."

"Now, what did you do?" Jerry protested. "How could you con him into this?"

"Wasn't too hard," she answered. "You know he's got this little problem?" She pantomimed tilting back a bottle and taking a drink.

"That's what they say."

"Well, when I was going into the office," Marjie said, "I noticed an opened pint of whiskey lying on the front seat of his car. I . . .

ah . . . made mention of it to him when I asked about the possibility of your being with me during delivery."

"Marjie, that's blackmail."

"That's right. It worked better than I figured. He was very cooperative. In fact, I think I could have gotten even more if I had pushed it."

"So you're going to make me come in and watch?"

"Not just watch, buddy boy," Marjie corrected. "This time around, you're going to be at my side, holding my hand, helping me push—"

"Oh, come on!" Jerry sputtered. "You can't expect me to—"

"You bet I can," Marjie insisted, "and I do. If you can help the cows when they're—"

"You can't compare the cows with—"

"Then don't buck coming in with me," Marjie said. "Settled?"

"All right. I give up," Jerry replied. "But nobody finds out about it, okay?"

"Sure."

"You're not going to blab it all over the county?"

"No."

"What's the deal? You're too easy on this."

Marjie laughed and looked up at Jerry again. "You're getting to know me pretty good. The doc said his one condition was mum's the word on it. He's afraid that if the word leaks out, he's going to have a parade of women dragging their husbands into the delivery room. I told him I thought that was a great idea."

"And he didn't agree."

"No. Not at all. But I got you in anyway."

"And you did blab your being pregnant all over the church at the wedding reception," Jerry added. "You almost stole the show from Billy and Ruthie. We're trying to congratulate them on their marriage, and they're trying to congratulate us on the baby. Then Ruth bangs on her glass with a spoon and gets everybody to stop talking and makes the big announcement. Man, I was embarrassed."

"You did get pretty red," Marjie teased. "Especially when she said that you were doing your part to fulfill God's command to 'Be fruitful and multiply.' "

Chuckling softly, Jerry added, "And when Chester piped in that I was trying to fill my quiver with arrows. I didn't know what he was talking about. Did you?"

"Not at the time," Marjie said. "Margaret told me later that was something King David said in the Psalms, but I still didn't get it."

"Me either," said Jerry. "When I heard that Margaret and Chester were going back to

Scotland soon, I guess I didn't care much. Kind of took the wind out of my sails."

"That makes two of us," Marjie replied, then sighed. "I'm sure Margaret will love being back with her family again, but still. . . . You know, if you hadn't introduced Chester to her, they wouldn't have gotten together, and now we wouldn't be having to say goodbye."

"And if I hadn't joined the navy with Chester, he might be dead, and I probably wouldn't have come to faith," Jerry added, shaking his head. "Who knows where we'd be today? No, this is a good thing. Chester will fit right in helping Margaret's father with the church services for the fellas overseas, though. So will Margaret. I'll never forget hearing her sing that first time in Glasgow. . . ."

"But Chester and Margaret fit in here, too," Marjie lamented. "Think of what might have happened if Chester wouldn't have been here to fill in for Pastor Fitchen when he had his stroke. Think of a Sunday morning service without Margaret's lovely singing. Think of—"

"I get your drift," Jerry said. "But they are leaving, and we can make it a lot easier on them if we're excited about their future. I got a feeling that God has something big in mind for them to do."

"I think you're right," Marjie agreed. "And I really am excited for them. But I'm not going to pretend I'm not sad. Just talking about them leaving makes me blue."

"So, let's talk about something else," Jerry said. "How about the way your mother and my dad were carrying on about the news of the baby? We sure lit their fires, didn't we?"

Marjie started to laugh and said, "I think that's all they talked about at the reception. Except when Benjamin was trying to explain to some of Ruthie's relatives that he was your father and yet now he's married to my mother. Now that was funny."

Jerry laughed as well. "And confusing. Those people didn't know whether to believe him or not. I think he enjoys seeing how people react to it."

"My mother seems to get just as big a kick out of it," Marjie said. "I'm so happy for her . . . and Benjamin. They've got a whole new life together."

"And Ruthie and Billy, too," Jerry said. "I really didn't think we'd ever see them make it to the front of the church. Can you imagine what she went through when he got cold feet?"

"If he had pulled that one on me, his feet would have gotten a lot colder," Marjie replied. "It's mighty cool out in the cemetery in late December."

"And you'd be just the one to put him out there," Jerry said with a chuckle. "Say, seeing as you gave me my Christmas present early, do you want yours?"

"What?"

"Do you want to see what I got you for Christmas?" Jerry asked. "What you gave me hasn't been the only gift that's been hard to hide. I've had yours since long before Thanksgiving."

"Are you kidding?" Marjie scolded, sitting up straight and drilling him with flashing brown eyes. "What did you get me?"

Jerry burst out laughing, enjoying the look of torment he'd raised on her face. "I'm kind of tired. Guess I'll be moving on to bed. Besides, you won't be able to use it now anyway."

"No you don't, sailor boy," Marjie insisted, grabbing him by the neck of his white T-shirt. "Nobody sleeps until this is finished. You asked me if I wanted to see my present, and I say yes. Where is it?"

"You gotta treat me nicer than this, or forget it!" Jerry retaliated. "Besides, it's not here in the house. You'd have found it in here."

"So pull on your boots and coat and go get it!" Marjie said, jumping up from the davenport.

"Maybe we should wait for Chris—"

"You started this, Jerry Macmillan," Marjie persisted. "Now where'd you hide my present?"

"I'll take you to it if you come with me," Jerry offered, a big smile beaming across his face.

"All I've got on is my pajamas and robe."

"That's more than I've got on under my robe," Jerry teased, standing up and stretching. "But if you run fast through the snow, you won't feel a thing."

Marjie followed Jerry to the mud room, and they quickly pulled on their boots and heavy work coats. Jerry went to the door and pulled it open, letting in a frigid blast of arctic air. The sky was crystal clear, and a swirling wind had kicked up since they had come home from the wedding.

"Wow! Won't feel a thing, eh?" Marjie asked as she passed Jerry and stepped onto the icy porch steps. "Where are we going, anyway?"

"Follow me," Jerry said, taking her arm and escorting her down the steps and sidewalk toward the barn.

"The barn?" Marjie asked as he headed her straight toward the milk room door. "You hid my Christmas present in the barn?"

"Where else?" asked Jerry. "Least it's warm inside."

Jerry pulled the barn door open, and Marjie turned the light on as she went through the doorway. She followed Jerry into the milk parlor where Jerry turned on the light.

Their Australian cow dog, Blue, was already on his feet with his tail wagging slowly and a bewildered expression on his face. Several black-and-white Holstein faces turned to see what was going on as well, and the long golden nose of a palomino saddle horse poked out of a stall with a nicker.

"Good evening, girls," Jerry called out to his host of interested onlookers. "Evening, Charlie, and to you as well, Blue Boy." He reached down and rubbed Blue's face and ears, prompting the small cow dog to sneeze repetitively. "Poor dog's got hay fever. And he's not as young as he used to be. I wish you'd let him stay in the house with us. Martha would love it."

"Hay fever, my foot," Marjie retorted as she walked over to scratch the horse's perked-up ears. "He's just not used to being waked up in the middle of the night. Now, what's up? Charlie here is dying of curiosity."

"Charlie, eh?" Jerry spread his arms, indicating the entire inside of the barn. "Well, I'll give you one clue. Look for something here that's abnormal. When you find that, you'll find the present."

"Abnormal like your brain?" Marjie teased, giving Jerry a push that almost toppled him into the nearly full gutter. "Why don't you just tell me where it is."

"No chance," Jerry persisted, crossing his arms. "This is a lot easier than you think. Just look around."

"Oh, you stubborn . . ." Marjie's words faded off as she gazed around the dingy inside of the barn. Besides the horse and the cattle, there wasn't much to look at—wooden gates, posts, sacks of feed, a big pile of gunny sacks draped over—

"That's it," declared Marjie, moving quickly toward the pile of burlap. "You buried something under here."

"Correct!" Jerry called out, grabbing Marjie's arms before she could pull off the top sacks. "Now you've got to try to guess what it is."

"Forget you!" Marjie cried, breaking free from his grasp and toppling the pile of dusty sacks to reveal a shiny brown Western saddle.

"Merry Christmas!" whooped Jerry. Blue caught his excitement and ran in circles, barking. A couple of the closer Holsteins slowly rose to their feet from the commotion.

Marjie stepped back in surprised wonder,

cupping her face with her hands. “For me?” she gasped.

“Who else?” Jerry piped up. “What do you think?”

“Goodness,” Marjie replied, touching the saddle horn and running her fingers down the soft leather seat. “It’s beautiful. Oh, Jerry! It’s been so wonderful to have a horse; I can’t believe I’ve got a saddle, too. I can’t wait to show Betty Hunter. But where’d you get it?”

“I worked a trade with our strange neighbor down the hill, Tom Metcalfe,” Jerry said with a satisfied grin. “Remember when I got the horse from him and he wouldn’t put the saddle in with the deal? Well, I figured he might be more willing now that it had gathered dust for a while, and I had a feeling he might be having some hard times. Anyway, he bit. And the price was right—a litter of pigs for the saddle!”

“That’s an incredible deal, Jerry,” Marjie said, turning to give him a big hug. “You’re wonderful!”

Chapter Two

Christmas Tidings

“He gave you a what?” Marjie’s mother asked with a laugh, looking up quickly from the pork roast she was slicing for their Christmas dinner. Her dog, Tinker, who sat perfectly still at her feet, swished a ropelike tail back and forth across the cold linoleum floor. "You're expecting a baby this summer, and Jerry goes out and gets you a saddle for your horse. What was he thinking?"

Marjie laughed as well and glanced through the kitchen door to the living room, where her fifteen-month-old daughter was enjoying a horsey ride of her own on Jerry's knee. Dark curls bouncing, little Martha squealed and giggled, then bounced to urge on her steed when the jiggling stopped. Instead, Jerry's father, Benjamin, reached over to take the little girl onto his own knee.

"He was thinking of me, of course." Marjie turned to answer her mother's question. "He didn't even know I was pregnant when he got the saddle. Besides, there's no law against pregnant women riding horses—unless you've written one lately."

"No laws, but a little common sense comes in handy," Sarah replied. "You'd better be keeping off that horse till you have the baby. No reason to risk it."

"Risk what?" Marjie asked, then she pulled out a chair and sat down at the kitchen table. "As long as I keep Charlie out on the regular paths, I'm not going to have any problems. A little bouncing up and down's not going to hurt the baby." She turned to give her mother a twinkling glare. "And don't tell me you always took it easy when you were pregnant."

"I sure didn't," said Sarah, shaking her head. She slid the last piece of pork onto the glass serving tray and covered it with a lid, then placed the whole thing into the oven to keep the roast warm. "Couldn't afford to. Besides helping your father with the chores and crops, I was trying to help pay the bills by taking in sewing from some of the richer women in the area. That got old real fast. Robert finally made me quit."

"Why? Were you getting too tired?"

Sarah took her cup of coffee off the stove and joined Marjie at the kitchen table. "Sort of," she said, motioning for Tinker to lie down on the rug by the table. "Tired of working my fingers to the bone and then to have some fuss-button refuse to pay because they weren't happy with what I'd produced. With some of the women, it didn't seem to matter what you did; it was never good enough. I ended up losing money on some of the jobs."

"Pa didn't care for that, I bet," Marjie said.

"That he didn't," Sarah replied, adding a chuckle. "You remember Mrs. Gimble from Spring Valley?"

"The wealthy old lady who smelled like a

walking perfume factory and had the squeaky high voice?"

"That's her," Sarah said with a nod. "She claimed that I must have done something to the fabric that she'd given me to make her dress. Said it didn't have the same sheen to it once the dress was made. She was storming around and demanding that I only charge her half price when your father stepped into the house with the same look on his face that he'd get when he caught one of you kids talking back to me. The living room windows were open, so he'd heard the whole story. She made the mistake of turning to Robert and pleading her case with him."

"And what'd Pa do then?"

"He put his hand up for her to be quiet and asked her how much the fabric was worth. When she claimed it cost her a dollar and fifty cents, he pulled his wallet out and handed her the money. Then he took my dressmaker's shears and, before Mrs. Gimble could rescue her precious material, proceeded to cut the dress in two from top to bottom. He looked straight at her and said, 'That should just about take care of your problem, I believe. Good day, Mrs. Gimble.' Then he smiled, turned around gracefully, and walked out of the house."

Marjie sputtered with laughter, almost losing the mouthful of coffee that she'd taken.

"So he left you to face the wrath of Mrs. Gimble?" Marjie asked. "How could he do that?"

"Seemed easy enough. Kind of reminds me of something you might pull on me," Sarah said, still chuckling to herself. "It really wasn't as bad as it sounds. Mrs. Gimble was so upset that she simply opened that big black purse of hers, stuffed in the precious buck and a half, spun around, and stomped out the door. She never said another word to me—ever. And that was, fittingly so, the end of my short career in the sewing business."

"Pa had a real touch with some people, didn't he?" Marjie joked. "I'll bet he went straight out to the barn and laughed the rest of the day."

"*Days*, Marjie, *days*. He laughed every time he stepped into the house for at least a week straight," Sarah replied. "He claimed that he could still see the cloud of perfume that had steamed off her face from the high heat."

Marjie burst out laughing again and shook her head. "He was a character, especially if he felt that someone was getting treated badly. Do you remember when we were in Lime Springs and Pa caught those two teenage boys who were tormenting Teddy by keeping his cap from him? They were tossing it back and forth, and Teddy was crying because he couldn't get it from them."

Sarah nodded and said, "Yeah. I thought your father would yell at them or grab one of them and give them a good shaking. Instead he said, 'It's okay, Teddy. Let them keep it. Maybe they need it more than you do.' Those boys were so embarrassed and ashamed. He took care of them about as quickly as he did Mrs. Gimble."

Marjie put both her hands around her coffee cup and looked out the kitchen window toward the gravel road with its thin covering of freshly fallen snow. An occasional gust of wind would twirl the white flakes into small piles, then another gust would pull them back apart. Thinking of her father, Marjie suddenly felt her laughter evaporate into the gray winter light.

"I miss him, Ma, especially at Christmas," Marjie said quietly, staring out through the frosted window. "Every Christmas Eve he'd come in from evening chores and claim that he saw lights going by overhead and that he heard bells ringing through the air. We'd dash outside and try to catch a glimpse of Santa Claus and his reindeer. It worked every time. That one year I swore I saw Santa, just like Pa said."

She turned a questioning glance to her mother. "Do you still miss him, Ma? Even now that you're married to Benjamin?"

Sarah looked down and rubbed the rough calluses that years of hard work in the barn and fields had left on her hands. Then she raised a hand to rub her forehead and sighed. "Sure, I miss him," she whispered. "There was no one else ever like him, and no one can ever replace him. Not even Benjamin. I still sometimes catch myself thinking he's come in the house when I hear the screen door shut. But . . ." Her lip trembled just a little. "Marjie, the Lord has been real good to me this past year, and I have a lot to be thankful for. But I think there'll always be a hole in my life where your pa used to be."

Reaching out and resting her hand on her mother's arm, Marjie felt the tears begin to pool at the corners of her eyes. In the years since the cancer had taken her father, she and her mother had seldom talked about what life was like without him. "Actually, it feels good to think about Pa again," she said, exhaling a large puff of air. "When you're growing up, it's so easy to take someone for granted. He really was a wonderful father."

"And a wonderful husband," Sarah spoke softly. She looked into Marjie's dark brown eyes. "And it's not just kids who take others for granted. Until someone's actually gone, it just doesn't seem possible to understand what you got. It's when the kids leave home, or someone you love dies or goes away for an extended period of time, then you realize the treasure you had. It can be mighty tough when it sinks in, especially if there was fighting or ugliness between you, and you could have done something about it before they left. Some folks can hardly live with themselves afterward."

Marjie nodded knowingly. "Makes me think of Teddy. I'm really glad that we were able to work things out with him before he left for the army. I was so angry with him 'cause of his drinking and the way he was treating you. Jerry's idea of a special going-away meal was a godsend. If it had been left up to me, I'd have been more likely to try out some rat poison on him."

Sarah laughed and looked out the window at her favorite lilac bush, which had been so lush throughout that whole summer of 1943. All that remained were a few brown leaves that flickered in the breeze. "Don't think I never thought those thoughts," she said. "The more that boy drank, the more awful he got. I couldn't hardly bear it. But even Teddy—even when he was so loathsome and mean that I didn't even recognize him as the boy I once knew—since he's left, I can't tell you how much I've missed him. You come to see things different after they go."

"What do you mean, different?" Marjie asked.

Sarah twisted her mouth and took in a deep draft of air. "Oh, I suppose I realized how much I'd taken advantage of him. After your pa died, you know, I'd have had to sell the farm if Teddy hadn't stayed on to help me. I knew he didn't like farming, but I just sort of ignored that. It really wasn't fair to expect him to stay on like I did, and I think there were times when I made him feel like he owed it to me. Guess it was my way of coping, but Teddy paid the price. That don't excuse his drinking, but he could have walked away at any time. He gave me some of the best years of his life so I didn't have to give up mine."

"My goodness," Marjie said, slowly shaking her head. "That's exactly what he did, didn't he? I didn't even realize how much he hated farm work until he tried to explain why he was leaving. Even then, I wasn't thinking about how long he'd already done it."

"That's what we fail to see about each other," Sarah said with a sigh and a pause. "We get all bent out of shape about something that's bothering us, but we can miss the big things that are staring us right in the face.

If we could just pull back a little from life, I think we'd be shocked by what we're really looking at."

"How do you pull back?"

Sarah laughed reflectively, shrugging her shoulders slightly. "You're asking the wrong person," she said. "If I could live the past thirty years over again, I guess I'd worry a lot less about getting things done and do all I could to enjoy the loved ones that God has given me. I'd spend a lot more time and energy on people. But . . . that's the past. Now I'm trying to live up to what I'm preaching. I think Ben is, too. I know he's been writing to that boy of his, Jerry's brother, that went out west so long ago. There was bad blood between them, although I don't know all the details. And so Ben's been trying to make up for that. He's a good man, Marjie. I'm a lucky woman."

Marjie nodded her agreement, then leaned in close. "So what's your life like now that you two are married?" Marjie asked, glancing again out the kitchen door to where the men were talking in the living room. "Do you mind me asking?"

"No, I don't mind," Sarah answered. "Compared to the past, you mean?"

"Yeah."

Sarah raised her hand and pulled on her

earlobe a couple of times, then rubbed her chin slowly. "It's . . . like a new life. I don't even try to compare Ben to your father, Marjie. I loved Robert deeply, and we raised you kids through some incredibly difficult years, and just when it looked like we might not have to work night and day to scratch out a living, he was taken away. My life with your father was far too short and left me feeling like I'd missed out on the best part.

"I was happy for my friendship with Ben," she continued, "but I never expected to fall in love with another man after your father. Then it just seemed to happen again. This has all been such a wonderful surprise . . . like a gift I don't deserve. Your pa was a very wonderful man, but I didn't realize how wonderful at the time. But I know what I've got with Ben. I appreciate him more. So I'd have to say I'm enjoying my new life with him more than I enjoyed life with Robert. Maybe it comes with getting older and having more time to do what we really want, but Ben and I are having a lot of fun together."

"No one deserves it more than the two of you," Marjie said soothingly. "I couldn't be happier for you. It is a gift, Ma. Don't ever feel guilty about it."

"You've been given some precious gifts, too," Sarah said, nodding her head as another set of squeals erupted in the living room. "Don't take them for granted, sweetheart. You never know. . . ."

The sight of a dark blue Hudson coming down the road temporarily broke Sarah's thoughts, and she and Marjie stared out the window trying to figure out whose car it was. It slowed down when it got to their driveway and stopped by the mailbox.

"Who is that?" Marjie asked.

"Don't recognize the car," Sarah replied. "I thought he was gonna stick something in the mailbox at first, but he appears to be reading the name. Strange on Christmas Day, ain't it?"

The car inched ahead and ever so slowly turned into the farm driveway. Tinker jumped up from her rug with a growl and made a dash for the front door with Sarah and Marjie following more slowly behind. Martha climbed down from Benjamin's lap when she saw her mother and ran to Marjie, who scooped her up and headed for the front window. Benjamin was already standing there, peeking out through a clear spot in the frosty glass.

"Who is it, Ben?" Sarah asked.

"Looks like one of the sheriff's deputies from Preston," Benjamin said as a man stepped out of the car. "I don't know his name, but I've seen him around town. Looks like he's got a paper or something that he's bringing in."

The tall, lean man with a clean-shaven face was not in uniform; he wore a large green parka and a fur cap. He tossed the cigarette he was smoking into the snow as he approached the old farmhouse door. Tinker began barking and jumping at the wooden door, her long ears flopping.

"Tinker! Get back!" Sarah ordered, grabbing the dog by the collar. "In there." She pointed back into the living room. The young dog attempted just one more bark under her breath as she reluctantly obeyed.

Sarah had opened the door before the man could knock. Caught off guard, he fumbled his cold fingers over the paper and looked as if he wasn't sure what to say.

"Merry Christmas," Sarah said with a friendly smile, motioning for him to come into the porch. "What can we do for you?"

The man stepped into the porch, where Benjamin and Marjie stood at the doorway. But his attention was on Sarah. "I'm sorry to bother you on Christmas Day, ma'am. But, are you Sarah Livingstone Macmillan?"

Sarah only nodded and crossed her arms.

"This telegram came into Preston this morning, and the sheriff asked me to bring it out to you," he said tersely, handing her the piece of paper. "I'm sorry to tell you that your son Paul has been shot in Italy."

Chapter Three

Sleepless Again

"So what more can you do about it?" Jerry asked, washing his hands after coming in from the morning chores. "You got your brother Teddy trying to find out more through his army-base contacts. You got Jacob Medlow down at the war-board office doing what he can. What else is there?"

"Nothing that I can think of," Marjie said, standing at the large dining room window in her long robe with her arms crossed. "I can't stand this waiting, though. You'd think they could tell you more."

Jerry sat down at the table to the hot breakfast that Marjie had already laid out for him. "You gonna join me, or are you gonna stand there staring out the window all day?"

Marjie shook her head and stretched her arms over her head. "Oh my," she mumbled and groaned, then she turned to Jerry and smiled. "I spent most of the night looking out on the valley," she said, then she took her coffee cup from the window ledge and plopped down in the chair next to him. "The moonlight shimmering on the snow crystals was just beautiful. If you had joined me, we could have made it romantic."

"I suppose so," Jerry agreed, taking a bite of his fried eggs. "Last night, and the night before, and the nights before that. It's been a week since you slept through the night, Marjie. I'm shot tired just from you getting in and out of bed all the time."

"That's why I stayed down here last night," Marjie said, rubbing her eyes. "Figured at least one of us should get a decent night's sleep."

"I appreciate it, and I did sleep better," Jerry admitted. "But I really don't understand what's eating you up so bad. The telegram came on Saturday, and we knew then that Paul was alive. When your mother got the call from the war department on Monday, they said he'd taken the bullet in his shoulder and that an army surgeon had removed the bullet and repaired what he could. Sounds like it could have been a lot worse."

Marjie took a sip of her lukewarm coffee and stared out the window. "They also said that serious damage had been done," she added. "What does that mean? He'll have an arm but not be able to use it? Maybe they'll wait a couple of days and then decide his arm should be amputated? What if it gets infected? Wouldn't that be dangerous, so close to his heart? Oh, Jerry, I'm thankful he's alive, but I can't stop thinking about all the things that can go wrong."

"Is this what it was like when I was gone on the *Wasp*?" Jerry asked. "Dad told me how worried he got about your health. Said you went for weeks on a few hours of sleep every night."

"Yeah, it was like this at least one time," Marjie replied. "That was when the mail got fouled up and I didn't hear from you for nearly two months. That was bad. I can't go through that again."

"Why don't you go back to bed this morning," Jerry offered, taking Marjie's hand. "I can take care of Martha when she wakes up. In fact, I was looking for a good excuse not to go back out there and clean the calf pens. Maybe if you get a few more hours' sleep, this deal with Paul won't look so bad."

"Maybe," Marjie said with a sigh. "But then maybe I won't be able to sleep again tonight. No, I appreciate the offer, but I think those calf pens are getting pretty full."

"My dad let you get away with this, didn't he?" Jerry asked.

"With what?"

"Torturing yourself," said Jerry. He put

down his fork and leaned over close to Marjie, reaching his arm around her. "I think you believe that if you're hard enough on yourself, somehow the situation will improve. You're so tired you can hardly wiggle, but you won't go to bed and catch up on the rest you've lost. I'm not going to let you keep on doing it."

"I'm not going back to bed, Jerry," Marjie protested. "I don't want—"

"You have two choices," Jerry broke in, standing up and looking down at Marjie. "You can go to bed on your own power, or I can you carry you up those stairs and put you to bed myself. But be assured, you will go."

"Let me check the mail first," Marjie said. "Maybe there's—"

"The mail won't be here for a couple hours yet, and you know it," said Jerry. "Now, which way would you like to go?"

"You're mean—"

"Up we go!" Jerry exclaimed, bending down and scooping Marjie into his arms.

"Okay! I'll go!" said Marjie. "Put me down or you'll kill your back!"

"Promise you'll go."

"I promise, I promise," Marjie assured him as he gently let her back down. "But only for a couple of hours. You realize that you're going to have to watch Martha close. She's fast on her feet, and there's nothing she can't get into anymore."

"Don't worry about her," Jerry said. "I'll bring in my secret helper."

"You're not gonna bring in the dog, are you?" Marjie sputtered. "He gets his hair all over the place."

"I'll take care of it," replied Jerry. "Martha loves playing with Blue. I suppose I could take her out in the barn and—"

"Okay, bring him in," Marjie conceded. "But you've got to sweep up the mess."

"Can't sleep, eh?" Jerry joked as Marjie stepped into the living room. He was lying on the davenport, and Martha sat on Blue. A look of patient martyrdom was etched on the cow dog's face. "You were really sawing logs when I peeked in."

Marjie gave a crooked smile and squinted her eyes against the noonday light that was streaming in through the window. "What time is it, anyway?"

"Quarter to one," Jerry said. "I was just about to get you up. Your mother's on her way over with a letter from Teddy. He apparently found out some news about Paul."

"You're kidding!" exclaimed Marjie, picking Martha up off the dog and dusting off some of the coarse black and gray hairs. "I don't think Teddy's ever written a letter in his life. What did Ma say?"

Jerry sat up and stretched, then he answered, "She just said there's some good news. She should be here any minute. Dad's got some pigs he's selling today, so she's coming alone."

"Why didn't you wake me up sooner?" Marjie asked. "You take your dog out to the barn, and I'll see if I can sweep up. Ahhh . . . when's the last time you changed Martha? She's soaking!"

"Would you believe five minutes ago?" Jerry asked, raising his eyebrows and jumping up off the davenport.

"Try three hours ago," Marjie countered. "Why are you men such knuckleheads when it comes to changing diapers? Maybe I should make you wear the same pair of underwear for a week straight and see how you like it. Or we could soak your pants and make you walk around . . ."

Marjie's words trailed off as the front door to the farmhouse clicked shut. Jerry had made his speedy exit with Blue before she could finish chastising him. He hadn't even bothered to grab his coat. Marjie thought about locking the doors shut, but then she remembered that she'd never seen a key to the front door.

By the time she got Martha's diaper changed, Marjie had heard the front door rattle and the sound of her mother and Jerry talking as they came in. She put Martha down on the floor and followed her out of the bathroom toward the front door.

"There's my little angel!" Sarah called out as Martha ran to her. She picked up her granddaughter and hugged her tight. "Feel Grandma's cold cheek," she said, pressing her frosty red cheek against Martha's. Martha gave a delighted laugh and wrapped her arm around her grandmother's neck.

"Must be some good news," Marjie called out. "It's good to see you smiling again. Christmas Day wasn't exactly the happiest time I've ever had."

Sarah smiled at Marjie and nodded that it was so. She reached into her coat pocket and pulled out a white envelope, then handed it to Marjie. "It's not as good as I'd like it to be, but all things considered, it's good news. Read it."

Marjie snatched Teddy's letter out of her mother's hand and sat down quickly at the dining room table. Sarah handed Martha to Jerry so she could take off her heavy coat. Then she joined Marjie at the table.

"My goodness," Marjie whispered as she

pored over the letter's contents. " 'The surgeon wanted to take Paul's arm off but he wouldn't let them.' That sounds just like Paul. 'He put the shoulder back together as good as he could, but it was shredded real bad. Paul won't probably ever be able to use his left arm.' Oh my. 'Rehab will be long and slow. They'll be bringing him back stateside as soon as he can travel.' "

Marjie stared blankly at the letter, then she looked up at her mother with wondering eyes. "This is good news, Ma?"

"He's alive, Marjie, and he's coming home in one piece," Sarah said soothingly, folding her hands together on the table. "Not every family is so fortunate."

"But what if he can't use his arm?" Marjie questioned, resting her forehead against her hand. "Then what? He won't be the same man."

"Paul's a fighter, Marjie," Sarah spoke quietly. "You know as well as I do that he isn't gonna let this keep him down. And who's to say he won't be the same? Maybe he'll be better!"

"What are you saying?" Marjie asked.

"Just think of what happened to Billy Wilson," Sarah continued. "Have all those burns on his legs and that bad knee made him less of a man?"

Marjie's frown relaxed, and she slowly shook her head. "No, that's true," she said. "Billy's a better man now than he was before the *Arizona* was bombed, even though he can't do everything he once did." She looked up, the doubt returning to her eyes. "But that doesn't mean it's going to be the same for Paul. I've heard stories. . . ."

"I've heard them, too," Sarah replied, sitting back in her chair. "But I've never known Paul to let adversity get the best of him."

Marjie sighed and rubbed her forehead. "I hope you're right, Ma. But Paul's never faced anything like this before."

Sarah nodded and said, "We might be surprised, sweetheart. He's watched his friends die. He's helped care for the wounded. Chances are he's had to kill some people. Marjie, he may have already faced things that were much more difficult for him to handle. We'll just have to wait and see. And trust."

Feeling some of her worries unravel in the face of her mother's quiet confidence, Marjie looked back down at Teddy's scrawled handwriting. She thought he must have written in a hurry because the letter gave no hint of the fine penmanship he had been noted for in country school.

"So, Teddy's not going to be in Texas anymore," Marjie said as she read on. "This is a switch."

"Where's he heading?" Jerry asked, putting a squirming Martha down on the floor.

"Says he's going to be stationed on some desert mountain in New Mexico," Marjie said. "Los Alamos. Wonder where that is?"

"Never heard of it," Jerry replied. "I thought sure he'd be on his way to Europe or out into the Pacific by now. Wonder what this is all about?"

Sarah shrugged her shoulders and smiled. "You remember when he was home at Thanksgiving how he chattered on and on about working with that electrical engineer? Turns out the guy was a science professor at the University of Chicago, and he requested that Teddy come along with him for this assignment. I don't think Teddy knows what he'll be doing, but he's tickled pink for the chance to keep learning from the man."

"Doesn't sound like he's going to get back here before they go," Marjie added, looking up at her mother.

"That's okay," Sarah said. "I'm just glad he's not heading overseas to fight. All I don't need now is to have another boy in harm's way."

"This really is good news, then," Marjie agreed. "At least Teddy's safe."

"We hope," added Jerry.

"You think the Japs are going to bomb New Mexico?" Marjie teased.

Jerry rubbed his cheeks and looked out the picture window toward the southwest. "I think . . . an assignment to help a scientist in the desert sounds a little fishy. I wonder what Teddy's getting himself into now."

Chapter Four

Chilly Blues

"So when's the next prayer meeting, Marjie?" Harvey Turner asked as he pulled his heavy winter coat up over his burly farmer's shoulders. "Me and Goldie hate to be late, you know."

"I'm aware of that," Marjie replied with her patented smirk, glancing over at Jerry, who was having a hard time keeping a straight face. The Turners were always the first ones to arrive at every meeting and the last ones to leave. "Two weeks from tonight, just like it's been since last fall. I expect you Turners to be here—on time."

Goldie Turner stepped out from behind the coat rack in the church's basement and pushed her gold wire-rimmed glasses back up on the bridge of her wide nose. "Wouldn't miss it," she called out, clutching her large black purse against her threadbare brown coat. "We got our Willard to pray for in England. And I don't care what they say about your brother, Marjie. I still believe it ain't luck that our boy's still flying missions across the Channel. I just know our prayers—"

"What's being said about Marjie's brother?" interrupted Jerry. Both he and Marjie's smiles had disappeared, and a deep frown was digging a trench across Jerry's forehead.

"There you go again, Ma," Harvey said, shaking his round head as he finished twisting the top button on his coat into place. "I told you to not talk about it. See, you got 'em upset already."

"I didn't—"

"It's okay," Jerry broke in again, holding up his hand before Goldie could protest back to her husband. "Nobody's going to get upset with you. But if people are talking about Marjie's brother, we'd like to know about it. Wouldn't we, Marjie?"

Marjie nodded and bit her lip. "If someone's talking about Paul, seems to me we have a right to know. But it's up to you. If you don't think you should tell us, I understand."

Goldie Turner's jaw relaxed a bit, but she still wasn't giving Harvey the happiest of looks. He simply shrugged his shoulders and kept shaking his head.

"I told 'em that I thought what they was sayin' was hogwash," Goldie announced, standing up straighter and looking directly into Marjie's eyes. "Got pretty riled up with them, I'll tell ya. Stupidest thing I've heard in a long time."

"What did they say?" Marjie asked.

"Oh, I told somebody we was comin' to the prayer meeting," replied Goldie. Her face was red, and her fingers tightened around the purse. "They said they thought it was mighty funny that your brother would be the one to get shot up after all the prayin' you and your ma done for him. Made me so mad I could hardly sleep last night."

"Mean and cruel, it was," Harvey said, setting his jaw and staring at Jerry. "They was lucky they wasn't talkin' to me. I woulda let 'em have it."

"Someone actually said that to you?" Marjie asked as she leaned back against Jerry and took his hand. She was glad that her mother and Benjamin had already left so they didn't have to hear this.

Goldie Turner pushed her glasses back up again and nodded. "Said they was just reportin' what somebody else mentioned to them. I straightened them out, though. Told 'em your brother may have taken a bullet, but at least he was still alive."

"Who said it to you, Goldie?" Jerry pressed. "I'd like to have a few words—"

"We don't want to know," Marjie said softly, turning and looking into Jerry's face. "It's bad enough that anyone would even think it. I don't want to know, Jerry."

"But it ain't right that they—"

Jerry hushed as Marjie put her fingers to his lips. "Please, don't," she whispered. "It would only make things worse."

"Don't you worry about it, Marjie," Goldie reassured her. "I gave 'em a tongue-lashing they won't forget for a long time."

Marjie nodded at Goldie and managed a half-smile. "I'm sure they won't," she replied.

It was the dry creaks of the hardwood floor that first woke Jerry; then he felt the heavy quilt being pulled back from the opposite side of the bed. Slowly opening one eye, he rolled over to meet Marjie as she crawled back under the sheets.

"Oh! You're freezing!" Jerry mumbled, pulling back just far enough to avoid touching the iceberg that had invaded his cozy haven. "Where have you been? Outside?"

Marjie tugged the quilt up around her neck and whispered, "Just go back to sleep, sweetheart. We can talk in the morning."

"What time is it?"

"Two-fifteen."

"Phew. You been up till now?"

"Just sleep. It'll wait till tomorrow."

Jerry reached his right arm around Marjie and began to gently rub her cold neck and shoulders. "You let what Goldie said get to you, didn't you? I told you not to—"

"It's not about whoever's talking," Marjie broke in, slowly massaging the temples around her eyes. "My head's killing me."

"Did you take something for it?"

"Aspirins," Marjie muttered. "My sinuses feel like there's a blacksmith in there hammering away. Rub your fingers up the back of my head and do the scalp. . . . There, that's better. Stay there now. It really hurts."

Jerry worked his strong fingers slowly back and forth around her head, being careful not to pull at her hair. "So, if you're not mad at the blabbermouths, why aren't you sleeping? And don't tell me it's because your head aches."

"I don't know," replied Marjie, shaking her head and offering a sigh. "It just bothers me."

"What?"

"Let's get some sleep. I'm so tired, and you gotta milk in a few hours."

"I'm plenty awake now," Jerry said. He

stopped the massage and pulled his arm away from her. "Tell me or I'm going to get upset."

Marjie rolled onto her back but continued to run her fingers over her forehead. "It's just that it might be true what they're saying."

Jerry was silent for a moment, then he chuckled out loud. "This is your newest trick, right? Jokes in the nighttime. Not very funny jokes, but still . . ."

"I'm not joking," Marjie said softly. "It's just what I was afraid would happen. Here I'm supposed to be in charge of a prayer meeting for the boys overseas, and look what good my own prayers have done. I knew I shouldn't have let them talk me into leading that thing."

"Come on," Jerry protested, looking at her face silhouetted against the bedroom window. Her eyes were shut and her lips pressed together tightly. "That's . . . well, that's just stupid. Even Goldie didn't believe it."

"Goldie hasn't walked in my shoes," Marjie spoke quickly. "Paul is the first boy we've been praying for who's been hurt. What does that say to you?"

"Doesn't say anything," answered Jerry. "Shoot! Don't you think that God answers our prayers in His own way? We don't know what God wants to do."

"So, it was God who wanted Paul to get his

shoulder blown to pieces?"

"Wait a minute," Jerry said. "You're making a mountain out of—out of something that's not even there."

"Paul may never use his arm again. I'd say that's pretty real."

"And Billy's legs will never be the same, and Betty Hunter's husband will never be coming back, and a lot of other things won't ever be the same. But that doesn't mean we should blame it all on God," Jerry reasoned, shaking his head. He reached out his arm around Marjie again and snuggled up close to her. "I believe He can bring good out of the evil, and war sure is evil. But I think war is man's fault. Or the devil's."

"Could He have protected Paul?"

"Sure."

"Well, we prayed, so why didn't He?"

"But how can we know that He didn't?" Jerry said.

"How can we know anything—for sure?" asked Marjie. "We can't. So why pray at all?"

"Oh boy," Jerry said with a groan. "You got it all wrapped up in one big knot. I suggest you get some sleep and see if it don't look a little different in the morning."

"Sleep sounds good," Marjie replied, stroking Jerry's arm. "Maybe if you hold me tight, I'll nod off. Can you watch Martha for a while tomorrow morning?"

"Sure. You wanta go back to bed after I get done milking?"

"Nope," Marjie said, then yawned. "I'm going up to see Fitch. He's gonna have to take over the prayer group or else find someone else to do it."

"No. You can't do that."

"I certainly can," Marjie whispered. "I'm done with it. It was foolish to think I should even try."

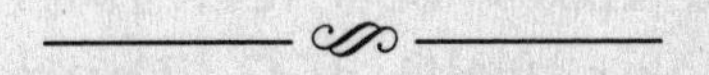

The old black Ford crept down the snow-packed driveway and came to a slow halt in front of the church parsonage. The wind had piled the snow in hard, crusty ripples, and it was impossible to tell where the parking spot was. Marjie shut off the engine.

"This stupid heater never did work," she muttered, pulling out the keys and taking a quick look in the rearview mirror at her bloodshot eyes. "I'm freezing, and all that thing can puke out is cold air. Why Jerry never fixed it . . ."

Marjie shoved the reluctant car door open and jumped out, then she made her dash up the partially shoveled sidewalk toward the large white house. "I wish I was in a better mood," she whispered as she knocked on the door, "but here goes."

As usual, the parsonage door swung open to reveal the narrow face and the friendly brown eyes of Dorothy Fitchen, the pastor's wife. "What a wonderful surprise!" she cried, reaching out a thin right arm and wrapping it around Marjie. "Come on in before we catch a chill."

"Is the pastor home?" Marjie asked. "I should have called before I came. I know it's rude, but I couldn't wait any longer."

"No, no, no," replied Dorothy as she closed the door with a loud thud. "It's fine for you to drop in anytime. Besides, Fitch isn't much on going out on these cold, windy mornings. Getting soft in his old age, I'm afraid."

"Maybe he's just getting smart," Marjie said. She took off her coat and handed it to Dorothy, then turned toward the footsteps she heard behind her.

"Well, well," Pastor Fitchen said, raising white, bushy eyebrows over a wide smile. "A little sunshine on this dull gray day. What brings you out of your warm house to see us old fogies?"

Marjie gave a twisted smile and shook her head. "I wish I was bringing some sunshine with me, but I'm afraid it's more like I've been eclipsed. I need to talk. I should have called but—"

"We got plenty of time to talk," the elderly pastor broke in, looking down at his watch, then he reached out a large, wrinkled hand and pointed to his study. "Nobody's here, and Dorothy makes sure that nobody interrupts. Some people don't even bother to make an appointment. Can you believe that?"

Marjie was so deep in thought that it took a couple seconds for the joke to sink in. "Yeah, I've met some of those folks," she said with a weak chuckle. "But you deserve them. You got that big salary, and retirement's just around the corner. Somebody has to make you earn your keep, and today it's my turn. Lead the way."

Pastor Fitchen shuffled down the hallway toward the door to the den. Although his speech and the mobility of his left arm had fully recovered from a mild stroke, his walk was much slower than Marjie recalled it being in the past. He closed the door behind them, and Marjie sat down in a large wooden chair that faced the pastor's cluttered desk.

Sitting down in his chair and leaning back, Pastor Fitchen folded his hands and took a deep breath. "Usually I ask people who come to talk with me what it is that's brought them here," he said quietly. "But I have to tell you that I know why you've come—at least what prompted it. I'm just surprised you weren't here earlier."

Marjie, who had crossed her arms when she sat down, leaned forward in her chair and shook her head. "Did Jerry call you?"

"No," replied the pastor. "Yesterday morning Dorothy was talking to someone who'd been listening in on a phone conversation. Goldie Turner was apparently chewing out somebody regarding whether your prayer meeting for servicemen was being effective. Said the party line was getting hot. I figured that story would get to you pretty quick. Goldie told you?"

Marjie nodded and looked intently into the pastor's saggy eyes. "Didn't sleep too well last night. Read my Bible for a while, then I tried praying about it, then I read the Bible some more, but nothing seemed to help. I'm sorry, but I'm here to turn the prayer meeting back to you."

"I can understand why you might want to do that," Pastor Fitchen said. "But I can give you a long list of reasons why you should keep it."

"Like my brother taking a bullet in the shoulder?"

"Yes, I think it is a reason, actually," he spoke gently and smiled. "I know you feel like a failure, but one of the reasons so many people are coming to your prayer meeting is because they know you've faced some of the things they're facing. They've told me that. I could lead the meeting for you, but I really haven't experienced anything like what you've faced with a husband in the Pacific, a brother in Europe, another brother—where'd you say he is? Arizona?"

Marjie laughed out loud and shook her head with her eyes closed. "I don't know a thing about prayer—never did. If they're looking to me, they got the wrong person. I warned you in the beginning, and you told me you'd bail me out if I got in water that was over my head. Don't back out on me now."

Pastor Fitchen reached up and rubbed his cheek, then turned and looked out his window for a moment. "I won't back out on you," he said. "But if I tell you a story from my past, will you think this whole thing over one more time before you decide?"

"Oh brother, you're gonna try to con me back into this, aren't you?"

"No," he replied, breaking into a laugh. "I'm getting ready to tell you something about my life that I've never told anyone else except my wife, and you think I'm trying to con you?"

"Yes."

The pastor laughed some more and shrugged his shoulders. "Well, you can take this story for what it's worth, but you're not getting out of here until I tell it."

"I'll listen," Marjie replied, "but no promises."

"It goes back to my very first pastorate," he said. "Seems like a lifetime ago. I'd been there for a year, fresh out of seminary, and I thought everything had gone so well—until I had my first run-in with our head elder.

"I had come to him thinking I had some good ideas for improving our Sunday school program. He quickly assured me that not only did I know nothing about running a Sunday school, but in his opinion I could best serve the church by giving more attention to my sermon preparation. I was, in his words, the boringest preacher he had ever heard. . . ."

Pastor Fitchen's voice trailed off, and he leaned back in his chair again and folded his hands. For a few moments, Marjie thought he looked older and gray, and his smile disappeared.

"If I didn't know some people who'd say just that kind of mean thing, I'd wonder if you were lying," Marjie said. "What did you do?"

"I, ah, believed him, unfortunately," the pastor replied, looking down at his hands. "I had been afraid that the congregation would find me boring, but I hadn't thought it was that bad. I nearly gave up the ministry over it."

"So when did you get over it?" asked Marjie.

"Oh, I managed to put my face back on again and kept on preaching," he said. "But I actually didn't get over it completely until I took my stand in that church meeting last fall for supporting the Bible project for the Dyaks. It took me way too long to learn my lesson."

"What exactly did you learn?"

"I'll tell you only if you'll reconsider the prayer meeting."

"It's a deal."

Pastor Fitchen leaned forward in his chair, and the sparkle seemed to return to his eyes. "I learned that no matter what else happens, the only thing that should concern me is whether I am doing the will of God. There are times when people cheer me on and tell me how good a job I'm doing, and there have been times when I knew people were booing me down and wishing I'd start looking for another church. I prefer the cheers, of course, and I truly hope that my ministry is pleasing and encouraging to my congregation. But I can't live for that, although I tried to for many years.

"All I can do," he added, "is what I feel God has led me to do. I may be applauded, or I may be ridiculed, but when it comes right down to my life, it doesn't . . . really . . . matter."

Chapter Five

Some Things Last Forever

"I can't tell you how much I've been dreading this day," Marjie told Chester Stanfeld when she met him on the stairs leading up to the Stanfelds' apartment. "I keep hoping you won't go."

Chester ran a big hand through his short-cropped brown hair and looked down at Marjie with a mixture of affection and amusement. "Don't tell Margaret that. She might change her mind—send me to the mission field without her."

"Don't count on it," Marjie told him as she squeezed by him on the narrow stairway. "I think you're both just dying to get on with your exciting life and leave us behind."

"Now, Marjie . . ." he began with a look of concern.

She cut him off with a half-smile. "Just kidding," she said as she disappeared around the landing. Then she called back as she heard the downstairs door open, "I think."

Chester and Margaret's tiny living room was cluttered with half-packed boxes and a hodgepodge of household items piled on the floor and on top of the furniture. The massive leather suitcases that Margaret had brought from her native Scotland had been shoved beneath the large bay windows. Margaret herself was sitting on the hardwood floor, her usually pale cheeks pink from the intense heat of the steam radiator that was percolating next to her. Enormous blue eyes fixed themselves on Marjie's dark frown.

"Hardly seems fair, does it?" she said with her lilting burr. "Just a wee bit over a year I've been here, and now it's time to pack me bags again. I hate it, too."

"That makes three of us," Ruth Wilson added, fixing her dark eyes at them both. She pushed aside the old brass lamp that she had been cleaning and leaned back in her tall wooden chair. "But if we're going to get all this stuff sorted and ready to sell and help Margaret pack what she wants to take back to Scotland, we can't be crying all day. And it doesn't take much to get me going—least since I started hanging around you, Marjie."

"Don't blame me," Marjie sputtered and

laughed, laying her heavy coat over a corner of the davenport. "I knew you were a live wire from the first day I saw you lay into Edna Miller in Sunday school. Somebody just had to help you discover all those tender feelings that were boiling just beneath—"

"You've accomplished that," Ruth interjected, shaking her head and smiling. "Now don't push it. I'd like to save my tears for when we actually say goodbye, if you don't mind. That's coming soon enough."

"True," Marjie replied. "And I hate it, I'm telling you." She scanned around the room. "So what can I do? Looks like you two already have a system going."

"Of course," Margaret said as her narrow, curving lips broke into a cheery smile. "Can you imagine anything not bein' organized with Ruthie around?"

The three women laughed, and Marjie's eyes misted as she looked at her friends. Between Margaret's arrival in Minnesota to marry Chester and Ruth's recent wedding to Billy Wilson lay a thousand memories of shared talk, shared schemes, shared laughter. *Just like having the sisters I always dreamed I'd have*, she thought.

"So, what's my job?" asked Marjie, clearing her throat. "I suppose you saved a really rotten one for me?"

"Like helping you can applesauce in that inferno of a kitchen of yours?" Ruth teased. "I'm still sweating from that particular Labor Day."

"I'll gladly just sit here if that's all you need," Marjie returned.

"Perhaps you'd be willin' to shine up those two maple end tables," Margaret said. "Mr. Edwards down at the thrift store is going to try to sell most of the furniture for us. Chester fixed some metal brackets for their store and did it for the cost of the iron, so Mr. Edwards said he'd do us a favor. I thought that if we polished the furniture well, we might get a fair price."

Marjie nodded and picked up the opened tin can of wax that perched on the corner of one of the tables. "That's kind of him. Be nice if you can get your money back out of the furniture. Nicer still if you could make a profit."

"Don't you get nervous about the future, Margaret?" Ruth asked as she renewed her efforts on the old lamp.

"You mean about whether we'll have enough money goin' to the mission field?" Margaret questioned.

"Yeah," Ruth replied. "Before we met Mr. Biden, I had never heard of anyone who simply trusted God to supply their finances. I still have a hard time putting myself in his shoes, especially with a family."

Margaret's blue eyes widened, and she shrugged her head. "No. The money is a worry, but not a big one for me. I've seen so many missionaries comin' back after spendin' most of their lives overseas; they always seemed to have enough money to do what they felt they were supposed to be doin'. But that doesn't mean I'm free o' worry. Not indeed."

"I'd be afraid of what it might be like to try to raise a family so far from home," Marjie said, pressing her waxy rag against the maple wood and rubbing hard.

"That is a worry," admitted Margaret with a sigh. "A big one. One has no idea what the living conditions will be. Will there be running water, houses, good food, medical care, schools, mail delivery, or decent roads to travel? What will we have to bring with us? Will it last? There are a thousand worries."

"Learning a new language and fitting into another culture—that would scare me," Ruth added. "I had a terrible time with languages in college."

"I couldn't do it," Marjie declared. "Jerry would end up shipping me back in a cage for loony people."

Margaret laughed but quickly grew somber. "I don't think they used cages, but what you've said is true. There have been missionaries who could not cope with what they faced, and some of them ended up returning . . . or worse."

"They went crazy?" Ruth asked.

"Some have, yes," Margaret said. "Others have been martyred. Some have barely arrived on their mission field and have taken ill from a tropical disease and died. But most of the stories I heard in our church were of those who had been successful, at least in part, and who were returning to the field to finish what they had started."

"My goodness," Marjie sputtered. "And here I've been trying to get out of doing the prayer meeting because a couple of people criticized me. I'd last about five minutes in another country."

"But that's what's so amazin' about God, Marjie," said Margaret. "I was ready to pack me bags and go home when I first met up with Chester's father. His harsh words and that terrible temper o' his just tore me inside. But God saw me through that time, and then He gave me so much more than I was even afraid o' losing! He'll see me and Chester through whatever He puts before us. I *do* believe that—despite how I feel inside. But to tell the truth, I always feel like a scared little bunny."

"I think we all do," Ruth said. "I was so afraid that Billy was going to back out on me before we got married. Everything inside me wanted to quit before he could hurt me again. It seems like anything that's really important to do has a huge price tag on it."

"But Billy was worth it, eh?" Marjie joked.

"Yes, ma'am . . . and then some," Ruth replied with a dreamy look. "And I thought he was just a good kisser."

"You're a wicked one," Marjie teased and laughed. "Still floating on the honeymooner clouds. Wait till you have a little Billy or two to chase around the house."

"So what about the prayer meeting?" asked Margaret. "I was sorry to hear about what was said. Your good mother must have been hurt, too."

Marjie shook her head and put down her rag for a moment. "I really don't think it bothered her, and I'm not sure why. She must have skin as thick as an alligator."

"We heard that you were going to quit the prayer meeting," Ruth said. "Is that true?"

"I thought about it for a long time," Marjie replied, looking from one friend to the next. "Would it bother you if I did?"

Margaret gave no hint of a change in expression, but Ruth nodded her head.

"Not about you," Ruth replied. "But . . . it would bother me that someone so right for leading the meeting was not doing it. I don't know if there's such a thing as a person having a gift of prayer, Marjie, but I'd say you come close. I mean that."

Margaret nodded her head but did not speak.

"Oh, phooey. I don't know," Marjie protested, but mildly. "I shouldn't have talked to the pastor, that's for certain. That old bird pulled on my heartstrings and convinced me to not give up, but I'm not promising anything. I wish somebody else would do it."

"That's how I've felt about me and Chester becomin' missionaries," Margaret said. "If somebody else did it, Chester could go to seminary, and then we could pastor a church right here in your gentle hills of Minnesota. But then, I guess that's the excuse Christians have given for centuries, the reason the old blind Dyak man wept so hard when Mr. Biden told him the Lord had come to earth long before his grandfather's grandfather. I have t' tell you, that story broke me heart in two."

Marjie swallowed a lump in her own throat and noticed that Ruth had turned her head away. All three applied themselves to their polishing, and no one spoke for a long time.

"I think it broke all our hearts," Marjie finally said. "Somehow I had just never realized how much of the world has never heard the gospel." She gave her table a couple more hard rubs before asking, "Margaret, will you think less of Ruth and me if we end up staying here—teaching or farming or whatever we do?"

"Ahhh, don't ask me such a question!" Margaret scolded. "I know yer hearts. God calls, and we answer. It's as simple as that, isn't it? Didn't Mr. Biden say that our Father is the Keeper of the harvest? It's His business to send us and keep us. Agreed?"

"Without a question," Marjie agreed. "I just wish He'd make it all a little clearer sometimes."

"Any idea of where you and Chester might go?" Ruth asked.

"After our trainin'?" Margaret asked.

"Yes."

Margaret's lips curled into a twisted smile, and she chuckled. "Me and Chester've been talkin' about whether we dared tell anyone."

"Come on, we're your friends!" Marjie exclaimed. "Where are you thinking about? And don't tease us, now. We want the truth the first time."

"Well . . . I'm glad you're both sittin' down," Margaret replied. "We've been thinkin' . . . we've been prayin' that if it's

God's will, we'd like to go to Japan when the war's done."

It took several moments for Margaret's words to sink in deep enough for Marjie to manage a faint "Wow!" Before she had thought it through, she blurted out, "But they're our enemies."

"I know," Margaret said softly, slowly standing up after having sat on the floor for so long. "They almost killed the man I love, remember. They *are* our enemy. But most of them have never had the chance to hear about the Savior's love, so they are also lost sheep. And who will go to them if we don't? Does our Lord love them less than He loves Mr. Biden's Dyak people? Or us?"

Ruth had stopped her work on the brass lamp and shook the cobwebs out of her head. "Still, my goodness, Margaret, I can't imagine it. All I see is the face of a brutal Japanese soldier with a bayonet fixed to slash innocent people to death. . . . I just can't imagine it."

"Me either," Marjie burst out. "You're sure?"

"No, we're not sure," Margaret replied, closing her lovely eyes. "But we are prayin' that way. Chester says that if we can just see beyond the war images, the Japanese are simply people like us. But they have lived under a false religion that corrupts and destroys them. They *need* the gospel. Should it go everywhere except to the Japanese?"

"No, I'm sorry," Ruth said. "That's not what I meant. I just can't see beyond the warrior's face yet. It's a bit overwhelming."

"Very," Marjie agreed.

"It is," Margaret continued, "and I'm not pretendin' that we're ready to do it. But I do think that someday we will be ready. And though it is so hard to leave the friends I've come to love like you, I think that getting ready to leave is helping me."

"How's that?" asked Marjie.

"Do you see all this . . . this stuff?" Margaret asked, sweeping her hand around the room. "In one year's time we collected almost everything here, but do you realize that none of it will last? Some of it we bought new, some of it came as gifts, and most of it came from the thrift store, but none of it is going to last forever, none of it. Someday it will all be in a junk pile somewhere."

She leaned over toward her friends, and her clear eyes shone with blue light.

"What's becomin' clear to me now," she added, "is that some things last forever. People last forever. I find that incredible and a little frightening. Americans, Brits, Germans, Japanese, Indians, Australians, Dyaks, whoever—every person lives on forever and ever, through eternity. I want to live my life making sure they've had the chance to take the Savior's hand as I have."

Chapter Six

Showdown

"Good evening, Deacon," Ruth piped up to Jerry as she entered the front door of the Macmillan farmhouse. "You got your guns all loaded for the big meeting?"

"Let me take your coat," Jerry said with a smile. "I don't know if I'm ready for this or not. Why didn't Billy come in?"

Ruth slipped off her coat and handed it to Jerry, then she greeted Marjie and Sarah and Benjamin, who were sitting at the dining room table. "The good Deacon Wilson thought that you and your fine-looking father, Elder Macmillan, could just as well hop in and ride with him. The car's nice and toasty—in contrast to some folks' cars."

Marjie tipped her coffee cup to Ruth in response. "What do you think of these boys getting elected to such prestigious positions, Ruthie? Think we can still put up with them?"

"Long as they don't get too bigheaded," Ruth replied, tapping Benjamin on the shoulder as she joined them at the table and poured herself a cup of steaming black coffee. "I'm still surprised that the three of them all got voted in on the same ballot. Then the pastor goes and calls a meeting right away for the elders and deacons to talk about whether the church is going to support Chester and Margaret."

"Well, the vote may be a surprise," Sarah said, "but not the meeting. I figure that Fitch was holding his cards, thinkin' these men would get the nod. He can use all the help he can get on this issue."

Jerry was putting on his coat. Benjamin took his last drink of coffee, then slowly stood up and stretched.

"These old bones would rather stay right here," said Benjamin, sauntering toward the coat closet. "But Sarah told me I'd be sleeping here tonight if I didn't stand up and be counted."

"Like you're one not to take a stand?" Marjie teased. "Everywhere you go, you leave buckets of hot water boiling. But just in case you suddenly get cold feet, I'm here to tell you that you're not staying in this house anymore. You sold it to us, and we don't let chickens roost here."

Jerry laughed and handed Benjamin his coat. "She means business, you realize," he said to his father. "So you ladies are going to be putting the finishing touches on plans for Chester and Margaret's going-away dinner?"

"Betty Hunter'll be here any minute, and then we'll get to work," Ruth replied. "We're going to see if we can outdo the dinner we threw when you came home. That's going be hard to beat, though," she mused. "Who would have thought that Chester was going to show up and blow the roof off the place. First time any of us had ever seen him. And I can still hear him calling out in that silent room, 'Jerry Macmillan saved my life! Stand up and help me give Jerry my thanks!' "

Everyone nodded and shook their heads at the memory, and Sarah even clapped her hands. "I was so shocked that I gave Benjamin my first hug that night!" she exclaimed, looking over at Jerry and Benjamin. "Chester's a part of us now. You tell the elders and deacons that it's time for the church to put its money where its mouth is."

"I think I get your point," Jerry said, stepping to the door and opening it for Benjamin. "Keep praying, okay?"

Jerry sat down in the hard wooden folding chair and rubbed his hands, but their chill was more from nervousness than cold. He and Billy were sitting together toward the back of the group, and Benjamin sat in the front with the six other elders. As they waited for Pastor Fitchen to arrive, Jerry looked around at the other men and wondered where they stood on this issue.

"Orville Manning's got his black suit and white shirt on again," Billy whispered to Jerry. "You'd think he's in charge."

"Isn't he?" Jerry leaned toward Billy and spoke softly. "He's the money man of the church. Nobody tosses more in the plate than he does, and everybody knows it. If he doesn't support this, what do you think's gonna happen?"

"I have no idea," whispered Billy, his green eyes focused on Manning. "He's had his way long before you or I were around. And he didn't like it at all when we got the church to help support the Bible project for Mr. Biden. I suspect Orville's still smartin' from that."

"If he would have had his way when Pastor Fitchen had his stroke, we would have a new pastor right now," Jerry said. "He found out he can't push Fitch around anymore, and he doesn't like it one bit."

Just then the elderly pastor made his slow entrance, carrying only his large black Bible to the lectern. A Sunday school blackboard stood to the left of the lectern, obviously brought in for the meeting. Pastor Fitchen quietly placed his Bible on the lectern, then he looked around the room at the men who had gathered.

"I . . . appreciate your waiting so patiently for me," he said, nodding his snow white head. "I wasn't feeling too good this afternoon, but I'm better now. We're all aware of why we're here tonight, and the idea of supporting Chester and Margaret Stanfeld on the mission field has already been debated, at least in part, in a meeting we had last fall—the night I had my stroke, if you remember."

A round of throat clearing circled the room, but the pastor seemed not to notice. "The Stanfelds are not requesting that we get behind them financially, and they know that there are peculiarities about their standing with our church and denomination that make it awkward even to discuss this," he continued. "But I know as well that there are many members in this church who would like us to commit ourselves to helping them. So, we're here to discuss the matter.

"If it's at all possible, I'm hoping we can talk about this in a manner that's consistent with fairness and Christian love. So let's try to listen to each other and not snipe or call names. I had the blackboard brought in so I could write out the pros and cons of the issue;

then we're going to vote. I have already stated my position, so let's hear what you have to say."

Lou Billingsley, one of the elders sitting next to Orville Manning, put up his hand. "The Stanfelds never even applied for membership in our church. Isn't that a problem for us? If we start supporting people who aren't members, where will it end?"

Pastor Fitchen had turned to the blackboard before Billingsley finished and started writing under the *CONS* column: *1. Not official church members*. But he was still writing when Benjamin spoke up.

"The reason they didn't take an official church membership here is because they feel their home church needs to be Margaret's father's church in Scotland," he announced. "Does that make them less of a member here? Chester has taught the adult Sunday school faithfully, and he preached when our pastor was ill. Margaret has sung her way into our hearts, and I know that some of our church members have come to faith through the Stanfelds. You don't consider them members of our church, Lou?"

"I just said they haven't taken a membership, that's all," Billingsley quipped.

Billy sat forward in his chair and was ready when Billingsley finished. "I'd like you to write down in the *PROS* column that many of us consider Chester and Margaret outstanding members of this church, whether it's written down on a piece of paper or not. You could put down as a number two that most of us are thrilled that a couple from our church is going to train for full-time Christian service. We think it's a privilege to support them."

Pastor Fitchen nodded and turned to write on the board again, but Orville Manning was already rising to his feet. Broad-shouldered and over six feet tall, he was shaking his bald head in disgust. "I don't care for this at all, Pastor. People work hard in this community for the few dollars they earn off their farms. I get real upset when we're asking them to give more and more and more and they ain't got it. Then to ask them to give it to someone who didn't even grow up here—I just can't believe we're even considering it."

The pastor had kept writing while Manning spoke. Then he turned around, raising his woolly eyebrows, and said, "I think you're still misunderstanding this, although you and I have talked this over, Orville. We are not talking about changing our budget or the amount of money that we give to the denomination. We're simply suggesting that we as a church set up a special fund for the Stanfelds that is totally a free-will offering. If some people want to make monthly pledges to that effect, do we see that as a problem?"

"You bet I do," Manning retorted. His smooth pate was gleaming in the light and starting to get red. "Those people are going to simply shift their giving from the general fund to the Stanfelds. The church will lose, and I'm opposed to it. I'd like to call our denomination's district superintendent in to look at this mess."

"Give him a call," Jerry suggested. "If I remember correctly, you told us the same thing about last fall's annual church sale. You said the general budget would be hurt if members could choose between donating items for it or for Mr. Biden's Bible project. But Mr. Biden got the money he needed to print those Bibles, and we went well over the general budget, too. Worked out pretty good for everybody. I'm sure the district superintendent would find that interesting. And Mr. Biden wasn't a member of our church; in fact, he was only in our church for one day."

"Emotionalism!" Orville barked. "Anthony Biden played on this church's emotions with missionary stories we don't even know were true. We don't even know if there were any Bibles. How can we trust—"

"That's enough!" Benjamin cried, standing up and turning to face the taller man. "Orville, you just went too far. I won't sit here and let you judge Mr. Biden, and I ain't gonna let you go after Chester and Margaret, either. I think we knew how we wanted to vote on this issue before we came in the doors tonight, so I make a motion that we stop any more discussion on it before people get hurt by what's said. I'm ready to vote."

"I second the motion," Billy called out from the back before any of the others could respond.

Pastor Fitchen set his piece of chalk down on the ledge of the blackboard and stepped back to the lectern. He surveyed the faces of the elders and the deacons, particularly those of Benjamin and Manning. Nodding toward the two men, he said quietly, "Please take your chairs, gentlemen."

As the two men sat down, the elderly pastor wrapped his long, skinny fingers around the corner of the lectern. "We have a motion from the floor to stop this discussion and to vote," he said. "All those in favor, signify by saying aye."

A chorus of voices from among the elders and deacons rang out. "Aye!"

"All opposed, signify by saying nay."

Orville Manning and a few others spoke out. "Nay!"

Pastor Fitchen reached back and rubbed his neck. "The ayes have it. If you could pass out the slips of paper and pencils that were on the edges of the rows, you may proceed to vote."

"Just a second." Orville Manning rose to his feet again. He folded his arms and looked around the room. "I have one question for you, Pastor. Are you still prepared to resign the pastorate if we vote against supporting the Stanfelds?"

"You're out of order, Orville," Pastor Fitchen said firmly. "Please take your seat."

"I know what's out of order," Manning sputtered, "and this meeting is out of order. You swayed the vote of everyone in this room by declaring you'd resign. That's out of order!"

Pastor Fitchen stood up taller and took a deep breath. "I have no voting power in this group assembled, and my words were given as any member of the church could have given at the time. Now, please sit down."

"If you can draw a line in the sand, then, so can I," Manning said, turning to the others in the group. "Our fine pastor failed to mention that the Stanfelds are talking about doing missionary work in Japan. In my mind that's aiding and abetting the enemy, and if this church chooses to support that, you may cancel my membership. You can bet there are other churches in this area that would be happy for my financial support."

"Sounds like blackmail, Orville," Benjamin said, looking up at Manning and then rising to his feet. "That's a desperate card to play, and I got a feeling you finally lost. Now, the pastor asked you to take your seat. I'm not asking you. Sit down or leave."

Orville Manning glared at Benjamin with his huge fists clenched against his barrel chest, as if he was sizing up his smaller opponent. "Jap lover," he muttered. Then he slowly turned away, pushed aside the empty chair in front of him, and walked proudly out of the room.

Chapter Seven

Winter's Day Ride

Marjie carefully pushed the front door of the farmhouse open, stepped into the unusually warm winter sunshine, and quietly closed the door behind her. Turning and shielding her eyes against the radiant sun rays glaring off the smoothly textured snow, she called out, "What a day for a ride! Can you believe this weather?"

"It's wonderful!" Betty Hunter exclaimed,

leaning forward in her Western saddle and rubbing the neck of her beautiful chestnut Appaloosa. "I guess we better enjoy it. They say Old Man Winter's going to roll back through tomorrow. Where's Jerry?"

"He and Martha are having their usual Sunday afternoon nap," Marjie replied as she came down the sidewalk and paused beside Betty and her horse Lucky. "And he told me I had to wear his navy coat or he wouldn't let me go. He says it's more protective than mine is. So . . . you think this monster will keep me warm?"

Betty burst out laughing as Marjie stretched her arms with her fingers barely poking out from the ends of the sleeves. Pushing her long blond hair back over her shoulders, Betty said, "When you first stepped out of the house, I thought you must have shrunk since we talked at church. I'd say it's a tad big in the shoulders, too."

Marjie laughed as well, shrugging her shoulders up and down. "Well, nobody's going to see me but you, so I guess we're all right. Go ahead and give Lucky a drink at the water tank if you'd like. I'll get Charlie from the barn. He's all saddled and set to go."

"Good," said Betty, turning Lucky toward the south end of the barn where the water tank stood. "I'll be with you in just a minute."

Marjie went quickly to the barn and stepped into the cavernous darkness. The warm air inside was heavy with the sweet smell of hay and cows. Jerry had saddled Charlie and put him in the wooden stall by the barn's north door. He whinnied as Marjie came up behind him and turned his golden face toward her as she stepped into the stall.

"How's it going, Charlie boy?" Marjie said as the palomino backed off gently from the side of the wooden stall so Marjie could get alongside of him. She lifted her hand and ran it down the horse's silvery mane and then down the white streak in the center of Charlie's face. "Ready for a little workout?"

She led the horse out into the farmyard and let Charlie stand for a few moments appraising the other horse. At first his ears had pricked forward and he sniffed the air carefully, but then he relaxed.

"Nice to finally have a saddle, eh," Betty said as Marjie mounted up. "Do you like it?"

"I love it," Marjie replied, pulling back the long sleeves of Jerry's navy coat, slipping on her gloves, and then taking her reins back in hand. "When Jerry said it came from Tom Metcalfe, I wondered if you might have helped Tom pick out this saddle when you were training Charlie for him."

"No. He already had the saddle," Betty

said, following Marjie as they headed toward the farm lane that led out toward the fields. "You know, that man and his wife were the strangest birds I've ever been around. Do you ever see them?"

"Never," Marjie said, shaking her head. "I've been here for almost two years now, and the only one I've ever seen is Tom. I met him when he ran over our dog with his car, and I see him every so often when he goes past on the road. Jerry says they have two children."

Betty pulled up alongside of Marjie as they plodded slowly down the farm lane. "Lovely kids," she said to Marjie. "A girl and a boy. But that woman is odd. I don't think she ever gets out."

"Well, I've never seen her," Marjie replied. "I know where their driveway is, but I've never even seen their house. I guess it's hidden back in the woods down at the bottom of the hill as you head north out of our driveway."

"You don't want to see it, believe me. . . ." Betty began as the two riders emerged into the open fields. Without a word, Betty dug her spurs into Lucky's side and took off at a gallop across the snow-swept hayfield. Marjie burst out laughing and felt an immense surge of power as Charlie responded to her push to follow. Their tracks sliced a nearly perfect diagonal across the unblemished rectangle of the field, then they turned and galloped back to the opening to the farm lane.

"Wow! Is he fast!" Marjie exclaimed to Betty as she reached the spot where Lucky had stopped. She was still laughing from the thrill.

"You two held your own!" she replied, laughing as well. She nudged Lucky to head down the hill toward the valley. "We just had a good head start on you."

"Don't you dare tell Jerry about our little run," Marjie said. "He's not much happier about me being on a horse than my mother is."

"As if he's not going to see the tracks?" Betty said, looking back at the evidence they had left behind and raising her eyebrows.

"Oops," Marjie said, nodding her head. "Guess what I need is another good snowfall."

The trail they were now following ran along the crest of the ridge that dropped suddenly to the creek below. There was silence for a time between the riders as the horses ambled slowly on, choosing their own pace. Marjie breathed deeply, enjoying the stillness and the beauty of the snow-covered landscape.

"Have you heard anything new about your

brother Paul?" Betty finally asked.

"Yeah," Marjie replied. "Ma got a letter saying that he's going to be sent back to the Vet's Hospital in Minneapolis as soon as he's recovered enough to travel. I can't wait to see him. I'm really worried about him. But at least he survived."

Marjie noticed Betty quickly turn away, and she instantly regretted her last words. Not only had Betty's husband been killed early in the war, but the two riders were nearly to the knoll that overlooked the farm fields in the valley below. It was here that Betty and Marjie had stopped on their first ride together, here that Betty had wept with deep heart sobs as she grieved his loss.

"Betty, I'm sorry. I didn't mean it the way it sounded," Marjie said as Betty stopped her horse underneath the two gnarly burr-oak trees that stood barren and gray.

"It's okay," Betty said, quickly dismounting and looping her reins over the wooden fence. Then she walked to the spot where she had sat and cried with Marjie the previous summer. "This is the place of healing for me, Marjie. On a warm Sunday afternoon on the eighth of August, I climbed back out of my shell to face the living again. Do you remember?"

"Are you kidding?" Marjie asked. She tied

Charlie alongside the Appaloosa and walked to join Betty. "I could never forget it. You had so much sorrow and pain. . . ."

Betty smiled and looked away again, her gaze scanning the valley below. "And I left a lot of it right here . . . with God," she said softly, glancing toward Marjie. "And you were right about what you said."

Marjie squinted and shook her head. "I'm sorry, but I don't remember saying much of anything."

"You said that God doesn't always give us explanations for what He does," Betty responded and gave a slight nod. Her almond-shaped eyes were clear and bright. "And He didn't, and He hasn't, but . . . I guess I don't worry as much about that now. Knowing His love is enough."

"Oh my," Marjie whispered. "I've had a terrible time feeling that ever since we got the news about Paul. I can't believe I was preaching to you about trusting God, and here I am . . ."

Betty wrapped her arm around Marjie and held her tight. Then she whispered, "Here's something else I learned from you, Marjie. Truth is always powerful when it comes from the heart. It set me free to live again. Thanks to you."

"No, it wasn't me, Betty," Marjie said, returning Betty's hug. "I was just here. God is good."

"God is very good," Betty said, letting go of Marjie. "And I'm glad you were there. And I'm going to be praying that you will feel His love again soon the way I've been feeling it." She gazed out over the valley and sighed deeply. "This really is a special place to me, Marjie. In fact, you know what I've been thinking? If I ever marry again, I'd like the ceremony to be right here."

Marjie looked up at her friend's smiling face. "Right here?"

"Why not? Benjamin and Sarah were married not far from here, weren't they?" asked Betty.

"Yeah, down in the field on the Seven Corners piece," Marjie replied. "But wouldn't you want to get married in the church? I can't imagine your folks going for a wedding on a farm lane under two sad old burr-oak trees."

Betty laughed and shook her head. "We did everything just the way they wanted on the first wedding. If there's a second one, I think it's my turn to plan what I'd like. Once Fred's memorial service was over, they never thought I should cry in public either, if you recall. And now they're mad about Chester and Margaret. They went to the church's goodbye potluck for them, and now Dad is furious that Chester and Margaret want to train to be missionaries to the Japanese. He says the Japs killed Fred, and they deserve to go to hell. I got so mad at him. We had a big fight over it."

"The Japanese did kill Fred, and they nearly got Billy and Chester and Jerry," said Marjie. "I'm sure it's really hard for them . . . and for you."

"It *is* hard, really hard. And the Germans nearly killed your brother," Betty replied. "But does that mean we condemn every German and Italian to hell? And then they turn around and condemn us for killing their sons and bombing their cities? Hate's a vicious circle, Marjie. I buried mine here, and I'm not about to take it up again."

"Well, then, I guess this would be the place to have the wedding," Marjie said. "Actually, I've got connections with the owner, and I think we can swing you a good rate, especially at this time of year."

Betty laughed and said, "It's a deal. But I can't guarantee the booking. We'll just have to see what happens. Do you want to ride down into the valley?"

"Sure. It looks beautiful down there," Marjie replied, stepping toward the horses. "Say, what did you think of Pastor Fitchen's message to Chester and Margaret the other night?"

Betty unlooped Lucky's reins from the wooden railing and quickly mounted, then she turned to Marjie and said, "I've never heard him speak like that before. It was like the man was on fire inside. When he warned them that they were headed for a war zone that's been held by the devil for centuries, it really frightened me for them. But I believe it's true. Do you?"

Marjie mounted Charlie and took a moment to get her oversized coat into place. "Yeah, I do believe it. I think the devil also has something to do with all the hate you've been talking about, and probably some of the worries that I've let torment me. 'He isn't a myth or a dream or a superstitious imagination'—isn't that what Fitch said?"

"Something like that," replied Betty as she turned Lucky's head downhill. "And he was right. You don't have to go to the jungles of Borneo to encounter the devil. He's doing a fair amount of trade right around us."

As they left the knoll and headed into the heavier part of the woods, Betty and Marjie fell silent again. Away to their right, a pair of blue jays signaled their presence with a sudden burst of shrill chatter. Large oaks and an occasional pine tree and endless clusters of gooseberry bushes crowded on each side of the cattle trail they were following.

They worked their way slowly down the path. The slope grew ever steeper and the horses now moved more slowly, placing each hoof with caution. Marjie could feel Charlie holding back, and the muted afternoon sunshine cast a strange lighting on the clouds of breath that billowed from his nostrils.

"Are you okay with this?" Betty called out, turning to look back at Marjie.

"We're doing fine, I think," Marjie replied, although she was having a hard time convincing the muscles in her stomach to relax. "It didn't seem to be this steep the last time we came this way."

"We just didn't notice it because the trail wasn't slippery," Betty said, pushing a snowy pine branch out of the way. Below them the rows of bent-over stalks from last year's corn crop stood placidly, awaiting the coming of spring. "Look at how deep and fluffy the snow gets down here where the wind doesn't blow."

Marjie had noticed. Along the last steep path that led to the creek, it appeared that the snow might be waist deep. "You want to go down all the way? Looks mighty deep down there."

Betty pulled Lucky to a halt and turned around to face Marjie. "The horses will be fine down there, but this last stretch of hill looks a bit nasty. You want me to go first and see how it goes, then you can follow?"

Marjie laughed and nodded. "Yes, I'm chicken enough to wait and see if you make it."

"I'll see you at the bottom, then," Betty said with a laugh. "Remember to lean your weight back and let Charlie find his own way down the hill. He's got good feet. You'll do fine."

With a nudge, Betty expertly steered the Appaloosa down the path with Marjie watching her every move. "You make it look so easy!" Marjie called out when Betty and Lucky had nearly reached the bottom without any problems. "How is it?"

"It's okay," Betty called back as Lucky got to the bottom and stopped in the deep snow alongside the buried farm creek. "Just don't rush him."

"Okay, Charlie. Your turn," Marjie said, urging him down the steep descent with her heels.

The palomino pawed the snow ahead, as if he wasn't any more confident than she was.

"Come on, big boy, down you go."

Charlie gave in and gingerly moved forward with Betty looking on from below. Marjie was relieved to find that the slope wasn't that much steeper than the one they had been on until about halfway down. They were negotiating their way along just fine, and Marjie managed to give Betty a wave. "This isn't so bad."

That happened just as they reached the steepest section. Suddenly Charlie slipped on a buried rock, and though he managed to right himself, Marjie could feel his panic. Staggering and lurching to find solid footing, the horse picked up speed and rushed down the last pitch toward the creek bottom.

Marjie clutched the reins and had all she could do to hang on as the wind rushed past her ears in a roar. As they almost reached the bottom, she knew that Charlie could never hold her weight up and that the two of them would go down together, with a good chance that the horse would roll on her. Then at the last second she noticed a spot where the snow was piled up at least a foot deeper than the rest of the area and heard Betty's muffled scream to "Jump!"

Instantly reacting, Marjie somehow managed to leap from the horse's right side and flew through the air toward the large puff of deeply piled snow. Head first, her entire body disappeared into its fluffy white cushion with a huge cloud of flakes spraying into the air as the only reminder of where she had gone. Meanwhile Charlie managed to keep himself upright and came to a stop some twenty yards across the creek bed. Blowing clouds of vapor, he looked back curiously at the place where his mistress had disappeared.

Jumping down from her horse, Betty raced to the spot where Marjie had been swallowed alive by the snowy powder. "Marjie!" she cried as her own legs got tangled in the deep snow and she fell forward toward the indentation in the snowbank.

Just then Marjie's white head popped back up through the snow, followed by her shoulders, and then by a huge shake that puffed clouds of glistening flakes into the sky around her head. Then Marjie's arms in their oversized sleeves came up and wiped the snow from her face to reveal a gigantic smile.

"What are you yelling for?" she asked her worried friend. "You think I'm deaf or something?"

Chapter Eight

Slippery Goodbyes

"Only God can see the future, Marjie," Jerry said, pushing the gas pedal down all the way to the floor as their old black Ford rumbled up a long hill on the highway that stretched between the towns of Preston and Chatfield. "We can't control this stuff."

"You think I'm not aware of that?" asked Marjie. Even with her heavy winter coat and Jerry's old wool car blanket wrapped around her, Marjie's teeth were chattering from the frigid air. "Why do Ruthie and Billy have to both get sick on the day that Chester and Margaret are leaving? I feel terrible for them."

Jerry shook his head and looked over at Marjie. "So do I. They're not even going to get a chance to say goodbye. But that flu really has knocked them out. Billy looked like death warmed over. And my dad and your mom have those sick pigs to tend. I'm glad that Mrs. Fitchen could watch Martha for us."

"Yeah, at least one thing worked out," Marjie groused. "The church dinner last Saturday was so perfect, then everything else falls apart. Just doesn't seem fair that we'll be the only ones there to say goodbye."

"No, it's not fair," Jerry agreed. "Like a lot of other things that we can't do anything about."

"Like everything that gets me worrying?" Marjie asked.

"That's not what I said, and you know it," Jerry countered, breaking into a grin.

"So you do think I worry too much."

Jerry broke out laughing and slapped his

hand on the steering wheel. "I didn't say a word about worrying. But if you really want to know, I think we all worry too much—including you. You're worrying right now, aren't you?"

Marjie's frown changed to a smirk. "You tell me."

Slowing down as he approached a corner with some icy-looking patches, Jerry nodded and replied, "You feel bad because Ruthie got sick, but what's really bothering you is that you now feel like you have to say or do something special for Margaret that you're sure Ruthie would have done if she had come along. And what you have to offer is never as good as Ruthie, so the argument goes. Correct me if I'm wrong."

Marjie pulled the tattered corner of the wool blanket up over her head and began to laugh hard. "Oh brother," her muffled voice said and then she pulled the blanket partially down from her face. "How'd you come up with that?"

"You think I was born in the barn or something?" Jerry teased, rubbing his forehead and laughing. "I'm not blind, you know. Every time you get stretched beyond what you think you can handle, you're looking over your shoulder for your best friend, Ruth, or the pastor, or Mr. Biden. And if they're not there to bail you out, you worry like crazy."

"Is it that obvious?"

"No," Jerry replied. "I'm your biggest admirer, you know, so I just happen to be watching you all the time. You *are* doing better, though."

"Thank you," Marjie said with a smile, letting the blanket drop back down and sitting up straighter. "I think I am, too. Believe it or not, Betty helped a lot the other day. But . . . I don't know. Sometimes I've felt like I couldn't possibly worry more than I do, and bingo, I look out the window and see another crop of cares growing up right alongside of the ones I've already got swirling around me."

"You just gotta keep preaching what you tell the prayer group," Jerry said. " 'Turn everything that is a care into a prayer. Let your cares be the raw material of your prayers.' "

"Sounds pretty good when *you* say it," Marjie said. "Wish it was as easy for me to live it. By the way, that quote's not from me. Chester showed me that in one of those books he found by that British pastor named Charles Spurgeon. He said something like, 'Baptize every anxiety in the name of the Father and the Son and the Holy Ghost and make it into a blessing.' "

Jerry whistled and nodded. "No wonder Chester's such a good teacher. He's pulling stuff out of those Spurgeon books and pretending like he thought it up."

Marjie laughed, "Probably. But I guess there's no sense reinventing the plow. If it's turning sod, you keep it in the ground."

"Do it then."

"What?"

"Turn today into a prayer," Jerry said. "All we're going up to do is say goodbye to our friends. Nobody's expecting you . . . or me . . . to work a miracle or say something they'll never forget. The only thing that really matters today is that we let them know how much we love them."

"I know," replied Marjie, rubbing her chin and staring down the road. "I just always feel like that's not enough."

"Guess it'll have to be," Jerry said. "That's Chester's folks' driveway up there on the right."

"Do you remember the first time we met Bill Stanfeld?" Marjie asked quietly.

"Phew! That was nasty," said Jerry, puffing out a big circle of air. "He called me a *fool.* A fool, Marjie. I was so mad at him. If Clare hadn't stepped between us, I hate to think what might have happened."

"How could one man change so much?"

asked Marjie as Jerry slowed the car down and turned carefully into the long snow-packed driveway.

"Same as us, I guess," Jerry said, shifting into second gear and then blowing Marjie a kiss. "Say, you're not going to get us all crying now, are you?"

"Not me," Marjie said, then smiled. "I hate crying. We're just here to say goodbye, right?"

"Right."

Jerry pulled the car to a stop in front of the Stanfelds' old brick farmhouse and turned off the engine. The midmorning sun glistened off the shiny glaze of the snow and made it nearly impossible to look toward the house.

"I can't go in there," Marjie whispered, shielding her eyes with a corner of the wool blanket. "I feel like we're going to a funeral."

"We only got about half an hour 'fore they have to leave for the train depot," Jerry said. He reached over and pulled the blanket from Marjie. "We better take advantage of it. Let's go."

Pulling her coat collar up as tight around her neck as she could, Marjie mumbled something that Jerry couldn't hear and reluctantly pushed her car door open. A sharp arctic breeze slapped her in the face, provoking more mutterings, and as she came around the front of the car, she slipped on a hidden patch of ice and nearly fell. Jerry half caught her and took her arm.

"Be careful of the ice!" Chester's voice called out from behind the partially opened front door to the farmhouse.

"Little late, buster!" Marjie yelled back, shielding her eyes to get a momentary look at Chester and Margaret standing in the doorway.

"Actually, it's pretty bad all the—"

But Chester's warning came too late. Both Marjie and Jerry found their feet flying out from under them as they stepped down on another patch of ice covered by a thin film of drifted snow. Marjie screamed as the two of them flew through the air and landed unceremoniously on their backsides.

"Are you okay?" hollered Chester Stanfeld as he ran carefully down the covered sidewalk toward them. The tone of his voice was of true concern, but with each step his muffled laughter got louder. By the time he reached them, he gave up on trying to hold it in. "That was some kind of landing!"

"Very funny, eh?" Marjie groused, still sprawled upon the ice patch and slowly trying to move. "I think I broke my rear end, and you stand there laughing at me like a donkey.

Here, help me up."

Chester stepped gingerly alongside Marjie on the slippery spot and bent over to take her hand, but as she took his hand, Marjie swept her right leg under his feet and pulled on his arm as well. Up went Chester's feet, and down plunged the rest of him, landing him hard next to Marjie.

Except for the rustling leaves from a nearby oak tree, for a moment there was silence. Then, just as suddenly, there was an explosion of laughter from both within the house and those who were spread across the icy sidewalk. Chester actually lay back on the ice and laughed and laughed.

"You don't mess with my wife," Jerry called out as he slid over and gave Chester a light shaking. "She's deadly."

Marjie was attempting to get to her feet and laughing so hard that the tears were streaking her red cheeks. "Somebody forgot . . . that I had two brothers I had to keep in line. That's one of the oldest moves in the book."

"Well done, might I add," Chester said between laughs, sitting up and watching Marjie dust the snow off her coat. "That . . . really . . . hurt."

"You're telling me," Marjie replied, turning toward the brick house and sweeping the snow from her backside as she walked away.

Jerry and Chester helped each other up off the ice and followed Marjie down the sidewalk. When Jerry slipped again, another round of laughter and yelling rang out.

Marjie stepped into the entryway to be greeted first by Margaret. She stood next to her pile of huge leather suitcases, her face a strange mixture of laughter and sadness.

"Oh, Margaret!" gasped Marjie, reaching out to hug her and hold her tight as they both began to cry. "I hate this . . . I hate this."

Bill and Clare Stanfeld stepped back toward the living room to make room for Jerry and Chester as they came into the entryway. All of the laughter evaporated as quickly as it had started, and Bill wrapped his arms around his wife and Chester.

Jerry put his arms around both Marjie and Margaret. Then he looked over at Chester, who stood next to his father wiping tears from his eyes and puffing his cheeks. Stepping away from the two women, Jerry went to his friend.

The two war buddies grabbed each other in a tight hug as waves of memories washed over them.

"You saved my life," Chester whispered, his head pressed against Jerry's.

"And you wouldn't give up on me," mumbled Jerry. "Guess you saved my life, too."

"I love you, friend."

"Same here. It won't be the same without you."

Marjie and Margaret continued to hug each other as well, and Marjie kept whispering, "I hate this . . . I hate this . . . I hate this."

"I know," whispered Margaret. "I know. I hate it, too. But we'll come back . . . someday."

"You'd better," Marjie said, "or I'll clip your husband's legs out again."

Margaret's hiccup of laughter was picked up by the others as they pulled back and swiped at their faces with fists and handkerchiefs.

"I'll never dance with you again," Chester said as he stretched his back muscles and arms. "It's like getting hit by lightning."

"You deserved it," Margaret said, still holding one arm around Marjie. "That will teach ye to laugh at yer friends' misfortunes."

"I guess," Chester agreed. "I'm just glad we're friends."

Marjie leaned her head against Margaret's shoulder and asked wistfully, "Can friendships be forever?"

"What?"

"Remember you said that some things last forever?"

"Surely."

"Do you think that friendships can last forever?"

"In heaven?"

"Yes."

Margaret pulled Marjie closer to her. "Oh, I do think so. Our Lord prayed, 'Thy will be done in earth, as it is in heaven.' If it's His will here today, why wouldn't it be His will forever? Surely we'll be together somehow in eternity."

"As friends."

"Why not? You're wantin' us for enemies, then?"

Marjie laughed and hugged her departing Scottish friend again. "No," she whispered, "but I'd like the Lord to give us some time together there to make up for what we're going to be missing here."

"Perhaps a century or two."

"At least," Marjie replied. "I think I'm going to be talking to Him about that real soon."

Chapter Nine

Stranger From Afar

"It was one of the strangest things I've ever experienced," Marjie said to Ruth shortly after the Thursday night prayer meeting had ended. Most of the large group were still gathered in small groups around the basement of the church. "We were just standing there waving goodbye and their car was rolling down that long driveway. I felt like I was watching a dream in slow motion, wanting to run after them, but I couldn't move. I wanted to call out for them to come back, but I knew that it was more important that they go."

"I don't think I could have taken it," Ruth said, shaking her head. "It's too much like sending somebody off to war—and I've done that too many times already."

"That's exactly what I felt, but I hadn't thought of it that way," Marjie said, putting her hand on Ruth's arm. "They really are going off to war, aren't they?"

Ruth nodded. "The more I've thought about it, the scarier it is to me. What the devil's done to this world is very real. Makes me very nervous for Margaret and Chester. They're thinking about invading a land that Satan's always controlled. I suspect he's not about to roll over and give it up without a fight."

"Well, I don't pretend to understand how much the devil does and how much people are responsible for," Marjie answered, "but I do think it's time we put Chester and Margaret on our regular prayer list."

Ruth nodded. "And not take them off."

"Say, do you know who that woman is who just came out of the bathroom?" Marjie asked, tipping her head toward the opposite corner of the basement. "I've never seen her before. She looks like she's about our age."

"I was going to ask you the same thing," Ruth replied, glancing over to where Marjie's eyes were pointing. "If she's from around here, she must be new. And I haven't heard about anyone moving in recently."

"Looks like she's coming over here," Marjie whispered. "She must know you."

"She doesn't know me," Ruth said, "and I have to go. That flu knocked me way behind in my class preparations. If I didn't feel so guilty about coming to your prayer meeting, I would have stayed home tonight."

"I don't—"

"Just teasing," Ruth interjected and laughed. Then she glanced back again and noticed that the other woman was standing politely, waiting for them to finish their conversation. "But I do have to go. See you Sunday."

"Wait," Marjie said, but Ruth was already on her way toward the coat racks. *Just like Jerry said*, she thought as she smiled at the stranger. "Hello, my name is Marjie Macmillan. I don't believe we've met."

"No, we've never met," the woman said. Her light brown hair was pulled back from a pale face, highlighting her delicate, soft features and hazel eyes. Her small nose and Cupid's-bow lips made Marjie think of an expensive china doll. "I'm from down in Lanesboro," she said, extending a thin hand, "and I've never been in your church before. My name is Agnes Humphreys. I'm pleased to meet you."

"I'm pleased to meet you, too," replied Marjie, taking the hand and giving it a shake. "You've come a long ways alone on a winter night. Do you know someone here?"

"No," Agnes replied, stepping closer to Marjie. "But I heard about your prayer meeting for loved ones who are off to war. I . . . just felt like I had to come. My husband left over two years ago, and I'd do anything to get him home safe. He's in Italy now, fighting the Germans."

"That's why you came?" Marjie asked, studying Agnes's wondering eyes. "Hoping that if you came, you'd be protecting your husband?"

"Not me, of course," the stranger replied softly. "God would."

"If you came, though?"

"It would help."

"If you came, God would see that you were

serious and make sure that your husband was protected?" Marjie asked. "Is that what you feel?"

Agnes Humphreys nodded. "I always figured that's how it works. I've never been a churchgoer, you see, but my nerves have gotten so bad that I can't take it anymore. I just started to go to church in Lanesboro, and when I heard about your meeting, this sounded even better."

Marjie looked around the room to see if Jerry or her mother were close by, but they were talking with their backs toward her. "Agnes, can we sit down for a moment?" she finally said.

"Sure. But I don't want to take all your time," replied Agnes as they sat down on the closest wooden folding chairs.

"I want you to know that prayer is very important," Marjie began carefully. "We really do believe that God hears our prayers and that He is caring for our loved ones. But . . . you need to know that you can't earn His protection. You can't bargain with God."

"A few weeks ago I told God that if He kept Howard safe, I'd go to church for the rest of my life," said Agnes, tightening her lips. "Are you saying that's wrong?"

Marjie put her hand on the stranger's arm and smiled. "I think I know something about what you're going through, Agnes. I spent what seemed like countless, endless nights tossing and turning, and I found myself trying to make deals with God to keep my husband safe. I really believe that God understood my heart. But I also believe that He loves us too much to make us bargain for His favor. His love and care for us is free, because He simply loves us first."

"It sounds too easy."

"Sure does," Marjie replied. "But let's say it's true that you must do things to stay on God's good side. How would you know when you've done enough? Is going to church once a week enough? Twice a week? If you give a dollar, would He be happier with two? Or should you give every cent you have? Does a one-hour prayer count for more than a five-minute prayer? Or should you pray all day? Where does it end? What if He's never pleased?"

"I can't imagine that He is, or that you'd think He is," Agnes said. "Don't you think that's sort of presumptuous?"

"Very presumptuous," Marjie agreed. "Unless God were to say it himself, right?"

"And you're saying God has spoken to you?" asked Agnes, shaking her head. "That sounds even more presumptuous."

"Or preposterous?" added Marjie.

"I guess," said Agnes, breaking her frown with a brief laugh. "I don't mean to hurt your feelings, but either way, I don't believe it."

"I didn't say that God had spoken to me alone," Marjie went on. "What if what God spoke was put down in a very clear, simple, written record for anyone and everyone to read and believe. Is that more believable?"

"I guess—if you can prove that God did that," Agnes replied.

"Here you go," Marjie said, handing Agnes her Bible with a smile. "This thing's got His handwriting all over it. I think you'll be amazed."

"I don't think so," said Agnes, taking the black leather book and staring at the shiny gold stamping on the front. "My father is a lawyer. He has no time for the Bible. Says it's no different than any other religious book, and they all can't be right."

"So you've taken his word for it and never read it?" asked Marjie.

"Father was right about almost everything," replied Agnes with a smile. "Besides, I never saw a reason to bother with it."

"Until now?"

Agnes nodded. "So you really believe that God has spoken and the words in this book are His?"

"Yes."

"I suppose you've always believed that?"

"No. It's been less than two years. I didn't have much time for the inside of a church either."

"Still, I don't think it's for me," Agnes said, handing the Bible back toward Marjie. "I—"

"Please," Marjie broke in, shaking her head. "You drove all the way out here tonight to pray for your husband. The Gospel of Mark is only sixteen chapters long. Surely it's worth giving it one shot. If you can read the book of Mark and come away still feeling it's not worth bothering with, I'll take the Bible back. But what if you discover that God is not silent? That you can know His thoughts?"

Agnes Humphreys looked deeply into Marjie's dark, confident eyes and finally gave a short laugh. "That's the strangest thing anyone's ever said to me. But how can I say no after a sales pitch like that?"

"You can't," Marjie replied, breaking into a grin. "But don't rush it. Give it a chance to be what it is."

"I'll do that," Agnes agreed. "And I'll let you know what I discover. But can I ask you one more question?"

"Sure."

"When people pray here, what happens?" asked Agnes. "Can you prove that what you ask for happens?"

"I can show you that many of the things we've prayed for actually worked out the way we asked," Marjie answered. "But not every prayer has been answered the way we requested it."

"Somebody mentioned to me about your brother," Agnes said.

Marjie nodded and took a deep breath. "Paul," she acknowledged. "We've prayed many times for his safety, but he was recently wounded in Italy."

"So it didn't work. The prayers didn't work."

"Not in the automatic way you're suggesting or the way I wanted it," Marjie answered. "God is a person, Agnes, not a wish-granting machine. I know this sounds really complicated, but there are times when we have to lay aside whatever our desire was and trust that God knows best. Sometimes His answer is no. Even God's Son, Jesus, found that to be true. He prayed that He wouldn't have to die, but He ended up dying anyway—for us."

"Is that in the book of Mark?"

"Yes. It's also in the books of Matthew, Luke, and John."

"Well," Agnes said with a sigh, "you've given me a lot to think about, and it sounds like I've got more reading to do than sixteen chapters. I can see it in your eyes that you believe what you're saying, but don't get your hopes up about me. To tell the truth, I think it sounds pretty strange."

"Coming from me, it may sound strange," Marjie replied, grinning again. "But what you read will not be strange. I guarantee that you'll discover something amazing."

"And that is?"

Marjie just smiled and said, "I'm not going to spoil it by telling you the story. Next time I see you, I expect you'll be telling me."

Two evenings later, Marjie was rocking Martha to sleep in the upstairs of the farmhouse when she heard Blue barking as a car came down the driveway.

"Great!" she whispered, looking down at her little girl's partially closed eyes. "You're just about out and here comes somebody to spoil it."

Marjie carefully stood up and kept rocking Martha in her arms as she went to peek out the bedroom window. She didn't recognize the car in the moonlight, but she could see that the driver getting out was a woman. "Who could it be?" she asked softly.

Walking over to the bedroom door, Marjie heard Jerry answer the knock on the farmhouse door, then heard him call out from the bottom of the stairs, "Marjie, you've got a visitor."

"Jerry," Marjie called back, "can you come up here? Martha's not quite to sleep yet."

"Da," Martha muttered in a sleepy voice.

"Yes, it's your daddy," Marjie whispered soothingly as she went to meet him at the top of the stairs.

"It's that woman you've had me praying for since the meeting the other night," he said softly. "She's got your Bible."

Passing Martha over to Jerry, Marjie quickly pushed back some loose strands of wavy brown hair and looked down at her everyday dress. "This old rag isn't even clean," she groused, scratching on a spot of dried carrots from Martha's supper.

"You look fine," Jerry spoke softly. "Just go down there. She's waiting."

"Talk about bad timing," Marjie sputtered as she dusted off the carrot residue and then headed down the steps.

Agnes Humphreys was standing on the throw rug by the front door as Marjie came through the stairway door. "I'm sorry if I've caught you at a busy moment," she said. "I could come back at another time."

"No, it's not a problem," Marjie answered, taking Agnes's coat and going to the closet to hang it up. "If you can put up with my crusty old dress, we'll get along just fine. How did you ever find our place?"

"I stopped at the parsonage," Agnes replied. "I figured they'd know where you lived. They seemed to think quite highly of you."

"Agh, I guess I've fooled them," Marjie said with a laugh, pointing toward the dining room table. "Would you care for a cup of coffee?"

"I would," Agnes said, "very much." She laid the Bible down on the table. "I've got some things that I need to talk with you about. Am I going to disrupt your evening plans?"

"No, not at all," Marjie answered, lighting the fire underneath the coffeepot to warm what was left over from dinner. "I was just going to do some reading is all."

Marjie brought a couple of china cups around the corner of the kitchen counter and set them on the dining room table, then she sat down across from Agnes. "I see you've brought my Bible with you. Did you get a chance to read it?"

"I sure did," Agnes replied with a smile, pushing the Bible toward Marjie. "I read what you said several times, and I think I'm finished with it. I appreciate you letting me use it."

"And did it live up to my billing?" Marjie

asked.

Agnes broke into a bright smile. "Let's just say you'll never be charged with false advertising. Your sales pitch was understated."

Marjie studied Agnes's expression. "Really?"

"Did you think it wouldn't?" asked Agnes.

"No . . . well . . . I wasn't sure how you'd react to what you read," Marjie replied. "So what happened?"

"Your coffee looks like it's boiling," said Agnes, pointing into the kitchen. "I could use a good stiff cup before I explain it to you."

"Coming up," Marjie said as she jumped out of her chair and went into the kitchen. She returned with the coffeepot and a hot pad for the table. Then she poured them each a cup and sat down.

Agnes took a sip of the hot liquid and set the cup back down on the table. "Were you praying for me the last two days?" she asked pointedly.

"I sure was," said Marjie. "Lots."

"That figures," Agnes said. "I stayed up really late reading through the book of Mark on Thursday, and it was as dry as dust. After I got my work done on Friday morning, I thought I'd give it one more chance, but I'd—well, I'd pretty much given up hope on it. Then I can't explain what happened, but I started to read and it was like a light went on inside my head. You're right; it is amazing. But it's confusing, too. Why would God become a man? What could possibly have compelled Him to become one of us and then willingly die such a dreadful death? Who could have dreamed up such a story? I was stunned by it."

"I still find it overwhelming," Marjie said, nodding her head. "I can't imagine ever figuring out why He loves us so. So, what did you do next?"

"I read and read and read some more," replied Agnes. "And the more I read, the more I saw; and the more I saw, the more convinced I was that it's true; but the more I believed, the worse I felt. I read about all those people Jesus met, and I saw the same sin and ugliness in my life. I didn't sleep much last night."

"You should have called," Marjie said. "God has an answer for that."

"Yes, I know," Agnes replied with another bright smile. "I did call the pastor of the church I've been going to. He was surprised, but he didn't seem to mind me coming over so late in the night. First he showed me some other Bible verses that explained exactly what I was feeling, then he asked me if I wanted to confess my sins and ask God to forgive them.

He said I could be forgiven because of what Jesus did on the cross. So I did ask for forgiveness. Is that what you did?"

"Yes," Marjie whispered, closing her eyes and nodding. "And you'll never regret it."

Chapter Ten

Rotten Cheese

"You can't do this, Marjie," Jerry said, placing the last of the silverware settings around the dining room table. "If it was anyone else, I'd be okay with it. But not the preacher and his wife."

"So what makes them off limits?" asked Marjie. She was tending several steaming pots on top of the stove in the kitchen. "You think they don't enjoy a good laugh now and then?"

"I think they probably do, but what if they get offended or something? The yarn in the muffins could really embarrass them."

"Not as much as the rotten cheese smell on Benjamin's silverware," Marjie said, breaking out into a laugh. "I can hardly wait to see what he does when he smells his fingers."

Jerry grinned. "It's been a long time since you pulled a trick like that on him. How'd you ever think this up?"

"Some things just come natural, I guess," Marjie said. "My grandmother used to put little pieces of yarn in cupcakes when she'd have visitors over. Then she'd sit there and wait for them to get the piece in their mouth and try to get it out without anyone noticing. I can still see her bouncing up and down in her chair, laughing so hard the tears would come down her face. But the spoiled cheese idea is mine. I think it's original, don't you?"

"I think it's one of the foulest odors I've ever smelled," Jerry said, laughing again. "After I doctored his silverware with it, I could hardly wash the stink off my fingers."

"Can you smell the silverware when it's sitting there?" asked Marjie.

"Not too much," Jerry replied. "If you go ahead and put the food on the table, Dad's not going to smell it."

"Good idea," said Marjie, pouring a large pan of green beans into a serving bowl. "They should be here soon. These beans are pretty powerful. We can set this bowl right in front of Benjamin's plate."

"Just in time. They're here already," Jerry called out, waving as Benjamin and Sarah's car drove past the dining room window. "Looks like they picked up the pastor and his wife."

"Quick!" Marjie called back, hurrying to

the table with the bowl of beans. "Let's get the food on before they come in."

By the time the guests had been welcomed in and were taking off their coats, Marjie was taking off her apron.

"Don't be bashful," Marjie called out from the corner of the kitchen. "You can sit wherever you like, but no complaints about the food—*Benjamin*."

"Starting right in on me, again," Benjamin played along, turning to the pastor and his wife as they walked to the chairs around the table. "Now you see why I moved out. I took that woman into my home when she didn't have a roof over her head, and she tormented me from the day she came. Shameful, ain't it, Fitch?"

"I reckon so," Pastor Fitchen said, wiggling his bushy eyebrows and patting his friend on the back. "Now I know that all those terrible stories you told me are true."

"You're gonna be sorry for any stories you've been telling behind my back," Marjie warned. "I—"

"Excuse me!" Sarah broke in. "Where is she?"

"What?" asked Marjie.

"Where . . . is . . . my . . . granddaughter?" asked Sarah, tapping her fingers on the top railing of her wooden chair.

"Oops!" Marjie cried, breaking into a laugh. "I knew there was something I'd forgotten. She's in the playpen in the living room."

"You're my own flesh and blood, and you forget where your own daughter is?" Sarah teased, grumping as she stepped away from the table to get Martha. "Have mercy on the second child, Lord."

"How've you been feeling, Marjie?" Dorothy Fitchen asked. "You look good."

"Go ahead and sit down," said Marjie, pulling back Martha's high chair. "I've felt a lot better this time around, thanks. Just about no morning sickness to speak of. I'm already starting to feel like a blimp, though. I can't believe it's going to take until July."

"Hundred degrees and high humidity," Jerry taunted, sitting down in his chair at the head of the table.

"Better hope she doesn't put you through the misery she did me," teased Benjamin. "Longest summer of my life."

"Go on," Marjie said to Benjamin as her mother came into the dining room carrying Martha. "You never had it so good."

Little Martha was greeted with the usual round of smiles and exclamations and a kiss from Benjamin before Sarah set her into the wooden high chair. Martha picked up the small spoon with the curved handle that Benjamin had given her at Christmas and promptly banged it down on the wooden tray. "Eeee," she demanded.

"Looks like the boss is hungry," Jerry said. "Pastor, would you lead us in prayer?"

Pastor Fitchen smiled and bowed his head. "Father in heaven, thank you for this food, and the hands that prepared it, and the dear fellowship you've given us. Amen."

"Wow!" exclaimed Marjie, reaching a cloth bib up around the baby's neck and tying it. "That was a shortie. I thought I'd have to tie Martha's hands to keep her quiet while you waxed eloquent."

"We had one rule about prayers at mealtimes when our children were little," Dorothy Fitchen said. "Short and sweet. No exceptions."

"It was a trial, I can assure you," the white-haired pastor said with a smile. He took a hot blueberry muffin and passed the basket to his wife.

"This roast beef looks mighty good, Marjie," Benjamin piped up, taking his fork in hand and dropping a big slab of meat on his plate. "She's a pretty good cook, Fitch, even if she does have a mean streak."

Marjie was busy mushing together some of the beans and potatoes for Martha, but she was watching Benjamin's movements as well. Glancing up at Jerry, who was sitting next to his father, she winked and pressed her lips together to stifle a giggle.

Jerry leaned over by Benjamin and took a couple of obvious whiffs at the air, then wrinkled his face. That he followed with a few more whiffs. "You . . . ah . . . did wash your hands, didn't you, Dad?" he said softly.

"What?" Benjamin replied, bursting out laughing. "Did I wash my hands? Sure I did. Why do you ask?"

"I got a whiff of something that smelled like . . . something," Jerry said, smiling but with a wrinkle across his forehead. Taking in another deep breath and shaking his head, he added, "Can't you smell it?"

Marjie was bouncing up and down in her chair, but fortunately for her, the others had turned their attention to Benjamin.

"Ah, it's just the green beans," Benjamin replied, still busy mashing his pile of potatoes.

"I don't think so," said Sarah, catching the scent as well and glancing over at Marjie. "Better check your hands, Ben."

"Oh, for crying out loud," Benjamin protested, setting his fork down and bringing his hand up to his nose. "You'd think I . . . ooooh . . . ooooh!" he moaned and his face soured.

"Oh my goodness!"

"What'd you bring in here?" Jerry cried, covering his nose and bursting out laughing.

A look of embarrassment crossed the Fitchens' faces before they realized that Jerry and Marjie and Sarah were laughing. Then they began to laugh as well. Benjamin slowly raised his right hand to verify that it really was as bad as he thought it was.

"Oh, brother, that is foul," Benjamin gasped, puffing out some of the contaminated air he'd taken in. "How in the world. . . ?"

"Better check your silverware," Sarah offered, breaking into a hearty laugh and looking over at Marjie again. "I think somebody's up to her old tricks."

Benjamin picked up his fork and stopped it a couple inches from his nose. "Bah! What is it?" he cried and grimaced again.

"Would you believe rotten cheese?" sputtered Marjie between laughs. "Isn't it terrible!"

"I can't believe you," Benjamin said, breaking into a smile and standing up with the fork in his hand. "This stuff had better wash off, or I may have to saw off my fingers. What do you think, Fitch?" Benjamin stuck the fork about six inches from the pastor's face.

"Ooh, that's wicked," he answered, covering his nose and laughing too. "I'm glad Marjie got you instead of me."

"You are lucky," Marjie said, turning her dark brown eyes on the pastor and noticing that he'd already buttered his muffin. "Say, how are the muffins? You might want to put a little more butter on them. Kinda dry, I'm afraid."

"No, they look fine," Pastor Fitchen replied cordially, picking up his muffin and taking a big bite. He smiled as the others looked on for his approval, but on his second chew he halted and frowned.

"Something wrong?" Dorothy asked, staring at her husband's strange behavior.

The elderly pastor tried to take another slow chew, but this time he raised his hand and covered his mouth. "Hmmm," he grunted while his tongue went to work, searching out the problem.

Once again Jerry and Marjie couldn't hold their laughter back, and Sarah and Dorothy and Benjamin joined in. Try as he might, Marvin Fitchen couldn't find a graceful way to solve his problem.

"It's my mother's old string in the cupcake trick," Sarah cried. "I haven't seen that one in years."

"Yarn!" Marjie blurted out, rocking in her

chair.

By now the pastor was laughing as well, but doing his best to cover his mouth. "Excuse me," he mumbled, rising to join Benjamin. "I'll be right back."

Benjamin went to work on his hand with a bar of soap in the kitchen sink, and Pastor Fitchen was relieved to clear out his mouth in the privacy of the bathroom. Both returned to find the group around the table still chuckling.

"Very funny, Marjie," said Benjamin as he sat back down at the dining room table. "May I eat now, or did you load my muffin, too?"

"Of course," Marjie replied with a smirk.

"You did, didn't you?" Benjamin railed, taking his knife and slicing the muffin into several pieces, then reaching in and pulling out a small piece of yarn. "Dorothy, you better check yours as well. Nothing's sacred in this house."

"I already found mine," the pastor's wife replied, holding up her piece like a trophy. "What a wonderful joke! I can't wait to try it on somebody. That would lighten things up around the parsonage, don't you think?"

"See what you started, Marjie," Sarah joined in. "People are gonna say you corrupted the pastor's wife."

"I'll bet you have some more tricks tucked

away, don't you, Marjie?" Dorothy asked.

"Not for this meal," Marjie replied, spooning in another mouthful of Martha's potatoes and green beans. "It's just too funny. I hope I didn't embarrass you too badly, Fitch."

The elderly pastor smiled and shook his head. "Not at all," he said, leaning back in his chair. "I love a good joke. I don't know how it happened to us, but Dorothy and I got too somber over the years. I suspect you noticed. I heard about a young teenager who was known to call me a *stuffed shirt*."

Jerry's face reddened, and he started to rub his forehead. "Is this a forced confession?"

"No," Dorothy cut in before her husband could speak. "Just the truth."

"I always said that preachers live too close to the church," Benjamin said. "It's like you never get away from it. Need a little fresh air and lots of space, I'd say."

"Probably would be a good idea," the pastor said as he carefully sliced his chunk of beef. "But lately, it hasn't seemed to matter."

"What do you mean?" asked Jerry.

"Well, maybe Dorothy can explain it better than I can," Pastor Fitchen replied. "But in the last months, especially since some of those difficult church meetings we had, I've had more people in my office asking for help than I've had in years and years of ministry."

"It's a very quiet thing," Dorothy added. "I don't think people are even talking to each other about it. But there's hardly a day when someone doesn't stop in. Fitch thinks it was the result of those meetings, but I think it was when he prayed with Mr. Biden."

"That's amazing," Marjie said. "What are the people asking about?"

"Boy, you name it," the elderly pastor replied, rubbing his eyebrows. "Some are coming to Christ for the very first time, although they've been church members for decades. Some have apologized for some things they had been holding against me. Others just need someone to pray with them."

"And all that's happening right here in Greenleafton?" asked Jerry.

"That's right," Pastor Fitchen said with a smile. "It's been like . . . a dream come true. While I was in seminary, this is what we talked about and hoped for. But it never seemed to work out this way for me . . . until now."

"We feel like it's an extraordinary gift," Dorothy added. "Like the Lord is making up for all the dry years when it didn't seem like Fitch's ministry was making any difference."

"Course, we've changed, too," the pastor acknowledged. "We didn't even realize those were dry years. We just thought they were normal." He paused to take a sip of water. "You know, I'd really like to tell the church about what's happened to me. Do you think I should?"

"Sounds like a great idea," Benjamin said. "Why wouldn't you?"

"I'm not sure," he answered. "It's very personal, for one thing. I'm afraid that I'll get all choked up. And I'm not even sure if I can describe what's happened to me or why. I just know that I've never experienced the peace of God so deeply in my life and that it's spilled over into my ministry. I finally have relaxed enough to let God do what He wants to do. It's an overwhelming peace. . . . I think I finally know what it means to say that God is in control, because He is my Father and He loves me."

"My goodness," Sarah said, rubbing her fingers together. "This is one sermon I don't want to miss."

Chapter Eleven

Reunited

"At least this car's got a heater," Marjie said, leaning forward in the front seat of Benjamin's car and scanning the roadway ahead of them. "Four hours in *our* car and we'd either be icicles or penguins by now. That's got to be the Veteran's Hospital up there. Look at all those buildings."

"Yeah, I remember seeing that when Chester and I got our bus ride out to Fort Snelling to sign up for the navy," Jerry replied. "Chester thought it was kind of spooky to drive us new recruits past the Vet's Hospital. He wondered if the navy was sending us a message that we'd better think about what we were doing."

"Did you?" Sarah asked from the backseat, where she was cuddled up next to Benjamin.

"Some, I suppose," Jerry said, slowing down to turn right on the road that led toward the large hospital complex. "At that point I was so lovesick for Marjie that I wasn't thinking too clearly about anything."

"And I was still crying in Rochester," Marjie added, still gazing ahead. "Suppose I'll be crying again today. Which building do you think he's in?"

"His letter said that he's in the main hospital," replied Benjamin. "Take the next left, go straight into the big parking lot, and he said the signs would be clear enough."

Signaling his turn, Jerry turned off the main road into the hospital's parking lot and slowed down, then pulled into an empty spot. "Whew!" he exclaimed, leaning his head back and giving a deep sigh. "We made it. And it's not even noon yet."

"You must be exhausted if you started milking at four," Sarah said as she pulled out her scarf to tie around her hair. "Glad you could get Billy to milk the cows tonight. It's going to be late before we get home."

"I'm glad that Ruthie could take care of Martha all day," Marjie added. "Don't feel too bad for Billy, though. He's gonna go down the hill and grab his younger brother to do the milking. There's no way his leg could take all that bending and lifting."

Benjamin pulled himself forward in the backseat and looked toward the hospital's main entrance doors. "You ready for this, Sarah?" he asked, then he took her hand and squeezed it tightly. "Two and a half years is a long time."

Nodding, she pinched her lips together and took in a deep breath. "I'm scared, Ben . . . really scared," she said softly. "I want to run through those doors and find him, but I'm afraid I won't know what to say to him, or I'll say the wrong thing. And I don't know what he thinks of me marrying someone he's never even met."

"I'm scared, too, Ma," Marjie said, turning around and looking into her mother's weathered face. "But not enough to sit here when

I could be seeing Paul. Let's go!"

"I'm right behind you!" Sarah exclaimed. Both women had pushed their car doors open and climbed out before Benjamin and Jerry had gotten grips on their car door handles.

"Wait up!" Jerry called out as he and Ben slammed their doors shut and hurried after them. But the mother and daughter didn't even look back. They pushed open the wide wooden entrance doors and headed straight through the busy visitor's lobby toward the main receptionist's desk.

"May I help you?" the brunette receptionist asked, looking up with a courteous smile.

"I hope so," Marjie replied, putting her hand on the top of the desk. "We're here to see a patient who's only been here a few days. His name is Paul Livingstone. Sergeant Paul Livingstone."

The attractive receptionist smiled and tapped her pencil thoughtfully on the desk. "Tall, muscular, wavy black hair, a strong, chiseled face, and gorgeous brown eyes just like yours?"

A look of bewilderment spread over both Marjie's and Sarah's faces. "That's Paul," Marjie answered. "You apparently know him?"

"Never heard of him," she replied with a

shrug of her shoulders, tapping the desk again, then she looked down and started searching through her pages of patients' names. "I just figured he might look like you and your mother."

"What?" sputtered Marjie, glancing over at Sarah. "How do you know she's my mother? Look, I don't know what your game is, but I don't think it's a bit funny. Would you please tell us where we can find Paul Livingstone."

The receptionist stopped smiling, leaned as far forward as she could toward Marjie's face, and opened her eyes wide. Then she turned slightly to look into Sarah's face and whispered, "He's . . . right . . . behind . . . you."

Marjie felt an arm wrap around her at the very moment a body pressed against Sarah from behind, but both were too shocked to turn. However, their lungs were working fine as they met the receptionist's bizarre stare with a simultaneous scream that turned every head in the lobby.

Benjamin and Jerry, who had spotted Paul sneaking up behind Marjie and Sarah, stood back watching as the threesome turned suddenly into one mass of arms and hugs and kisses and crying and laughing. The two Macmillan men roared with laughter and joined several onlookers who started clapping their hands and calling out their congratulations. It was a scene that had been played out many times in the Minneapolis Veteran's Hospital lobby over the past two years.

It was several minutes before the wave of emotion subsided. Stopping between moments of laughter and tears to look at her brother, Marjie was surprised by what she saw. He had lost a lot of weight, as she had expected. But instead of wearing a hospital gown and a bathrobe, Paul was decked out in his army dress uniform. His left arm was tucked inside the dress coat and appeared to be held up with a sling.

With his mother's head buried against his chest, Paul leaned over and spoke softly into her ear, "I made it, Ma. They couldn't kill me."

Another round of tears erupted, and the two women clung to him and squeezed him as tight as they dared. Marjie could feel her brother tremble as the tears streamed down his face. Since they were small children, she couldn't remember Paul ever displaying his feelings like that, not even when he had left for the army six months before the war began.

Other hospital visitors had come in and

were waiting to speak to the receptionist, so Jerry stepped forward. "Maybe we better move out of the way. There are some chairs back over in that far corner. Why don't we go over there?"

Without letting go of each other, the threesome stepped away from the desk and moved silently toward the corner.

"Are you with them?" the receptionist asked Jerry as he started to turn away.

"Yeah," replied Jerry with a polite nod. "He's my brother-in-law."

"You got five bucks?" the woman asked, tapping her pencil again. "He said he'd pay me full price if I could fool your wife. He owes me, don't you think?"

"I reckon he does," Jerry said, shaking his head and laughing again. As he pulled out his billfold and handed her a couple of bills, he said, "Here's five, and the other's a tip. Did you ever think of acting?"

"Nope," she said with a smile. "This pays better."

Jerry laughed and turned to join his reunited family. Fortunately for them, another family had just cleared out from the corner of the lobby, leaving half a dozen metal folding chairs for them to take. Paul and Marjie and Sarah sat down on three chairs bunched together. Jerry and his father pulled two other chairs up close and joined them.

"It's great to see you, Paul," Jerry said, reaching out and shaking his right hand. "You look good."

"Thanks," replied Paul, placing his right hand back down on top of Sarah's hand. "I'm mighty glad to see you, too. Marjie wrote me that they couldn't kill you either."

"I'm still kicking," said Jerry. "I didn't see the action you did, though."

"How's my little sister treating you?" Paul asked, stepping down on Marjie's shoe. "I think she's lost her tongue."

Without lifting her head from Paul's chest, Marjie muttered, "Get off my toe or I'll pull your hair, you big bully."

Paul burst out into a hearty laugh, and the others joined in. "Nasty as ever, aren't you?" he said. "And you an expectant mother, too. I thought you'd be nice to me at least for the first day."

"Why's that?" Marjie asked, pulling her head back and staring into his dark brown eyes. "You go and get caught behind the German lines, then you get shot up and scare us half to death. I'm mad at you."

"Good," said Paul, laughing some more. "Nothing's changed, then."

"A few things have," Sarah spoke softly, taking Paul's right hand in both of hers and kissing him lightly on the cheek. "I'd like you to meet your stepdad, Benjamin Macmillan."

"Pleased to meet you, Paul," Benjamin said, reaching out to shake Paul's hand. "I've heard a lot of good things about you."

Paul had to pull his hand away from Sarah in order to meet Benjamin's. "I'm pleased to meet you, sir. I've heard a lot about you as well—or read a lot, anyway. You get high marks from Ma and Marjie. I'm happy for the two of you. Ma deserves a good man. But I have to admit your getting married did surprise me a bit."

"Surprised us all," Benjamin followed, returning Paul's attentive gaze. "I never expected to remarry after Jerry's mother died. But I didn't do very well as a bachelor. Marjie rescued me."

"You can say that again," Marjie agreed. "He's the worst cook I've ever seen . . . followed by his son."

"You're not as old looking as Marjie said in her letters," Paul said, glancing over at Benjamin and smirking.

"I never said that," Marjie sputtered, sitting back in her chair. "Now stop teasing and get serious for a minute. I want to know about your shoulder. I thought you'd be all bandaged up."

Paul smiled and leaned back. "You forget

it's been over three months, Marjie. I'm about as healed as I'm gonna get. Do you wanta see it?"

"Well, I guess," Marjie spoke haltingly. "Do you mind?"

"No," Paul replied, unbuttoning his green dress coat with his right hand and pushing it back to reveal his left arm and hand for the first time. He was wearing a white shirt, and a cotton sling held his arm in position. His closed left hand looked a bit blue in contrast to the white shirt. "I can put a shirt on by myself now and get it off as well," he said as he unbuttoned the shirt and worked at tugging it out from underneath the sling. "Can you help me with this, Marjie?"

Reaching over, Marjie took the fabric of the shirt that was pinched at the top by the sling and gently tugged it loose. It fell back to reveal a deep dent in Paul's left shoulder and upper arm. Red, purplish scar tissue had healed over the crevice left behind by the German bullet.

"Oh my goodness!" Marjie gasped, covering her mouth and moving back. Tears once again formed at the corner of her eyes.

Sarah laid her hand on Paul's motionless left hand and mumbled softly to herself.

"That hand's cold, ain't it, Ma?" Paul spoke quietly. "Circulation's not so good.

Probably shoulda let that surgeon take the arm, but I had to try. Doesn't look like I'll ever use this arm again, though."

"Does it hurt?" asked Jerry.

"It aches, but it don't hurt like it did," said Paul. "Feels like a dull headache, except it's in my shoulder. I can live with it."

"What about rehabilitation?" asked Marjie. She lifted her hand and gently ran her fingers across the wound. "We thought—"

"That's what I'm doing," Paul broke in. "They're teaching me how to get along with one arm."

Sarah continued to rub his cold hand. "Can you feel my hand?" she asked, looking up at her son.

"Oh yeah," said Paul. "I can feel. I just can't move it. The muscles and everything in my shoulder are all shot."

"If you can feel, then it's not useless," Sarah said. "I love this hand."

Paul smiled into his mother's face but couldn't speak. All he could do was keep nodding.

"You're welcome to come live with us, Paul," Benjamin offered. "Your room is still there, and if you think you want to take over the farm, Sarah and I can work out a deal with you."

Shaking his head, Paul took a breath and

said, "That's a mighty fine offer, but I'm not interested in the farm. I've been thinking about what I'm going to do ever since the nurse told me I wasn't going to die, and I'd like to try to find work here in Minneapolis. I figure there must be some factories that need a tough sergeant like myself to make sure their employees are working hard. I already started checking around. There's a lot of jobs here if I can just figure out how to get my pants on without some nurse's help."

They all broke out laughing, and Paul reached up and pulled his shirt back over his damaged shoulder.

"Ma said you'd fight your way back through this," Marjie said, helping him button the shirt back into place. "I really didn't expect you to be able to joke about it, though."

"You either joke about it or you cry," Paul replied, leaning back as she did the top button. "I've watched too many men die to do much crying over this. And if you saw the mangled bodies I've been seeing since I got shot, you'd understand why I'm thankful still to be in one piece."

"We're thankful," Jerry added solemnly. "Thanks be to God."

"Yes," Paul continued, smiling again, "thanks be to God! In fact, I'd like to celebrate."

"What?" asked Marjie. "How?"

"I heard there's a great steakhouse in downtown Minneapolis. Murray's, I think they call it," Paul said. "I'd like to treat you all to the biggest steaks we can get our mitts on! How about it?"

"If you're paying, let's go!" Marjie exclaimed, kissing her brother on the cheek. Then she stepped on his toe as she jumped to her feet.

Chapter Twelve

Mud Puddles

"Only in Minnesota, eh?" Marjie piped up as Pastor Fitchen opened the parsonage door to welcome her in. "One day it's a frozen tundra; the next the roads turn to a slimy ooze."

"I love the warmer weather," he replied, stepping out of the big white house onto the concrete steps and stretching in the early spring sunshine. "It's supposed to get up near sixty today. Bet it won't last, though."

"The road's going to be a disaster if the temp drops back down," Marjie said, turning around and pointing down the gravel road toward the west. "Look at those ruts. They're so deep, I wasn't sure if I was going to get through."

"The first snowstorm we had came before the ground froze—that's why it's so soft," the elderly pastor said. "It's going to be a few weeks before the roads dry up . . . if we're lucky."

"You'd better talk to the deacons about getting some fresh rock on your driveway," Marjie said. "Looks like it's been a few too many years of pinching pennies."

"Why don't you put a good word in to your husband?" Pastor Fitchen replied. "He and Billy Wilson can pull some strings. Two good truckloads of gravel would make a big difference."

"I'll see what I can do," Marjie replied. "I thought the pastor from Lanesboro would be here by now. Did you hear anything more from him?"

Pastor Fitchen looked up the road and shook his head. "Nope. He should be here anytime now. I think he's bringing along an elder from his church, too. We may as well go in and get comfortable."

"Where's Dorothy?" Marjie asked as they made their way down the long hallway toward the pastor's study.

"She's getting ready to go to Preston," Pastor Fitchen replied. He followed Marjie into the study and removed a small stack of books from a chair so that she could sit down. Then he moved to his desk and sat smiling at her over unruly piles of papers and study books. "She hates to drive, but she hates waiting for me to go along even worse. I'm afraid I drag my feet a bit when it comes to shopping. There's nothing tires me out faster than walking around stores looking at stuff I don't need."

"That sounds familiar," Marjie said with a laugh. "Jerry's not been in a store since he got out of the navy!"

"He's a man after my own heart," the pastor responded.

"So just what are we supposed to talk to the Lanesboro pastor and elder about?" asked Marjie.

"He called and asked if you and I would get together with them to outline how you've organized and run the prayer meeting for loved ones who are in the war," Pastor Fitchen replied. "After what happened with Agnes Humphreys, I guess they sat up and took notice. I wouldn't be surprised if some of the other pastors in the area knock on your door and ask about your prayer meeting."

"Ahhh," Marjie murmured, shaking her head and turning away for a second. "So what's the big deal? You don't need some kind of fancy program. Just call a meeting, get together, and pray. That shouldn't take long to discuss."

"It shouldn't, but it probably will," said the pastor with a smirk. "Most of us pastors like outlines and details and time frameworks. But I think you underestimate some of the things that you've done to make the prayer meeting successful."

"Like what?" Marjie asked. "Serving coffee?"

Rubbing his index finger along the bottom of his lip, Pastor Fitchen nodded and said, "I think that's helped people relax and be themselves. Actually, you're going to think this is funny, but I've made a list of things that you've done that you're probably not even aware of."

"You're serious?"

Pastor Fitchen lifted a piece of paper from one of the piles on his desk and waved it at her.

"Let me see that," Marjie demanded, leaning forward and reaching out her hand.

"No chance," the elderly pastor replied, breaking into a laugh. Then he opened one of the desk drawers and dropped the sheet of paper into it. "These are my notes for the meeting. If you look at them now, you'll try to deny that they're true and spoil what could be a helpful time for these men from Lanesboro."

"You are as ornery as an old mule," Marjie sputtered, half joking and half serious. "Give me a hint, at least, or I'll go home."

"You're not going anywhere," Pastor Fitchen replied. "And I'll tell you this much about my list. There are some things you've done with the prayer meeting that help make it work better than any prayer meeting we've ever had in the church. But I think what's more important, and the part these people are going to want to know about, is the kind of person who's in charge of the meeting."

"You think they're going to want to know about me?" Marjie asked, sitting back in her chair.

"Yes. And I'm going to tell them," the pastor replied. He was all smiles again as he pointed down at the desk drawer.

"Now I'm really nervous," Marjie said. "Why didn't you warn me?"

"You didn't ask."

"But I already told you that I don't know beans about prayer," Marjie protested. "Now you're going to let them embarrass me—"

"They will not," Pastor Fitchen broke in. "I keep telling you it's not about how much you know, although that's helpful. It's a lot more about how friendly you are, how caring, how sincere. I'd think by now you'd be thanking me instead of getting all worried again."

"Why?"

"Think of Agnes Humphreys," the elderly man reasoned, leaning forward on the desk. "You nearly quit the prayer meeting before she had a chance to come."

"So."

"So . . . come on, you're too smart for this," he continued. "Your meeting provided her with an opportunity to have a personal need met, and through that she came to discover what faith means. Did you answer all her questions about prayer?"

"No."

"So, did she walk away?"

"No, but—"

"Don't you see that however much you did or didn't know, you made a difference in that young woman's life?" Pastor Fitchen asked. "You have a gift for this, Marjie, and it's not something everyone has. I think it's a wonderful gift, and you almost gave up before Agnes opened her heart to you."

Marjie gave a deep sigh and rubbed her cheek. "Every time I come in here to talk, you sucker me in deeper and deeper. I think you're just buttering me up so I'll do more of your work for you. We pay you too much, you know."

The elderly pastor laughed and closed his eyes for a moment. "I'm an old man," he said softly, "so you need to remember to give me more respect. My fees are high because you're benefiting from all of the wisdom I've gained over the years . . . and because I have to put up with so much ingratitude."

"Okay, you squeezed it out of me," Marjie said with some laughter of her own. "You were right about sticking with it, and I am really grateful for that. But I reserve comment on what you're going to say to these men about me today. It better be good, or I'll let you have it."

The creaking of the wooden floor in the hallway outside the pastor's study brought their bantering to a temporary halt, and a light knock on the door was followed by the sight of Dorothy Fitchen's cheerful face in the doorway.

"I'm leaving now, so I thought I should say goodbye," she said to her husband with a bright smile. "I didn't want to interrupt, but it sounded like you must be telling jokes in here. What's all the laughing about?"

Pastor Fitchen raised his bushy eyebrows and replied, "Marjie's giving me a hard time—like she did when we ate over at their house. First she tries to choke me with a piece of yarn, and now she tells me that I'm getting paid too much."

"And you love every minute of it," Dorothy said, winking at Marjie. "Keep it up, Marjie. He's been on the grouchy side lately, so he needs all the laughs he can get. See you later."

Just as quickly as she appeared, Mrs. Fitchen was gone and down the hallway. The sound of the front door shutting returned the house to silence.

"I don't deserve a woman who's so good to me," Pastor Fitchen said, shaking his head as he glanced out the window. "I haven't been much fun to be with the last couple days."

"I noticed your desk looks like it's piled to China," Marjie observed. "Something wrong?"

"I don't think so, but Dorothy does," the pastor replied. "I'm so tired all the time. Feel like I'm dragging this old body around against its will."

"You been to the doc?" asked Marjie.

"No. What's he going to tell me except that I'm getting old and feeble? If he was giving out pep pills, I'd go today," he replied, glancing back out the window and then slowly standing up. "Oh no, Dorothy backed up too far. Looks like she's got the back wheels stuck. I'd better get out there and help her."

Hearing the revving of the car's engine and

the whir of tires, Marjie followed the pastor out of the study and down the hallway. She thought his steps seemed heavy and measured as he plodded toward the front door. Neither of them bothered to grab their coats as they stepped out into the warm spring sunshine.

"Hold it!" Pastor Fitchen called out to his wife, waving his hands for her to stop spinning the tires.

Dorothy Fitchen rolled down her window as Marjie and the pastor came alongside the idling car. "Guess I went a little too far," she said with a sheepish grin.

"I can't argue with that," Pastor Fitchen agreed. "But it doesn't look too bad. Now wait until I get in back of the car to push. And this time, you have to rock the car back and forth, or else she's going to drop down. You know what to do, right?"

"Yeah," Dorothy replied, nodding. "I should have thought of it in the first place."

Pastor Fitchen stepped around a couple of large mud puddles, then moved onto the soggy lawn in the back of the car. Marjie was right on his heels. "No, you don't have to help, Marjie. Let me get it."

"Just be quiet and move over to the other side," Marjie teased, giving him a slight nudge. "You're going to need all the help you can get."

"Well, you're probably right," he answered, putting his hands up against the back of the car and leaning against it like he was too tired to push. Then he called out, "Okay, Dorothy. Try it. Back off when the tires start to spin."

Marjie readied herself to push, and Dorothy carefully edged the car forward, then quickly reversed when the back left wheel started to spin. After the fourth cycle of rocking, the car felt like it had enough motion to come up out of the divot the spinning tires had dug.

"Give it to her!" Pastor Fitchen called out as his wife was shifting into first gear again.

Dorothy responded by shoving down the accelerator, which caused the left wheel to spin at a hundred miles an hour. With the motion and acceleration, though, the car had enough traction to creep up off the lawn and onto the driveway. But Dorothy didn't let off on the gas, and the left rear wheel was still whirling when it dropped into one of the huge mud puddles. A wall of brown water sprayed straight backward from the car, soaking the front of Marjie's skirt from the waist down.

Marjie's scream was partially muffled by the roar of the car engine and the continued spinning of the tires as the car finally caught hold of gravel and lurched down the driveway. Then the car crunched to a halt and the engine quieted as Dorothy Fitchen flung the door open.

"Don't you dare laugh, and don't you dare say a word!" Marjie called out her warning to the pastor. His mouth was wide open, but only the slight trace of a smile was cutting its way across his face. "Oh, look at me!" Marjie cried.

Her white maternity blouse was speckled with wet mud, but the real damage was to the cotton plaid skirt. Big clusters of mud clung to the fabric, and the brown water had soaked through to her skin. She stood there, frozen in place, with muddy drops falling down onto her waterlogged shoes.

"Marjie, I'm so sorry!" cried Mrs. Fitchen, jumping out of the car and walking quickly back toward them. Pastor Fitchen still hadn't moved or spoken. "It's all my fault. I—"

"It's okay, Dorothy," Marjie interrupted. She reached down and tried to wipe away some of the greasy mud, but succeeded only in smearing it around worse. "It was an accident. It'll wash out, I think. Besides, I won't be able to fit into this skirt much longer, anyway."

The sound of wheels turning into the parsonage driveway caught their attention, and they looked up.

"Oops," the elderly pastor said softly. "Looks like it's the people from Lanesboro."

"And you said I wasn't going to be embarrassed by these guys!" Marjie exclaimed. "Try again, Fitch."

Chapter Thirteen

Fox Trot

"It's a long walk down there if those baby foxes aren't out like you say they will be," Marjie protested as she finished buttoning Martha's light coat.

"The years must be creeping up on you, Mother," Jerry taunted, standing in the front doorway of the farmhouse. "Wasn't so long ago you were walking all over this farm. Now I have to drag you out on the most gorgeous spring day we're going to get."

Marjie silently tucked Martha's pants legs into her boots, then whispered in her ear, "Okay, you're ready. Go to Daddy!"

"Da!" the little girl called. As fast as her clomping boots would allow her, she ran across the dining room floor and leaped into Jerry's arms. He scooped her up and gave her a big hug and kisses. Since the day that she had taken her first steps, Marjie wondered if Martha ever actually walked. Everything Martha did she seemed to do at a flat-out gallop.

"Have a nice walk," Marjie said, smiling and sitting down at the kitchen table. "I believe I'll take advantage of this and have myself a nice nap while you're taking care of sweetie pie."

"Come on, we gotta get out there soon," Jerry insisted. "The mother fox seems to stick around right after lunch. That's when I've seen them out of the den, playing around. Five pups."

"You go on," Marjie replied, glancing out the window at the budding elm trees. "I'm over six months' pregnant, *Pa*. I need my rest."

"Okay, I shouldn't have called you *Mother*," Jerry confessed and laughed. "But you need your exercise, too."

"Chasing that little whirlwind all day doesn't qualify as exercise?" Marjie asked, slowing rising from the wooden chair and lightly running her hands over her extended abdomen. "And if you ever call me *Mother* again, you're on permanent dish duty. Do you understand what that means?"

"Get your coat."

"Try again."

"Please get your coat," Jerry said, breaking out in laughter. "Do it for me. I really want you to get a chance to see the baby foxes. With the warm breeze and the sunshine, I'm sure they're out."

"Okay, you win," Marjie said. She went to the closet and grabbed her red sweater rather than a coat. "I'd kinda like to ride Charlie out there. Maybe you could—"

"Let's just walk it," Jerry interrupted, pushing open the farmhouse screen door and letting Marjie go through first. "If we're going to get close enough to spot the foxes, we need to be as quiet as possible. Besides, you've been taking Charlie out almost every day since the ground firmed up. It's not like the poor horse isn't getting any exercise. I think—"

He was interrupted by Martha's excited squeal. "Boo!"

"So what about old Blue Boy?" Marjie asked as the Australian cow dog came racing up from the barn. "I suppose he's going to be real silent, too. I'll bet Martha won't say a peep either."

"Get back to the barn, Blue," Jerry ordered, pointing toward the open door to the milk room. Blue's tail and ears dropped simultaneously, and his large brown eyes looked up in a sincere beg. "Forget it, Blue.

We have to lock you up for a little while. You'd spoil it for sure."

"Boy, you're serious about this, aren't you?" Marjie said as Blue turned quickly and trotted back into the barn with his tail still dragging. "No dog, no horse, no noise. What if Martha spoils it with some interesting chatter?"

Shrugging his shoulders and pushing the barn door shut, Jerry replied, "If she does, she does. We'll just have to chance it."

"Slim odds, sailor boy."

Jerry put Martha down on the ground and took her one hand while Marjie took the other, and the threesome headed down the farm lane.

"Didn't you say the den was hidden in the woods beyond the Seven Corners hayfield?" Marjie asked.

"Yeah, just below the ridge that leads down to the creek. We can get pretty close without being seen. The female usually stays around the den and watches, but today might be the day."

"The day for what?"

"Wouldn't it be fun to have a fox for a pet?" Jerry asked.

"You're not serious."

"I sure am," replied Jerry, breaking out into a laugh. "Dad claimed that my grandpa caught a baby skunk once and kept it in the barn as a pet. Said it was a better mouser than any cat he ever had."

"And he never got sprayed?"

"Nope," Jerry said matter-of-factly. "He did a little surgery on the pair of glands near the base of the skunk's tail. So much for that problem."

"Sounds pretty strange to me," Marjie said, pushing back her long wavy brown hair after a gust of wind blew it into her face. "So you think you could tame a baby red fox if you caught it?"

Martha began to fuss about walking, so Jerry picked her up and swung her up on his shoulders.

"I'd like to try," Jerry said. "Why not?"

"Why?"

"For the fun of it."

"A fox belongs in the wild where God put it," Marjie said. "If I start raising chickens, I'm sure that a fox hanging around the barn would be a great combination."

"I still think it'd be fun to try," Jerry replied, kicking an oak branch to the side of the farm lane. "Actually, I did catch one a long time ago, when I was just a kid, but it got away. Guess I was trying to be like Jack. When he was ten or eleven, he caught this baby raccoon and tried to keep him as a pet.

He called him Bandit because of his black mask. But the older he got, the wilder he got. By the end of the summer, the only way Jack could handle him was with big leather gloves."

"Boy, that does sound like fun," Marjie teased. She put a hand on Jerry's arm as they cut down the hill toward the Seven Corners hayfield. "No wonder you wanted to be just like your big brother. You could've gotten your hands torn to shreds too."

"Well, Jack should have let him go earlier," Jerry replied. "But he'd been so much fun when he was little that I guess it was hard to give him up. You should have seen him when Jack put a marble in the bottom of a glass jar of water. He'd reach his paw down in the water and stir and stir, trying to get his paws around that marble. We'd laugh so hard, but he wouldn't give up."

Marjie laughed along with Jerry, and she shut her eyes momentarily as the warm spring breeze massaged out some of the tiredness she had been feeling. "Where'd your brother keep the coon? In the barn?"

"Yeah," Jerry answered, laughing again. "When we were milking, he'd come walking past, and I'd squirt him right in the face with a blast of warm milk. He loved the milk, but boy, he hated having his face dirty. He'd sit down and lick and lick and lick. Once he'd get all cleaned up, Jack'd give him another shot."

"That's mean," said Marjie through a chuckle. "Sounds like the time I caught a little sparrow that was just out of the nest and couldn't fly yet. Paul and I thought we could teach it tricks and maybe have a circus act with our prize bird. We kept it in a wooden box in the old chicken coop and made a little wire trapeze that we hung from the roof. Every day we'd drag that terrified little sparrow out of the box and set him on the trapeze. He'd just sit there, and we'd swing the wire back and forth."

"Did you feed him?" Jerry asked.

"Oh sure," Marjie said. "We had a tuna can of water in his box, and we brought him crushed corn and any bugs we could catch. He must have been eating something, because he survived a week of our torment. After a couple days we got him to fly from our hands to the trapeze, and we thought we were on our way to the big top. But one day Teddy came and opened the door to the chicken coop just as Paul was taking the bird out of the box. That little sparrow cruised straight out the door and past Teddy's head so fast we hardly knew what happened. Paul beat on poor little Teddy, and I cried like I'd lost my best friend."

Jerry and Marjie both were laughing as they approached the edge of the woods. Placing Martha back down on the ground, Jerry lifted the barbed-wire fence as high as he could stretch it and helped Marjie pass safely underneath it. Then he helped Martha scoot down and crawl underneath it as well, following her with a roll of his own that got him past the barbs without catching.

Taking Martha's hand, Jerry started into the woods. "Okay. We're going to come around the side of the hill, and we have to be quiet now. There's a ridge that we'll crawl out to the edge of, and if the foxes are out of the den, we should be able to see them below us. The female usually sticks pretty close to the den. We'll follow this cow path around the hill."

Coming to the first cluster of prickly gooseberry bushes sandwiched between a couple of huge burr-oak trees, Jerry picked Martha up and carefully pushed away the branches as they made their way down the path deeper into the woods. Marjie had to stop and pull out a branch of sharp needles that got tangled with her sweater, but she soon caught back up as they came around the side of the hill to where the sun was shining brightly.

"There's the ridge," Jerry whispered, carefully setting Martha down on the ground and taking her hand. She looked up at him and giggled as he put his finger in front of his mouth and said, "Shhh. Gotta be quiet, sweetheart."

"I better take her," Marjie said softly as she took Martha's hand from Jerry's. "You lead the way."

Marjie and Martha slowly followed Jerry toward the ridge. When he got within ten yards, he fell down on his knees and crawled, motioning for Marjie and Martha to get down as well. Marjie managed to get down on her knees, and Martha seemed to think it was a game and followed suit. Together they crept through the brown grass and weeds until they were alongside Jerry.

Inching forward, Jerry maneuvered his head over the edge of the ridge and peered down the steep slope. "Look!" he whispered without turning his head toward Marjie. "Quick!"

Marjie poked her head up over the ridge and scanned down toward the creek. Just as Jerry had said, all five red fox pups were out of the den enjoying the warmth of the sunshine. Two of them were lying fast asleep some twenty yards or so from the partially exposed hole in the ground that led to their den. Two other pups were chasing each other up and down a knoll that was even farther away. Marjie spotted the mother lying on a rock that was several yards up the hill from the den, and then she noticed a fifth pup way off on his own exploring the edge of the creek.

"What a sight!" Marjie whispered with a grin as the two pups on the knoll wrestled down the grassy slope, rolling over each other. "Martha, look."

Martha had been distracted by a stick she had found while crawling to the edge of the ridge, but she quickly popped her head up over the ridge and looked down as well. Whether it was the sight of the animals or simply the steep slope to the creek that excited her, Martha let out a scream so loud that the two sleeping foxes actually leaped into the air.

But just as quickly as Martha screamed and all six of the foxes raced for the den, so did Jerry. He was on his feet in a flash and running down the rocky slope toward the hole before Marjie could cry out for him to stop.

"You're going to break your neck!" Marjie yelled.

Five of the six foxes dived through the opening to the den before Jerry could beat them there, but the one baby fox that had been farthest away did not make it. Jerry tripped the last couple of steps before the den, but recovered his balance just enough to ready himself for the little red streak that was headed straight toward him.

Diving to Jerry's left to try to get past him, the baby red fox dodged in exactly the direction that Jerry thought he would. With a swift, strong swoop of his left arm, Jerry caught the fox in his hand and fell down on top of it. Quickly wrapping his large right hand around the back of the baby fox's neck and clamping down his left hand on the fox's front paws and upper body, Jerry managed to immobilize the little animal with a minimum number of bites and scratches.

Marjie had picked up Martha and was slowly making her way down the steep incline as Jerry shouted, "I got him! I got him! Marjie, look! I got him!"

Standing motionless by the fox den, Jerry was beaming with delight as Marjie and Martha came alongside him. Marjie couldn't help but laugh at the sight. Jerry had the look of a triumphant ten-year-old, and the bushy-tailed, sharp-snouted young fox was growling up a storm in between loud pants for air. The fox's large, pointed ears were bent out of position, and its eyes were flashing in the sunlight.

"Boy, is he strong!" Jerry exclaimed, pushing the little fox out for them to see better but keeping his iron grip on it. "I told you this was going to be my day."

"I can't believe you caught him," Marjie said with a laugh. She reached out and took hold of the fox's red-orange tail and let Martha feel it as well. "You're a wild man."

Jerry broke out laughing. "I don't know if I can hang on to him all the way home."

"You're not serious about trying to make a pet out of him, are you?" Marjie gasped. "Look at that poor little baby. How can you even think it?"

"I caught him, that's why!" Jerry exclaimed. "He's all mine now. I'll keep him in the barn and train him."

"To do what?" Marjie protested. "Go get the cows for you? Serve Blue his dinner or something? As old as this fox is, you'll never tame him. He'll pace around that barn until he gets his chance, and then he'll be gone in a puff of smoke. But then he won't know how to survive in the wild, either."

"Ah, you always spoil my fun," Jerry said, his shoulders sinking a bit. "Wouldn't it be fun to try it, though?"

Marjie shook her head and said, "You can't take this poor little thing from its mother and just hope everything will work out. You know it won't. It's not right, Jerry. You have to let it go."

Jerry finally gave up on trying to stare down his wife and smiled. "So here I go and catch a fox barehanded, and my wife won't let me keep him. He might have been worth some money."

"We can survive without the money," said Marjie. "He's too cute to take from his brothers and sisters. Let him go."

Jerry turned toward the foxhole and slowly bent over and held the baby red fox out to release his grasp. "This is gonna be trick—ouch!" he cried as the little red ball exploded from his grasp, getting in a good nip as it exited for the safety of the den.

As the last of the red tail descended into the darkness of the foxhole, Jerry looked down at the bleeding gash the fine, sharp teeth had left behind. Then he looked up at Marjie disgustedly and said, "Just let him go, right. Thank you, thank you, thank you."

Chapter Fourteen

It Is Well

"Jerry, we've got to hurry!" Marjie called up the stairway toward their bedroom. She and Martha were dressed for Sunday morning church and waiting for him.

"I'm coming!" he called back, running the brush through his short blond hair one more time, then hustling out the bedroom door and down the stairway. Marjie was already out the front doorway with Martha by the time he caught up. "Man, I hate Sunday mornings. One thing goes wrong when you're milking, and you have to run the rest of the morning."

"And I wanted to get there early today," Marjie sighed. She hurried into the car shed and got into her side while Jerry ran around and jumped in on the driver's side. "I'm so excited about Paul coming this morning. Ma said he caught a ride with somebody who was coming down to Spring Valley from the Vet's Hospital late last night."

Jerry quickly backed the car out of the garage and spun gravel as he rolled down the farm driveway. "This should be a great service. Didn't the pastor say that he was going to talk about all those little things he told us have been happening lately?"

"Yep," Marjie said, trying to wiggle Martha a little bit forward to get some of the weight off her stomach. "It should be good. I'm concerned about Fitch's health, though. When I was up in his office the other day, he wasn't well. And Ma said that Dorothy told her she thinks it's getting worse. She can't talk him into seeing the doctor about it, though. He's as stubborn as your pa was."

"He does look sorta gray to me," Jerry said, turning the corner onto the county road that led to Greenleafton. "I noticed it the night they were over for dinner. His coloring reminds me of someone who hasn't seen the sun for about a year. I thought he was in good spirits, though. He sure laughed about the stinky cheese trick."

Marjie laughed and said, "Yeah, and he got a real kick out of Dorothy plastering me with mud. I caught him smirking about a dozen times when we were talking to the pastor and the church elder from Lanesboro."

"Guess he thought you looked pretty snazzy in his robe," Jerry teased, pushing down on the gas pedal as they rolled down one of the hills. "I wish I could have been there to see that."

"No, you don't," Marjie warned with a smile. "I'm getting so big I couldn't even get Dorothy's robe to fit right. If it would have happened anywhere but at the parsonage, I would've been fit to be tied. Can't this old rattletrap go any faster?"

"I got it to the floor," said Jerry. "I suppose you could get out and push."

"Not again, thank you," she smirked. "Guess I'll just have to be patient."

By the time they got into the church and Marjie had dropped Martha off with the two women who were taking care of the nursery, it was nearly time for the service to start. Coming down the stairway from the nursery, Marjie stepped into the foyer and immediately spotted Paul dressed in his army dress coat. He stood with Sarah and Benjamin, surrounded by a number of people who were meeting him for the first time. Jerry was also standing there with Billy and Ruth.

"Wow!" Ruth exclaimed, taking Marjie by the arm and batting her dark lashes in mock flirtatiousness. "You didn't tell me how tall and handsome your brother was. He might have given Billy a run for his money. Those big brown eyes are—"

"That's enough!" Billy sputtered. "I was here first, so don't go getting any ideas about the new guy on the block."

"Maybe you could introduce him to Betty Hunter," Ruth suggested, scanning the church for the tall, slender widow.

"Not a bad idea," Marjie replied, scanning the foyer for a glimpse of bright blond hair.

"He doesn't look like he needs help from either of you," said Billy, pulling Ruth away. "Let's find a place to sit before the organ starts playing."

"Hey, big brother," Marjie said as she

wrapped an arm around Paul. "Glad you could make it."

Paul was all smiles and hugged her back with his good right arm, then he leaned against her and whispered, "I'm going crazy meeting all these people. What did you tell them about me?"

"Everything I could think of," Marjie joked, taking his arm. "Come along, handsome, and I'll show you the best seat in the house."

The organ began playing as an usher led them down the center aisle to an empty pew toward the front. Marjie and Paul scooted down the row, followed by Jerry and Sarah and Benjamin. When they were all settled into their spots, the pastor and choir made their entrance through the side door and sat down as the organ continued to play.

"The war department must have brought him out of retirement to take some young guy's spot, eh?" Paul whispered to Marjie, but she didn't offer him the smile he was expecting.

"He's not much to look at, that's for sure, and he's not the best speaker you're ever going to hear," Marjie spoke softly back to Paul. "But if you listen to his words this morning, you're going to be surprised. He's truly a man of God, and we love him a lot."

"Yeah, I sorta got the same message from Ma," whispered Paul.

Just then Pastor Fitchen looked out at the congregation and noticed that Paul was with the Macmillans. He smiled and nodded, then glanced back down at his notes before the organ music ended. Then the elderly pastor stood and stepped slowly to the wooden pulpit.

Lifting his hands, Pastor Fitchen raised his eyes to the vaulted ceiling and spoke out loudly, "O sing unto the Lord a new song: sing unto the Lord, all the earth. Sing unto the Lord, bless His name; show forth His salvation from day to day. Declare His glory among the heathen, His wonders among all people. For the Lord is great, and greatly to be praised: He is to be feared above all gods. Psalm 96, verses one to four."

Then the white-haired man closed his eyes and placed his hands back down on the sides of the oak pulpit. His bushy eyebrows seemed to droop completely over his eyes, but it was clear that his lips were moving in prayer. Those who were seated closest to the front could hear him repeating the phrase, "We sing to you with all our hearts, for you are worthy to be praised."

It was clear to Marjie that this was going to be another Sunday morning where the order of the service found in the bulletin was not going to be followed to the letter. Over the past months, she had come to expect the unexpected from Pastor Fitchen, and this morning he would not disappoint her.

"The Lord is great!" Pastor Fitchen called out loudly, opening his eyes again and slowly scanning the faces of his congregation, "and greatly to be praised. Today, we have an answer to our prayers seated in our midst, and I am here to bless God's name for the life He has spared. Paul Livingstone, the oldest son of Sarah Macmillan, is alive and well, although his shoulder and arm have been seriously damaged by a German bullet. He fought for us in northern Africa, Sicily, and Italy. Paul, I don't mean to embarrass you, but would you stand up?"

Glancing quickly over at Marjie, who could only offer a smirk, Paul coughed nervously and stood to his feet. He smiled at the elderly pastor and mouthed a "thank you," and then tried to sit back down.

"One second, Paul," Pastor Fitchen urged. "Most of the folks here have never seen you before, but probably everyone here has prayed for you. Could you turn around and let them get a good look at you?"

Paul chuckled softly, then turned around in the narrow aisle and looked around at the congregation. Other than his own family, there were only a few faces he recognized. "Thank you for praying," Paul spoke out, surprising Marjie. "If you knew how many times I should have died, and how fortunate I am to be standing on two feet, albeit with one bum arm, you . . . ah . . . you would know how powerful God is. I don't know why He spared me, but I plan on finding out."

Before Paul could sit down, Pastor Fitchen began to applaud, saying again, "Sing unto the Lord a new song. Bless His name forever." And his clapping was followed by a loud rush of applause and quiet acclamations of praise to God from many in the congregation.

Not knowing quite what to do, Paul just stood there, and to Marjie's added amazement, he started to laugh. He shut his eyes for a few moments but kept right on laughing. When the applause finally subsided, he raised his good arm and said, "If I could clap my hands today, mine would be the loudest here. Thank you." And with that, he turned and sat down.

"I told you you'd be surprised by the old guy," Marjie whispered in Paul's ear.

"Shocked would be a better description," Paul said in return. "What's he going to pull next?"

"Just hang on for the ride," Marjie suggested, but she wasn't sure what was coming next either.

The rest of the service, though, was truly incredible. After the choir had sung and the announcements had been read, Pastor Fitchen cut out the other portions of the service and started in like a storyteller describing his life journey. Stepping back into his late teen years, when he had first met and courted Dorothy, the elderly pastor recounted the high points and the low points of his many years of ministry. It was a story the congregation had never heard.

When he began to relate some of the stories of the past year, the old pastor choked up several times and wiped tears from his eyes, and there were few dry eyes in the congregation. "It's been like all of the things that I've ever hoped would happen have happened," he said. "You who have tasted of the good things of the Lord with me the past few years know what I'm talking about. We've gone from a dry and weary land to a place of abundance that I had long since thought could only happen in heaven.

"I know it's going to sound silly coming from an old goat like me," he continued, "but I hope you can believe me when I tell you that it's wonderful to know that God is your Father. To know Him, to know Him, to know Him . . . is peace like a river . . . is joy like a fountain . . . is unspeakable and full of glory. Can you hear Him calling?

"He says, 'Ho, every one that thirsteth, come ye to the waters, and he that hath no money; come ye, buy, and eat; yea, come, buy wine and milk without money and without price. Wherefore do ye spend money for that which is not bread? and your labor for that which satisfieth not? hearken diligently unto me, and eat ye that which is good, and let your soul delight itself in fatness. Incline your ear, and come unto me: hear, and your soul shall live; and I will make an everlasting covenant with you, even the sure mercies of David.' "

Pastor Fitchen's eyes were glistening as he quoted from the book of Isaiah, and he stopped to catch his breath. "Ever since I was a young man, I've sung a wonderful hymn, 'It Is Well With My Soul.' But when Margaret Stanfeld sang it in the last service before they left for Scotland, that hymn got stamped somewhere deep inside me. 'Whatever my lot, Thou hast taught me to say, It is well, it is well with my soul.' I wonder if you'd open your hymnals with me this morning and join in singing those words before we close. It's . . . page two fifty-six. Please stand."

The organist had been given no warning, and it took her a minute to get ready to play. Meanwhile Marjie looked down the aisle at her loved ones and shook her head in amazement at the powerful things that Pastor Fitchen had said. She wasn't sure how much Paul had understood, but she could see that Benjamin and her mother had been deeply moved.

As the first verse began, the congregation entered enthusiastically into the singing. Marjie thought that every voice except for the pastor's was giving it all they had. But Pastor Fitchen was not even mouthing the words, which was odd for him. He seemed content to simply drink in the words of the anthem.

As the chorus to the first verse ended and the organist was about to begin the second verse, Marjie saw the elderly pastor suddenly turn and look at the large stained-glass windows on the west side of the church. His eyes widened, as if he saw something strange or wonderful. Then, without warning, he collapsed to the floor with a dull thud and was gone.

Chapter Fifteen

Another Goodbye

"Doc Sterling said that Fitch was dead before he hit the floor," Jerry said as he turned the old black Ford's lights on to indicate that they were part of the funeral motorcade. Then he pulled their car up behind several others that were idling behind the hearse. "I don't think he felt a thing. What a way to go."

Marjie took a deep breath and watched as Benjamin and the seven other pallbearers carefully lifted the unadorned wooden coffin into the back of the large black hearse and slid it into position. A cold gust of wind mixed with ice pellets caught one of the men's hats and nearly blew it off before he could catch it. Then the tall, black-suited funeral director closed the door of the hearse, and the eight pallbearers quickly made their way into the two cars behind it.

"I hate death," Marjie said quietly, leaning against her brother Paul's disabled left shoulder and staring ahead as Dorothy Fitchen stepped out of the church, followed by her son and daughter and their families. Dorothy wore a long black coat, and she held one hand tightly against the side of her black hat to keep it in place as they climbed into the two cars directly in front of the Macmillans. "Even a glorious death is still a death."

Sarah Macmillan, who was wedged into the backseat next to Ruth and Billy Wilson, rubbed her hands to keep them warm and said, "I hate it, too. I hate everything that surrounds death. But I've been having a hard time getting angry about this one. With my own two eyes, I saw our friend step from this world to the next. I still wonder what it was that Fitch saw when he turned toward the stained-glass windows."

"He saw something profound," Ruth spoke up, holding Billy's hand. Her voice was raspy, and her eyes were very red. "Even though my mother was a believer, ever since she died, I've dreaded the thought of dying. She coughed and coughed. I thought I was going to go crazy listening to her, trying to help her. But nothing seemed to make a difference, and then she finally stopped breathing, and it was all over. But . . . the look on Pastor Fitchen's face . . . I'll never forget it. It gave me a sense of anticipation of what was on the other side."

"I've seen that look before—many times, too many times," Paul said as the hearse finally inched forward, followed slowly by the cars that had been waiting. "I've watched men dying in the field; I held some of my friends. And it was the same in the hospitals. You cannot describe what it's like when some people die. I did all I could to dismiss the chaplains and what I knew of religion, but when I came face-to-face with death, I didn't have any more room to doubt the supernatural."

Billy Wilson was nodding in agreement from the backseat. "But they're not all good deaths," he said. "When I came to in that hospital in Hawaii, it wasn't just my legs that were on fire. I heard men dying in terror of the dark, cursing God and blaspheming. I still sometimes wake up at night hearing them cry out. It was awful."

"It's worse than awful," Paul added with a shudder. "I caught an occasional glimpse of heaven in some men's eyes, but I peeked over the rim of hell with others. Hell is the only word for where they were."

The long motorcade moved west through Greenleafton, heading up the gravel road that led toward the church's cemetery, and the cars started to pick up some speed. The cemetery was about a half-mile out of town, on a site that had been located next to the original church building.

"I hate seeing the snow and cold again," Marjie said, not caring much for the topic being discussed in the car. An early spring snowstorm had roared through southeastern Minnesota the night before, blanketing the greening fields with a couple of inches of wet snow. Fast-moving low gray clouds continued to dominate the sky, with occasional snowbursts and ice pellets and a miserable wind. "A couple of days ago I was outside in a sweater. Besides, my coat won't button in the front anymore."

"I'm glad they got that canvas shelter up for Dorothy and the family," Sarah said. "Least it'll cut down the wind."

"What do you think Dorothy will do now?" Ruth asked.

"Oh, I think she'll move close to her daughter and family in Illinois," Sarah replied. "That was their plan for when Fitch reached retirement. She's got his pension, and I think they did a pretty good job of saving over the years." She paused and sighed. "Still, it's going to be hard on her to be alone after all these years. Money ain't everything."

The hearse made a right turn into the cemetery driveway and continued up the road nearly as far as it could get. The burial plot was on the cemetery's north end, in the shelter of a large pine tree that had been planted by settlers two generations before. A large canvas canopy surrounded the grave, and enough steel folding chairs had been set up inside for all the family members. One by one cars that followed the hearse came to a stop and the engines were turned off.

No one in the Macmillan car moved or spoke for a few moments while they waited for the pallbearers and family to get out of their cars. The wind whistled against the car windows and even rocked the car a bit, intensifying the eerie feeling that seemed to always surround the old graveyard.

"Just in case you're wondering," Marjie finally said as the cars in front of them began to empty, "I hate cemeteries, too."

For the moment, at least, the heavy mood in the car was broken, and everyone laughed as they shared Marjie's sentiment. Then, with a reluctant, grim-faced resolve, the passengers of the Macmillan car shoved their car doors open and stepped out onto the snowy grass. Huddling together in groups of two, they marched to the grave and did their best to get close to the protective canopy, but the biting wind still found its way past the canvas. Marjie pulled her coat around her expanded middle as best she could and tried to fill in the gap with her long scarf.

Marjie guessed that about two hundred people from the packed church had chosen to brave the elements at the gravesite. Bodies pressed closely together in universal misery as a sudden burst of wind-driven ice pellets peppered down upon the mourners.

With the flapping canvas and the haunting whoosh of the wind through the towering pine tree, Marjie could not hear a word that the preacher was saying to the family members and pallbearers who were gathered within the canopy area. To her thinking, it was just as well. She had thought the funeral sermon was stiff and impersonal. It was hardly the preacher's fault. Assigned by the denomination to do the service, he had hardly known Pastor Fitchen. Still, something inside her had protested at the pat phrases that had little to do with the man she knew and loved.

Leaning hard against Jerry, Marjie spoke softly to him, "Your pa saved this funeral, didn't he?"

Jerry's head moved up and down, but his shoulders were locked in one position. He whispered in her ear, "I'm glad Dorothy asked him to speak about their friendship. I don't know how he could say what he said without choking up. He was terrific."

Marjie looked at her father-in-law, who stood in the row of men behind the seated family members. He was staring out over the fields and hills to the far horizon, his gaze was stoic and fixed. *I thought he was the one we'd be putting in the ground first,* she mused. Then she thought, *I wonder if he's thinking the same thing.*

By the time the gravesite ceremony was over, most of the mourners were too frozen to think of trying to offer their sympathies to the grieving family members. Sarah did step into the canopy enclosure and give Dorothy a hug, but the majority of the people decided to talk with the family at the luncheon in the church basement that was to follow the burial.

They met up with Benjamin again once they were back in the warm church basement. The inviting smell of coffee and sandwiches and a variety of cakes filled the room, and it didn't take long to leave behind the remaining memories of piercing wind and snow. After offering their sympathies to Dorothy and her family, Marjie and Jerry rejoined the others at a big wooden table.

"Boy, this coffee tastes good," Marjie said to Sarah, who was holding Martha.

"Tastes or feels?" asked Sarah. She was breaking off pieces of her sandwich and feeding them to Martha bit by bit.

"Both," Jerry declared. "But feel is more important than taste at this point. That was pure misery out there today. I should have stayed with Martha."

"Where'd Benjamin wander off to now?" asked Marjie, scanning around the crowded basement. "I don't see him down here."

"He's not," Sarah replied, handing the next piece of sandwich to Paul who dropped it in Martha's mouth. "Said he had some unfinished business to attend to."

"Today?" Marjie asked. "Where?"

"At the cemetery," Sarah said quietly, turning so only Marjie could hear. "But I don't think he wanted anyone to know."

"He went there by himself?" Marjie continued.

"Yes," replied Sarah.

Marjie leaned back in her chair and tried to figure out what Benjamin meant by having unfinished business, and then she recalled that distant look in his eyes. The longer she sat at the table, and the louder the conversation and laughter got around her, the more it bothered her. Finally she decided she had to at least check on Benjamin.

Standing up and motioning for Jerry to follow her, Marjie walked back toward the bathrooms but stopped by the coat racks. Turning to Jerry, she whispered, "I'm going to go see how your pa is doing. I'll be back shortly."

"What?"

As she pulled on her coat, Marjie said, "I'm going out to the cemetery to check on your pa. I'm worried about him."

"Why?"

"I just am," Marjie said. "You stay and make sure that Martha doesn't run my ma ragged. I'll probably only be gone a few minutes."

"I should be the one to go," Jerry offered, reaching for his coat. "You can—"

"No, let me do this," Marjie insisted. "I can't take the noise down here right now, anyway."

The hearse had already left the cemetery by the time Marjie got there, but she could see Benjamin's car up by the canopy as well as the gravedigger's car.

"I gave him five more minutes," Harlan Shetling said, rolling down his car window as Marjie walked past. "I gotta get that grave closed up before dark, you know."

"Thank you for your patience, Harlan," Marjie answered with a nod.

Stepping around the corner of the canopy, Marjie saw Benjamin who was sitting on a chair close to the grave. The wooden coffin had been lowered to the bottom; an assortment of flowers and some dirt lay on top of it already. Benjamin greeted her with a thin smile and motioned for her to join him.

"Are you okay?" Marjie asked, sitting down on a chair next to him and wrapping her arm around him. "I don't want to be here unless you want me here."

"I'm glad you came," said Benjamin, but his eyes held the same distant look that she'd noticed during the burial. "I just wanted to say one last goodbye. I couldn't do it with all those people around."

Marjie nestled her warm cheek up against her father-in-law's cold face and held him tight, then finally she said, "So, why don't you say goodbye?"

"I can't," Benjamin whispered, shaking his head, but that seemed to be all the help he needed to let go of his pent-up grief. His shoulders began to shake first, and then he started to sob. And he was not alone. Marjie's tears quickly joined his and mingled with the black earth that would soon cover their friend's wooden casket.

Chapter Sixteen

Top Secret

"The weather this year has been murder for getting the crops in," Marjie said to her mother as she pushed the screen door open and stepped out onto the front steps of the white farmhouse. She sat down on the steps next to Sarah, who was watching Martha play at her little wooden table with two little chairs. "It's already May sixteenth, and he's finally sowing the oats. Jerry's been prowling around here like a caged animal."

"Ben has gotten a little edgy himself lately," said Sarah, leaning back against the side of the house. "Can't tell if it's because the fields are so wet or if he's still grieving over Fitch. That first week after the funeral he was really low. I think he's doing better now. I'm glad that Jerry asked Ben to come over and work on the corn planter. Ben's not wanted to go anywhere lately. Good to get him out of the house."

"Hopefully this nice weather's going to hold," said Marjie. "If Ben can get the corn planter working right, Jerry hopes to have the corn in by next week."

"Jerry did a fine job on the chainlink fence around the lawn here," Sarah said. "I can't believe he put it in himself. Why didn't he call and ask Ben to help on that?"

"Oh, it was one of those deals that he kept starting and stopping on," Marjie answered. "He'd try to get in the field to work, but it was too wet. So then he'd work on the fence for a while. Then he'd check the field again. He was so frustrated. To say the truth, I was glad he had the fence to work on. It kept him out of my hair for a while."

"Well, it's a wonderful play area for Martha," Sarah said, nodding toward the little curly-headed girl who looked up from her doll when she heard her name. "And for number two, here," she added, gently tapping Marjie's stomach with her elbow.

"That's for sure," Marjie agreed. "I can just send her out here to play and not worry about how far she's going to wander. I figure I've got about six or seven weeks to go on number two."

"I could have used a fence like this when number two came along for me," Sarah commented. "You were the dickens in the yard. Every time I turned around, you were heading for the creek, or climbing to the top of the pine trees, getting your clothes full of pine sap, or heading for the sinkhole with Paul."

"It was all Paul's fault, of course," Marjie joked, looking over at her mother. "We had a lot of fun together when we were little. I'm glad he's back close to us. So he got a job in Minneapolis?"

"A job, an apartment, and a girlfriend," Sarah announced with a bright smile. "He started dating one of the nurses he met, and her father owns a big bakery. And it just so happens that the bakery was looking for someone to supervise their truck deliveries around town. Sounds like a good job for

Paul, doesn't it?"

"Perfect," Marjie replied. "Sounds like he's getting a little chummy with the family, though. Maybe he'll marry the baker's daughter and make us all rich."

Sarah laughed and nodded. "He better hurry, though. I'm not getting any younger. What's that racket I hear coming?"

"Sounds like a big motorcycle," answered Marjie, looking down the driveway but unable to see down the road because of the pine trees. "Nobody around here owns one. Wonder who it is?"

Marjie and Sarah listened as the low roar from the motor suddenly stopped, and Marjie thought she heard voices.

"They stopped down at the corner," Marjie said quietly. "Sounds like a man and woman talking and laughing."

"You must have bat ears," Sarah teased, standing up and walking past Martha out to the edge of the new fence. "I don't hear a thing now. Where's Blue?"

"I'm sure he's out in the field with Jerry," Marjie answered. Then the motor came to life again, and it sounded like it had turned up the road toward the Macmillan farm.

Suddenly a Harley-Davidson motorcycle with two riders wheeled around the corner of the driveway and zoomed down the farm driveway past them. Both riders had on army coats, sunglasses, and old leather helmets. Rounding the corner by the barn, the speeders kept right on going and disappeared down the farm lane to the fields.

"What was that all about?" Benjamin called out, stepping out of the machine shed with a big wrench in his hand. "Where'd it go?"

"To the fields," Marjie yelled back, walking around the corner of the farmhouse and raising her hands in disbelief. She opened the new fence gate and walked out into the middle of the driveway. "There were two people on the motorcycle, but I have no idea who they are."

"Here they come again!" Benjamin hollered, turning around as the thunder returned down the farm lane. Shooting out into the open farmyard from between the trees, this time the riders began to whoop and scream. Sarah raced over and picked up Martha, who had started to cry as the motorcycle sped right past Marjie and rolled down to the end of the driveway. There it braked and turned around again, but this time it came slowly down the driveway toward Marjie.

"Teddy Livingstone!" Marjie shouted when the riders finally got close enough for her to get a good look at the driver. "I'm going to kill you!"

The shiny motorcycle with leather side bags draped over the back wheel came to a halt and the engine went quiet, but the laughter from its two passengers only got louder. Pulling off his leather helmet, Marjie's brother Teddy tried to wipe away some of the tears and catch his breath. "You should have seen your face!" he cried between gasps for air.

"You creep!" Marjie shouted, grabbing him by the neck of his coat and shaking him. "You scared the wits out of me!"

Just then the Macmillans' small Ford tractor came rolling out of the farm lane with Jerry almost standing up and Blue racing behind it. "What's wrong?" he called out. "What's going on here?"

"See what trouble you cause?" Marjie said, starting to laugh as Blue pulled up alongside them, barking and huffing and puffing and slobbering all over the place. Pointing to Ted, she said to Blue, "Go ahead and slobber on him. He deserves it."

"Is this any way to welcome my wife to the family, Marjie?" Ted said with a huge smile, stepping up over the motorcycle's gas tank and turning toward the other biker, who was pulling off a leather helmet to reveal a tousled cap of auburn hair.

Marjie's jaw dropped as the woman carefully lifted off her dark sunglasses and looked up to reveal clear cobalt blue eyes over high, elegant cheekbones. "Pleased to meet you," she said to Marjie, still chuckling to herself and holding out her hand. "I'm Lavonne."

Taking Lavonne's hand, Marjie couldn't say anything, but she did start to laugh. Sarah came up behind her carrying Martha, and Benjamin and Jerry approached as well. Finally Marjie said, "I'm very pleased to meet you, Lavonne. You'll have to forgive me for asking, but Teddy is the biggest joker around. Is this for real?"

"From what I've heard, he's only second best," Lavonne deadpanned, "but I'm afraid this isn't a joke. 'Till death do us part' and all that." Then she stepped up over the bike and wrapped her arms around Ted. Marjie looked up at her brother, whose face was beaming like a lighthouse, and she finally believed it.

"Ma!" Marjie screamed. "This is Teddy's wife!"

"For goodness' sake!" Sarah gasped as Jerry took Martha from her arms. "I can't believe it."

"You better!" Ted declared with a laugh, wrapping his arm around his mother and pulling her close. "Lavonne Livingstone, this is my mother, Sarah Macmillan."

"I'm happy to meet you, Sarah," Lavonne said, taking her mother-in-law's hand. "Teddy wanted to surprise you."

"Teddy doesn't believe in surprises, honey," Sarah replied. "He's a shocker, not a surpriser."

Everyone laughed again, and Marjie introduced Jerry and Martha and Benjamin to Lavonne. She was not quite as tall as Marjie, and she was very friendly.

"You up and eloped and rode this thing all the way from New Mexico?" Sarah was asking Ted as Marjie finished her introductions.

"They gave us a week's pass," Ted said, looking down at the motorcycle. "This thing is faster than the buses and trains, and a lot more fun!"

"Not when it's raining," Lavonne muttered under her breath, bringing another round of laughter.

"You're a brave soul to marry this nut," Marjie told her. "How'd you meet?"

"At the base," answered Lavonne, running her fingers through her hair and fluffing it out. "I joined the Wacs a year ago and got a really tough job. I'm a military driver. I get to chauffeur some of the top dogs around. That's how I met Teddy."

"Teddy's a top dog?" asked Marjie. "Dog, I can believe."

Lavonne laughed, and Ted answered for her. "I work for a guy who's a top dog, which made her think I was a big shot. I managed to fool her, too, until she got a good look at my stripes. She liked my motorcycle, though."

"So how long have you been married?" asked Sarah.

"Three days and . . . four hours," Ted replied, looking down at his watch. "The base chaplain married us. He's a Presbyterian, if that means anything to you. I've been going to church to hear him preach every Sunday since we met. What do you think of that, Ma?"

Sarah smiled wryly and shook her head. "I suspect a certain pair of blue eyes had something to do with that. You update me in a year on how you're doing with church, and then I'll let you know what I think."

"I told you Ma was sharp, didn't I?" Ted said to Lavonne, grinning.

Nodding, Lavonne asked, "Would you mind if I went in the house and freshened up a bit? I feel like I've got three or four layers of dirt on my face."

"Come right in," Marjie replied, turning toward the house and leading the way. "We have an extra room, if you two newlyweds would like to stay here."

"Thank you for offering," Lavonne said, walking beside Marjie. "But I think Teddy was going to ask your mother about staying with them. And he wants to make a fast trip to Minneapolis to see your brother. Teddy did tell me, though, that you have a horse. I hate to be so forward, but I was hoping you might let me ride him while I'm here. I grew up on a farm in Pennsylvania, and I haven't had a chance to ride since I left home."

"I'd love it if you rode him," Marjie responded, holding open the iron gate and heading up the sidewalk. "Charlie loves to run, and I haven't been able to do much with him lately." She cast a rueful glance down to her expanded middle. "He could use a good workout, and he could use a good brushing, too, if you feel like it."

"Boy, would I!" Lavonne exclaimed.

"Hey Marjie, do you have anything to eat around here, or should we head over to Ma's?" Ted called out as he and Sarah and Benjamin came through the front gate.

Marjie held the front door open for Lavonne. "The bathroom's around through the dining room. Make yourself at home." Then she turned to Teddy and said, "You can put your order in, but the best I can do for dinner is baked chicken, mashed potatoes and Ma's gravy, green beans, and all the apple pie you can eat."

"Yahoo!" Ted cried, wrapping his arm around his mother again. "I hit the jackpot."

"There's just one condition, *Theodore*," Marjie added.

"What's that, *Marjorie Belle*?" Ted asked, settling down a notch.

"I want to know what you're doing in New Mexico," said Marjie, grilling him with her eyes. "Everything."

Ted stopped in his tracks and shook his head. "Oops," he said seriously. "You already know more than you should know. I told you things about the guy I'm working with that I didn't know would become important. Joking aside, Lavonne and I can't tell you a thing more. Please don't ask. Okay?"

"Jerry was right," Marjie said softly to herself, staring at Teddy and knowing he meant business. "It's top secret, then?"

"No comment," Teddy replied. "But I'd like some chicken."

Chapter Seventeen

The Little Girl

"I drove all the way out here to help you with your garden," Ruth Wilson said, pushing back her cup of coffee and leaning forward in her chair as if she was going to stand up. "I've got the whole day and the sun is shining, so let's hit it, lady."

"It's too hot, I feel and look like a whale, and this baby's driving me up the wall," Marjie said, rubbing her extended abdomen and groaning. "Besides, that garden is a disaster zone. I got part of it in, and Jerry's been too busy in the field, and I just don't care about it anymore."

"You'll care in the middle of the winter," replied Ruth. "Look, all you have to do is show me what you've got for seed and what you're still missing, and it's done. I'm lightning in the garden. Just bring me out a glass of water every once in a while."

Marjie laughed and groaned again. "You're lightning no matter what you do, Ruthie. So you'll get my garden all put together, and then I won't be able to take care of it for the rest of the summer. Sounds like a lot of work that's going to end up as a lot of weeds. This is June 1, and I'm hoping for July 1 on the delivery, meaning that the rest of the summer is going to be one mother's desperate quest for survival. Forget it, Ruthie."

"Listen to me now," Ruth argued. "I've got the summer off from school. I'm coming out this way regularly to help my dad with things around the farmhouse, so I'll just add you to my list. What Jerry can't get to, I will."

"I don't know, Ruthie," Marjie stalled. "I hate to take advantage of your kindness. Besides, I've got enough tomatoes and apples from last year's canning to make it through another winter. I can buy the other stuff at the store."

Ruth just shot her a sideways glance and stood up. "I know where the hoe is, and I'm going to start cleaning up those two rows of raspberries. You can sit there all day if you like. But after I get the weeds out, I'll find your seeds in the shed and you'll soon be guessing about what's coming up where in the garden. See you later."

With a taunting laugh, Ruth zipped across the dining room and out the back door before Marjie could get out of her chair to protest. Instead of following Ruth, Marjie went to the dining room window and looked out to see how Martha was doing. "Good," she whispered, seeing that Martha was holding a jabbering conversation with her one-armed doll, a grungy bear, and Blue, who was stretched out full length in the warm sunshine attempting to nap.

"Okay," she sighed, "now to catch up to the other whirling dervish." She grabbed a couple of sacks of seed corn and peas from the corner table and headed out the farmhouse's back door. True to form, Ruth was already cruising down a raspberry row, and the weeds were flying.

"This isn't half as bad as you made it out to be," Ruth called out, standing up straight and taking a short break as Marjie tossed the seed sacks down along the edge of the garden. "Where did you hide the spuds?"

"No spuds this year," Marjie replied. "I had to twist Jerry's arm to dig them last fall, so I thought I wouldn't bother."

"Where'd you hide them?"

Marjie laughed and turned toward the shed. "They're right inside the door. If you'd walk instead of run, you couldn't miss them."

Stepping inside the shed, Marjie grabbed the pail full of potato eyes that she had cut from last year's potatoes, and she pulled out a couple of wooden stakes and some string for making rows. The sound of the tractor coming up the lane caught her attention, and Marjie waited to see what Jerry was doing.

Jerry waved as he wheeled the tractor up to the machine shop and stopped. "Looks good," he called out as he jumped down from the Ford. "Sorry I can't help with the garden."

"I'll bet you are," Marjie teased. "What's up?"

"I ran out of fenceposts down by the

creek," Jerry replied, standing with his hands on his hips by the tractor. "Every post in that section of fence was rotted."

"There's hot coffee on the stove," Marjie said. "Why don't you take a break and play with the baby for a little while?"

"You talked me into it," Jerry answered. He peeled off his gloves and set them on the fender of the tractor, then started toward the house. "We got hay that's almost ready to cut. And the corn's already popping up."

"Get a little heat and things really speed up," Marjie said. "I hope that'll happen in the garden, too."

Marjie turned around and headed back to where Ruth was hoeing her way back down the second row of raspberries. Heaps of weeds lay strewn in her wake.

"You're almost getting me into the mood for this," Marjie said, setting down the pail of potato eyes and looking over the plot for where she wanted the rows to go. Just then she happened to catch some movement out by the end of the pine-tree windbreak. "Ruthie, who's that little girl out on the road? I've never seen anyone walking past here."

But the child was half walking, half running, and when she saw the two women in the garden, she began to cry out and wave her arms.

"I think that's Tom Metcalfe's little girl. Something's wrong!" Ruth exclaimed, dropping her hoe and taking off on a run toward the child.

Marjie tossed her wooden stakes and string to the ground and cried out, "Jerry!" Then she followed after Ruth as fast as her increased bulk would let her, hoping that Jerry had heard her. She could see the little girl rushing to Ruth, who immediately took her into her arms.

When Marjie got there, Ruth was holding tight to the weeping child, crooning to her, patting her back, trying to calm her down. She looked to be around six, barefoot, her filthy dress torn in two places. Her thin little face was a smear of tears and dirt.

"What is it, sweetheart?" asked Ruth, gently stroking the girl's matted hair. "Try to tell me again."

"Momma!" cried the little girl, still gasping to catch her breath.

"Something's wrong with your mommy?" Ruth asked.

The little girl shook her head up and down. "You've gotta help!" she sputtered, tears pouring out. "Daddy said I had to get help!"

Ruth took the little girl's face in her hands and looked straight into her bloodshot eyes. "What's wrong with your mommy, sweetheart? It's very important that you tell me what's wrong with her."

The little girl was shaking so hard that Marjie didn't think Ruth could coax any more information out of her, but the girl managed to mumble in a whisper, "She's lying on her bed, and Daddy says she's real sick. You've gotta help!"

"We've got to get down there!" exclaimed Ruth, glancing up at Marjie. "Here, you take her and wait for me. I'll get the car."

Marjie pulled the little girl up against her and hugged her tight as Ruth ran back toward the farmhouse. When she was almost to the house, she met Jerry with Martha in his arms coming out to see what was wrong.

"Something wrong with Tom Metcalfe's wife!" Ruth cried on the way to her car. "Call the doctor and tell him he has to come as fast as possible. Marjie and I will take my car and see what we can do."

"I'll be down there just as soon as I call!" exclaimed Jerry, turning back toward the house. "But be careful. Metcalfe's driveway is down nearly to the bottom of the hill past the dump. There's a gate you have to open, and the driveway is real rocky and steep."

Ruth had her key in the ignition before he had finished talking. Gunning the engine hard, she spun the tires of her green Plymouth and threw dirt and gravel all the way down the driveway. She barely kept control as she turned left onto the county road and then slid to a stop alongside Marjie and the Metcalfe girl. Marjie pulled the car door open and helped the girl into the front seat. Then she clambered in beside the little girl, and Ruth roared down the road, leaving a huge cloud of dust to roll through the ditches.

"You have to slow down!" Marjie cried as they sped toward the hill that ran steeply down toward the woods. "The corners down by the dump are horrible."

Despite Marjie's warning, Ruth was still going too fast when they came over the ridge. They shot down the sharp descent with Ruth stomping the brakes and the Plymouth fish-tailing over the rough limestone rocks. Coming to the first curve, Ruth let off the brakes and fortunately had slowed the car enough to handle the turn. She pressed the brake down again and the car shuddered some more, but it slowed down to a near crawl.

"Wow!" Marjie gasped, still clutching her door handle with one hand and the little Metcalfe girl with the other. "I think I wet my pants, Ruthie."

Ruth was shaking too hard to laugh, but managed to shift into first gear and let the car creep past the steep embankment on the right-hand side of the road where people threw their junk and garbage. Marjie shuddered to think what would have happened if a truck had been parked at that spot.

"The driveway's down there on the right," Marjie said, pointing ahead. "See the mailbox?"

"Yeah," Ruth replied, looking straight ahead and tapping the brakes again, coming to a complete stop before the gate. "Can you get the gate? Or should I?"

"I think I can get it," Marjie replied, pulling open the car door and walking over to the big wooden gate. She thought it felt good to have her feet on the ground rather than to be flying over it in the car. Unlatching the iron catch, Marjie was relieved that the gate swung freely on its hinges instead of having to be dragged across the driveway.

Ruth pulled the car through the gate and stopped. Marjie closed the gate and latched it to keep in any of Tom Metcalfe's livestock that might be grazing nearby. Then she hurried back into the car, noticing that the little girl was clinging to Ruth again.

"I've never been back in here," Marjie said as Ruth started forward. "It looks a little rough."

"Jerry said it's pretty bad," replied Ruth, puffing out a big breath of air as they started to climb a short rocky knoll that curved to the left and then dropped off straight down to the creek below. The driveway was only wide enough for one car, and there was no way to see up over the ridge.

"Whew!" Marjie gasped as they topped the rise. The driveway was clear ahead except for more rocks and some huge tree ruts.

"Hang on!" Ruth warned as the Plymouth pitched off one of the ruts and spun on the loose limestone. "I hope it's not much further."

Bouncing from side to side, they came around another sharp, blind curve in the driveway and breathed a huge sigh of relief as it opened up into the farmyard. But then relief turned to shock at the condition of the property. There was hardly a hint of paint ever having been on any of the buildings, and a couple of the sheds had already collapsed in upon themselves. Except for a path wide enough for a hay wagon to get through, the yard was piled deep with old, rusty machinery.

Ruth pulled the car up by the house behind the Metcalfes' rusted-out auto. There was no sign of the little girl's father, but three black nanny goats were grazing along the south side of the house. The front door of the house was hanging open, and at least a dozen cats of assorted shapes and colors were lying around the front porch.

"Where's your daddy, sweetheart?" Ruth asked, putting her arm around the little girl.

"He's in the house." She spoke softly.

"Maybe I'd better go in and see what's wrong," Marjie offered. She pushed open her car door and began picking her way over to the dilapidated farmhouse. The concrete porch was cracked and had sagged off to one side, and the windows were so rotten that several panes had fallen out and the openings were stuffed with rags. "I think it's better if you stay with her out here," she said to Ruth. "I'll call you if I need you."

Ruth nodded her head, and Marjie walked quickly to the house. Several of the cats scooted away from the front door as she approached; the others she had to step around. Peeking inside, she saw no movement, just shapes in the gloomy half-light. She was able to make out a table and some chairs and what looked like piles of trash.

"Mr. Metcalfe? Tom?" Marjie called out, suddenly realizing that she didn't know the first name of his wife or of the little girl in the car. There was no response, so she tried again, "Is anyone home?"

Marjie thought she could hear some noise inside, but she couldn't make out what it was or where it was coming from. So she stepped inside what she thought must be the dining room.

"Oh my goodness!" Marjie groaned, caught off guard by the stench of rotting food and old tin cans and boxes with who knows what in them. A wave of nausea swept over her, and she covered her mouth as she gagged. Fortunately nothing came up. She paused before moving on, hoping her stomach would settle down, and looked around.

To her right, an open door led to the kitchen, but Marjie could see that no one was in there. More mounds of trash and moldy food were heaped on the floor and the counters. Listening closely, Marjie thought the noise she had heard was coming from behind the closed door into another room.

She picked her way around the trash in the dining room and stopped to knock on the closed door. But there was still no answer. When she turned the large white knob and slowly opened the door, the source of the noise became apparent.

A large wooden radio stood against the far wall, but all that was coming out of the speaker was a continuous stream of static. And there, sitting in a big wooden rocking chair in front of the radio, was a hollow-eyed man staring straight into the radio's lighted dial.

Chapter Eighteen

Lily Metcalfe

"Tom," Marjie called out again, knocking on the door and waiting in the doorway for a response from the man she had met only once before. Silhouetted against one of the wide living room windows, Tom Metcalfe obviously hadn't shaved in several days; a rough stubble covered what Marjie thought she remembered to be a badly pitted face. His oily brown hair was bunched into irregular piles that made his head look oversized and lumpy. His big hands were wrapped tightly around the ends of the rocking chair's wooden arms and he gave no appearance of having heard Marjie call his name. He just continued to rock the chair in a slow, rhythmic manner.

As Marjie stepped into the room, a loud groan and the movement of a body from behind the door caused her to jump. Glancing around, she saw a skinny little boy who was napping on a tattered davenport. He had rolled over onto his stomach, and his arm was draped down off the edge of the cushion.

Food was crusted around his mouth, and his yellow pajamas were heavily soiled. He looked about two years old.

"Dear Lord, please help me," Marjie whispered, wondering if there might be other children in the house. She forced down panic. First she had to find out where Mrs. Metcalfe was.

Picking her way around the heaps of old dirty clothes spread out around the living room floor, Marjie approached Tom Metcalfe carefully, afraid of how he might react to her. When she got within a couple of feet but still out of arms' length, she spoke loudly, "Tom! This is Marjie Macmillan. I've come to help your wife. You sent your daughter to get us."

The reclusive farmer stopped rocking the chair. His dull, glazed-over brown eyes opened wide and turned slowly up toward Marjie, but his head did not move. For what seemed like several minutes, he appeared to be trying to focus in on her face, squinting at her and then opening his bloodshot eyes wide again. Finally his head moved up toward her as well, and he said flatly, "Where'd you put my shoes and socks?"

"What?" gasped Marjie, caught off guard. Then she glanced down at his feet and noticed that, oddly enough, he was barefoot.

His long pale toes were wiggling up and down.

"I can't find my shoes," he said, looking straight at Marjie. "My feet are cold."

"Tom, where . . . is . . . your . . . wife?" Marjie asked firmly. "Your daughter said she needed help."

"Ellie," Tom responded, finally releasing one hand's grip on the wooden rocker and reaching up to scratch the whiskers on his neck. "My daughter is Ellie. She's a good girl."

"But where is your wife, Tom?" Marjie demanded, anger replacing whatever fear she might have had.

"Right where I left her, of course," said Tom without any change in expression. "She's upstairs in the bedroom. You're not going to wake her up, are you? Don't you wake up Lily."

"You stay right here!" Marjie commanded, pointing to the chair. "I'll bring you your shoes."

A crooked smile crossed Tom's face. "Oh, thank you. My feet are cold."

The open door to the rickety stairway was on the opposite side of the living room. As fast as she could move, Marjie climbed the stairs and stood staring down the narrow hallway. All three bedroom doors were shut, and an eerie silence made Marjie shudder. "Maybe I should've stayed in the car and let Ruth check out the house," she muttered.

Taking hold of the first white doorknob, Marjie slowly opened the creaking door and peered into the dark room. A wool blanket was draped over the single window, smothering the bright daylight from the outside, and when Marjie clicked the wall switch, the light in the center of the ceiling did not come on. From the dim light of the hallway, Marjie could make out what she thought was a human form in the full-sized bed.

"Mrs. Metcalfe!" Marjie called out into the shadows, but the only response was more silence.

Rather than going to the bed, Marjie stepped to the window and slowly tugged the blanket loose from the top. As the light began to stream in, she turned toward the bed and gasped, "Oh no! Dear God!"

One glance had told Marjie all she needed to know. Lily Metcalfe lay perfectly still in the bed, flat on her back with a blanket neatly tucked in around her neck and a pillow beneath her head. Her eyes were closed, and her face held the same yellow and gray shading that Marjie remembered from when her own grandmother had died.

"Oh no," Marjie whispered again, stepping

to the bed and looking closely at the ashen face of the farm woman she had never seen. Lily Metcalfe's hair was matted against the pillow, her face was gaunt, her eye sockets sunken. Her lips were thin and cracked, and the skin around her neck was loose and wrinkled. Marjie would have guessed the woman's age at sixty-five, but from the age of the children, she figured that Lily was probably not much older than thirty years old.

Reaching out her hand, Marjie put her fingers gently on Lily's cold cheek and sighed loudly. There was nothing she could do for the poor woman now. Death had long since stolen away her life, and Marjie was left to wonder what had happened and if it could have been prevented. She held her hand on the clammy skin for several seconds, then turned and walked slowly out of the room.

Marjie descended the stairs and stepped back into the living room. She was relieved to see that the little boy was still asleep on the davenport. Tom Metcalfe was staring into the light of the radio dial again, and Marjie approached him guardedly.

"Tom," she said gently, then she decided to risk it and put her hand on his arm. "I visited your wife, Tom. She hasn't been well. Tom, she passed away."

"What's that?" he asked, blinking his eyes

and wrinkling his forehead. "Yes, I know she's sick. I sent Ellie to get help."

"Tom, your wife passed away," Marjie spoke clearly in his ear. "She's *dead*, Tom."

Looking back at the radio, Tom swallowed hard and said, "I'm glad she's sleeping so well. I tucked her in. You aren't going to wake her, are you?"

"No," Marjie finally replied, shaking her head. "I won't wake her."

"Good," he whispered with a slight smile as he started rocking the chair again. "Did you find my shoes?"

"No, but I'll look some more," answered Marjie, walking away.

"Thanks," he added. "I got a lot of field work to do. Haven't planted a thing yet."

Marjie went through the doorway into the dining room and hardly noticed the smell from the rotting food or all the trash in the way. By the front door she stopped when she spotted the Metcalfe's telephone on the wall. "Why in the world wouldn't he call somebody?" she whispered angrily, but when she picked up the receiver, the line was dead. She wanted to slam it back down, but she was afraid she might wake the little boy in the living room.

Stepping out of the gloomy house, Marjie let her eyes adjust back to bright sunshine.

She could see that Ruth had gotten out of her car and was seated on an old car seat in the shade of an old cracked willow tree, holding little Ellie Metcalfe in her lap. Marjie could tell from the grim expression on Ruth's face that she already knew the story.

"It's not good," Marjie said to Ruth as she walked up to them. Ellie did not look up but kept her head buried in Ruth's shoulder.

Ruth kept stroking the little girl's back. "She told me her mother wasn't breathing. Did you find her?"

Marjie nodded slowly and sat down beside them. Leaning back on her hands, she said, "Yeah, she's upstairs in her bed. She's been dead for a while. There's a little boy sleeping in the living room. Tom's there, too, in the rocking chair. He's . . . ah . . . not all there. But I don't think he's going to do anything."

The little girl began to cry hard, and Ruth hugged her tightly. "It's going to be okay, sweetheart," Ruth whispered as she began to sob. "We'll take care of you and your brother."

"Her name is Ellie," said Marjie, choking up at the little girl's grief and wondering what would happen to the children. Then she remembered that she hadn't checked the two other bedrooms upstairs for other children. "Ellie," she spoke soothingly, "do you have any other brothers or sisters?"

To Marjie's relief, Ellie shook her head no, then buried her head against Ruth's shoulders. "Thank goodness for that," Marjie whispered to Ruth.

The roar of a motor down the treacherous driveway signaled Jerry's approach, and the rattling of the fenders as the old black Ford came wheeling into the farmyard was a welcome sound to Marjie's ears. Jerry pulled around the two parked cars and found a spot for the Ford between a couple of broken-down hay wagons.

Scooping Martha into his arms, Jerry jumped out of the car and raced toward the women. "The doc's on his way!" he cried, slowing down as he realized that neither Marjie nor Ruth were jumping up to meet him. "Is everything okay? I had a terrible time trying to reach the doc, but he's coming now."

"That's good," Marjie said. "We're going to need him." She drew him aside so that Ellie wouldn't hear. "Jerry, Mrs. Metcalfe is dead, and Tom's in pretty bad shape, too. I think he's had a nervous breakdown or something."

"No!" Jerry gasped, setting Martha down on the ground next to Marjie. "Lily's dead?"

"Yes," Marjie replied. "She's upstairs in bed."

"What happened?" asked Jerry.

Marjie shrugged. “Hopefully the doc can tell us that. I have no idea. And Tom thinks she’s sleeping.”

“Where is Tom?” Jerry asked as Marjie picked up Martha and held her tight. “And what about Timmy? Should we get them out of there?”

“They’re both in the living room,” said Marjie. “I think it would be good if you could carry the little boy out. He was sleeping on the davenport. I’d hate for him to wake up alone and go upstairs to see his ma. But I think that Tom’ll be content to stay in his rocker.”

“I’ll get Timmy,” Jerry declared, turning toward the house, “but I’m going up to see about Lily first.”

“Be prepared for the smell,” Marjie added. “And tell Tom that you’re going to look for his shoes.”

Jerry looked at Marjie strangely, then shrugged his shoulders and hurried to the house. The cats cleared a path as he approached the front door, and Marjie noticed that Jerry stopped in the same spot she had when he stepped into the house.

“I’ve never seen a house in worse shape than that one,” Marjie whispered to Ruth.

“I wouldn’t have thought anyone lived there,” replied Ruth. “Looks like it could fall in at any time."

"I didn't mean the outside, Ruthie," continued Marjie. "You wouldn't believe the mess inside. There's trash and dirty clothes and rotting food everywhere. Looks like the cats come and go as they want. I thought I was going to throw up from the smell. It's not fit for humans in there."

"Two kids live there, Marjie," Ruth said quietly. "Tom's always been a strange man. What are we going to do?"

Marjie could only whisper, "I don't know."

Chapter Nineteen

The Eyes of Tom Metcalfe

"Finally, he's here," Marjie sputtered to Ruth as Doctor Sterling's shiny yellow Lincoln Continental coupe turned slowly into the Metcalfes' crowded farmyard. For more than an hour since Jerry had arrived, Marjie had been watching Martha and Timmy, who were playing together by the side of the house while Ruth continued to hold Ellie.

Hearing the automobile, Jerry stepped out of the house and onto the porch. After he had given up on trying to make sense out of what Tom was talking about, he had gone to work cleaning in the dining room, but the kitchen remained untouched.

"Good thing you gave me those directions," the doc muttered to Jerry as he hopped out of the car and grabbed his medicine bag. "You'd never guess that was a driveway I just came down. Looks more like a trail for the stagecoach. Where's Mrs. Metcalfe?"

"She's upstairs," said Jerry. "But there's no rush, Doc. She's been dead for some time."

The doctor's shoulders sagged, and he stopped alongside the long car and moaned. "Shoot! What happened?"

"All we know is that she was sick," Jerry said. "We thought you might be able to figure out what took her."

"What did Mr. Metcalfe tell you?" Doc Sterling asked, walking up to the porch. "He didn't—"

"No, no, no," Jerry broke in, shooing the cats away from the open door and pointing inside. "Tom's a strange one, but he didn't do anything to her. You can ask him and see if you can figure out what he says."

"What's that supposed to mean?" the doctor asked, stopping in his tracks in the doorway. "Don't tell me that smell is—"

"No!" Jerry cut him off again. "But the house is a pigsty, and I think Tom's cracked.

He's blubbering away in the living room and won't get out of his rocking chair."

"Great," Doc Sterling mumbled, holding his nose as he stepped into the house. Waving at Marjie, Jerry turned and followed.

"Looks like Ellie fell asleep," Marjie said, sitting down next to Ruth. "Poor little thing."

"We don't even know what she's been through," replied Ruth. She tried to stretch her back muscles as far as she could without bothering the little girl. "What if she was there when her mother died?"

Marjie shook her head. "Even if she wasn't there, she's going to need a lot of love to get her past this. As horrible as it is inside that house, the worst thing is that her mother is gone forever. It might not affect Timmy so much. He may not even remember her."

"He seems to be doing all right," Ruth said, glancing over at Timmy and Martha, who were making a vain attempt to catch one of the black nanny goats. "I can't believe those goats don't give those kids a good butting."

"I think they're so used to the kids that they hardly notice," Marjie observed. "They act like pets. I wonder if they've been spending time in the house. Smelled like it."

Fifteen minutes later Jerry emerged on the porch again and took a deep breath of the fresh air. Covering his mouth and shaking his head, he walked over to Marjie and Ruth and sat down beside them on the old car seat.

"He thinks her appendix must have burst in the night," Jerry said. "He got Tom to talk a little bit, and he said Lily's been sick for days. She kept complaining about having pain in the lower right side of her abdomen. Tom doesn't believe in doctors, so my guess is that she's been in that bed for a long time."

"What's the doc doing now?" asked Marjie, looking up at the desolate house.

"He's up in the bedroom examining Lily as best he can," said Jerry. "I had to get out of there. He wanted me to help lift her up, but I started getting sick on him. I never touched a dead person like that."

"An appendicitis attack doesn't explain all the trash and filth in the house," Ruth observed. "Sounds like she's been sick for months."

Marjie nodded, but Jerry shook his head. "Lily was a dreadful housekeeper," he said. "When I came down here and helped get Tom's corn out of the field a couple years ago, I went home to eat. The house was so filthy that I hated to drink her coffee. She was a pleasant woman, but in her own way she was as odd as Tom. She never went out. Whatever she needed, Tom would get it when he made a trip to Preston. I never saw her in public."

"Strange that Tom would've bought Charlie for Ellie, isn't it?" asked Marjie, looking down at the little girl. "She must have only been about three. No wonder she got scared of the horse. And no wonder you got a good deal on him."

Jerry nodded. "Pretty odd, like everything else down here. I wonder what the doc's gonna do with Tom? He won't move out of that chair, and I don't feel like wrestling him out of it. Tom is a brute for strength."

A cry from Martha brought Jerry to his feet, then he laughed. One of the small goats had finally taken enough taunting and sent her rolling with a solid head butt to the rear. Her look of comical indignation was enough to grant them all a moment's relief from the tragedies of the day.

Another twenty minutes elapsed before Doctor Sterling emerged from the farmhouse, and he surprised them all by leading Tom Metcalfe to the long yellow Lincoln and helping him into the front seat on the passenger's side. Rolling down the window, the doctor then closed the door and walked over to where they were sitting.

"How did you get him out of his chair?" Marjie asked.

Doctor Sterling smiled. "I used the oldest

medical trick in the book. I brought him his shoes and socks, and he was as happy as a lark. His feet were cold, you know."

Marjie laughed, but with a sad shake of her head. "So where are you taking Tom?"

"Well, I sure can't leave him here alone," the doctor said. "Unless he's got some family that you know about, I'm going to have to find a place for him to stay for a while and see if he comes out of this."

"A mental institution?" Marjie asked.

"Possibly," the doctor responded, shaking his head. "We can keep him at our hospital for a few days and see. Do you know if he has any relatives around here?"

"I'm pretty sure he doesn't," Jerry said. "His parents died when he was in his early teens. He was an only child, and he traveled all over the place before settling here. I don't know a thing about Lily, except that he met her out east someplace."

"This don't sound good for the little ones," Doctor Sterling lamented. "They're always the ones who suffer the most. I suppose I better take them along to town and drop them off with the people in the courthouse."

"No, please. They can stay with us, for now at least," Marjie offered. "They know us now, and there's no sense getting them more upset than they already are."

"Well," the doctor mumbled, "it's not what I'm supposed to do in this situation, but . . . well, it's probably better than what I'm supposed to do. This is only temporary, you understand."

"Certainly," said Jerry. "You let us know what we should do."

"What about Mrs. Metcalfe?" asked Ruth over Ellie's sleeping head. She glanced up at the bedroom window.

"Oh, I'll have a couple men come out and get her this afternoon," the doctor replied. "I got a hundred dollars that says she burst her appendix, but I'll have to check that later. Right now I'm more concerned about old Tom. I appreciate you taking the kids for now."

Doctor Sterling turned around and walked back to the car. Jerry and Marjie got up and followed him to the car and went around to the passenger's side to say goodbye to Tom.

Tom Metcalfe had his hands firmly planted on his knees and was staring straight at Marjie and Jerry as they came up to his window. His eyes were opened wide again, but the rest of his haggard face was expressionless. "I found my shoes," he said serenely.

"Good," Jerry replied. "Don't you lose them. We'll see you later, Tom. You do what the doc tells you, and you'll be just fine."

"Lily's sleeping," Tom said. "Don't go waking her up, now."

"She's not going to wake up, Tom," Marjie said softly.

"Needs her sleep," he replied with a nod. Then he squinted his bloodshot eyes and stared deeply into Marjie's face. "You take good care of the kids, Lily. They're all we got in this world. I'll be back tomorrow." Then suddenly his jaw went slack and his eyes went blank, as if someone had turned out a light inside.

Marjie took an involuntary step back from the car. Grabbing Jerry's arm, she leaned against him and fought another wave of nausea. For fear that Tom might react, she restrained the cry that was screaming inside her.

"We'd better go," Doc Sterling said, letting out the clutch and slowly backing the big Lincoln away from the house. "I'll call you about the kids."

Tom Metcalfe's blank gaze had turned away from Marjie, and he seemed oblivious to them again. The yellow automobile quietly rambled down the driveway and disappeared around the sharp blind curve that led to the county road.

"That was awful," Marjie gasped at last, shaking her head and clinging to Jerry's arm.

"Did you see it?"

"See what?" Jerry asked, holding her tight. "I saw him talking to you like you were his wife."

"No, Jerry, didn't you see his eyes?" Marjie cried. "There's no one inside him. It was like he's gone."

"Boy, I hope not," Jerry said. "Those kids over there need a father."

Ellie had finally woken up, and she let go of Ruth for the first time since they had driven into the farmyard. Ruth took the opportunity to stand up and stretch her very stiff joints and limbs. Timmy, still in his soiled pajamas, came running and jumped on Ellie.

As Marjie and Jerry walked back to them, Ruth pushed back her black hair and straightened her shoulders. "My body aches everywhere," she said. "Why don't we take the kids and go? There's nothing more we can do here."

"I'm going to shut the door and keep those cats out of there," Jerry said, turning toward the house.

Marjie still felt a bit numb, and she replayed the bottomless look that she had seen in Tom Metcalfe's eyes.

"Are you okay, Marjie?" asked Ruth, stepping to Marjie and taking her arm.

"Yeah, I think so," she whispered back. "We need to get the kids back to our house and set up some beds for them."

"Marjie, I want to take them," Ruth said. "You've got enough to handle without two extra children who are going to need a lot of attention."

"But he told me that I was supposed to take care of them," Marjie replied, taking a ragged breath.

"What?" asked Ruth. "Jerry told you—"

"No, when we were by the car, Tom started to talk to Marjie like she was Lily," Jerry said, coming back alongside Marjie. "It was scary."

"I really feel like I should take the children," Ruth said, looking into Marjie's eyes. "You're eight months' pregnant, and you've got Martha and a house to take care of. I have the whole summer off. And I think Ellie sort of—anyway, I really want to take them."

Marjie nodded and took a deep breath. "My, I must be tired," she mumbled, rubbing her forehead. "For a second there, I found myself believing a crazy man."

"Let's go home," Jerry said. "There's a lot here that I'd like to forget."

Chapter Twenty

Timmy and Ellie

"So how are you feeling this morning?" Jerry asked as he sat down at the dining room table for breakfast. "Rough night, eh?"

Marjie gave a half-smile and pushed the maple syrup across the table for his pancakes. "Not if you enjoy a good boxing match. This kid's a slugger. I hope you're all set to drop everything and head for the hospital."

"Did you sleep at all?"

"Oh, some," said Marjie, spinning her empty coffee cup with her finger. "It's not just the baby that's keeping me up. There must have been nearly a hundred and fifty people at the prayer meeting last night; everybody seems to have so much fear and worry and heartache. It's overwhelming. With Pastor Fitchen gone, the prayer meeting is about their only source of comfort."

"Everyone knew that sooner or later we'd cross the English Channel and attack the Germans," Jerry said, "but who could have imagined all those men landing at Normandy?" He looked out the dining room window and stared blankly toward the western horizon. "One hundred and eighty thousand of 'em, it said in the paper—and that was just the first day. It's no wonder so many families in the church are coming to pray. It's hard to imagine not knowing someone who's involved with the fighting there."

"Or the dying," Marjie added wearily, "or the wounding, or the missing in action. Every time I listen to the radio I keep hearing the casualties from Utah Beach, and Omaha Beach, and on and on it goes. And it's only been a week since D-Day. When's it going to end?"

"Not soon enough," Jerry replied. "But Hitler's really getting a taste of what our boys can do. And they say that Stalin's armies are attacking him on the Russian front. Hopefully this is the road to the end."

"Hopefully," Marjie agreed, then she leaned forward with her elbows on the table and rested her head on her left hand. "So what about today?"

"About Timmy and Ellie?" Jerry asked.

"Yeah," said Marjie. "Everything seems to be happening so fast. I'm afraid that if we don't do something, those kids are going to slip into the county's hands."

"I don't think so," Jerry replied, cutting a third and fourth pancake into pieces. "Ruthie's checking everything out. She's not going to let something bad happen to them if it can be prevented. Besides, you can't rule out Lily's mother. She may want the children."

"There's no chance of it, Jerry," Marjie argued. "When the police found her, she didn't even know or care where Lily's been all these years. All she seemed to care about was that she didn't have to pay for shipping the body back east. If she cared about the children, she could have made it out here by train for the funeral today. I'll bet they'll never hear another word from her."

"What did Ruthie tell you about Tom?" Jerry asked. "Did they take him to Rochester?"

"Yesterday, I guess," replied Marjie. "Sounded like the doc waited a couple days too long. Tom used some of that brute strength you talked about and knocked one of the nurses around pretty bad. They couldn't keep him restrained."

"The orderlies at the state mental hospital in Rochester don't have that problem," Jerry commented. "I've heard that's a pretty rough place. Seems like once you hear about people going in there, you don't hear about them getting out again."

"So what about the kids?" Marjie asked again. "The Metcalfe farm is not worth a plugged nickel, and the county's probably going to use whatever money there is to pay for the burial plot and all the other costs. They're going to put the children into the system faster than you think."

Jerry laid down his fork and leaned back in his chair. "I know what you want me to say, Marjie, but I can't," Jerry reasoned. "Timmy and Ellie play with Martha like they're family already, and I think that if anyone could give them a good home, we could. But, I don't know, the timing's so bad. Think of how much time and work Martha requires. How can we add our brand-new baby *and* two little children who've just lost their parents? I don't see how we can do it."

"The timing's not so hot for those kids either," replied Marjie. "We'd just do it. People have survived a lot worse stuff than this."

"Is it the best for the kids, though?"

"Compared to what?" Marjie reasoned. "Would we love them? Yes. Could we provide for them? One way or another, we would. It would just be pretty lean."

"But is your heart in it?"

"What?"

"Is your heart in this?" asked Jerry. "Are you convinced that this is what God wants us to do, or would we be doing it because we're afraid no one else who really cares will do it?"

Marjie shook her head and frowned. "I don't think that's a fair question. There's so much going on here—so many confusing problems—I can't analyze everything. You do what you have to do, I think. And we've got to do something."

"But you can't do everything," countered Jerry. "And what if the thing you're able to do is actually the wrong thing, even though you meant it as a good thing?"

"Then it's a bad thing, I guess," Marjie sputtered, shaking her head. "But how do you know if it's what God has for us?"

"Maybe by answering my first question," Jerry replied. "Is your heart in this, Marjie? If it is, I'm willing to search my heart again and ask the Lord to make it clear. But I gotta tell you that my heart isn't there, although it bleeds for those kids."

Marjie stared into Jerry's blue eyes and saw his compassion. "I can't believe I was so lucky to marry you," she whispered to him, then she looked away. Sitting back in her chair, she lightly massaged her extended abdomen and knew that it was not in her heart to adopt the Metcalfe children either. But the knowledge did nothing to alleviate her heavy heart or the tears that began to fall.

The funeral service for Lily Metcalfe was held at the cemetery and was very short. Pastor Chiles from Cherry Grove had agreed to perform the service, although he had never met the Metcalfes. He mostly read Scriptures and gave a brief sermon on death and the resurrection. Of the few dozen people who came, most were neighbors who had had some dealings with the Metcalfes.

Throughout the service, little Ellie Metcalfe remained glued to Ruth's side, her eyes big and hollow, a faraway look on her face. Marjie realized that she was probably the only one out of the whole gathering who truly mourned for Lily Metcalfe and felt her loss in a personal way. Her brother Timmy, too young to understand, fidgeted the whole time. Billy had all he could do to control the two-year-old for the service's brief duration.

When the service was concluded and those who wanted to offer their sympathies to the children had done so, Timmy and Martha were released from the strong arms that held them, and they immediately took off running down the long rows of tombstones. Shouting and giggles followed, and then of course the two children began attempting to climb the oddly shaped granite rocks. Martha picked a tall gray tombstone with a couple of good toeholds and was quickly perched atop it.

"Get down! Get down! Get down!" Benjamin called out, chasing after the two mischief-makers while the others watched and laughed.

"He's on the cemetery committee," Sarah said. She chuckled as Benjamin managed to get Martha down while Timmy successfully reached the summit of a big tombstone farther down the row. "They get complaints about people who let their children climb on the tombstones."

Ruth leaned over to Ellie. "Why don't you go help Mr. Macmillan, sweetheart. He's got more than he can handle there. You can play tag with Timmy. But keep him off the tombstones if you can."

Ellie nodded without speaking and took off after her brother.

"How's she doing, Ruthie?" asked Sarah as the group walked slowly down the driveway toward their parked cars.

"Not very good," answered Ruth, taking Billy by the arm. "Part of the day she'll be fine, but there can be several hours where she either pulls into a shell or just wants to sit on my lap and cry. She really wanted to see her dad, so we took her one day, but that was terrible. He didn't even know who she was. But it seems like setting up a school time has helped her some."

"What's that?" Jerry asked.

"Oh, I discovered that Ellie's missed a

whole year of school," Ruth said. "I'm not sure how she didn't show up on the county records, but Tom apparently didn't want to send her, and nobody checked. So she's already a year behind. I've been taking a couple of hours every day and working with her on the basics. She likes it, and she learns quickly, and it helps get her mind on something else."

"She has a hard time sleeping, too," Billy added. "Ruth's been up and down almost every night. And Timmy's like a race horse. He's got you running every direction."

"Did you hear anything new from the county office?" asked Marjie.

Both Ruth and Billy nodded, and Ruth said, "A couple things. They appreciate what we're doing, but they want to start the process to find a home for the kids—or homes. The administrator doesn't think it's too likely they'll find someone who'll take both kids."

"Oh my goodness," Marjie gasped, crossing her arms and leaning against the back of their old Ford. "That can't be. Those children have to stay together. They're all the family they've got."

"That's what we told them," Billy agreed. "And they asked us if we had anybody in mind who'd take them in. And we did."

Marjie groaned and shook her head. "I'm so sorry, Ruthie. I shouldn't have said what I did on the phone the other day. I really wanted us to try to bring the children into our family. But Jerry and I talked it over, and . . . I don't think we can do it. Not with the baby coming. And hearing about what you've been through the past couple weeks . . . well, I just can't."

"I don't think you were supposed to do it," Ruth replied. Her black eyes began to flash. "There's another couple we know who don't have children and really want to make a home for them. They've already talked with the county administrator, and I think it's going to happen."

"What! Who?" exclaimed Marjie, catching a burst of energy and grabbing Ruth by the arm. "Why didn't you tell me?"

"Because I wanted to make sure you had a chance to work through your feelings about it," Ruth explained. "I didn't want you to regret it later."

"So who is it?" Marjie cried. She gave Ruth a good shaking, and they all laughed. "Tell me!"

Ruth looked at Billy, then back at Marjie with a beaming face.

"You?" Marjie gasped in disbelief as they nodded. "You've only been married half a year. And what about teaching school?"

"I can take a few years off from teaching,"

Ruth said. "This is more important than a career. And we'll add our own children in the years to come. Billy always said he wanted a lot of kids!"

"Hallelujah!" Marjie shouted, attempting to hug Ruth and Billy in the same motion. But her stomach got them first and sent them both flying backward.

Chapter Twenty-one

A Little Too Late

"That breeze felt good last night, didn't it?" Jerry mumbled, sitting on the edge of the bed after having turned off the alarm clock. The bedroom curtains were swishing from side to side in the gray predawn light as he stretched and yawned. "Feels like it drove the humidity down. Maybe I can get some of my hay to dry today."

Marjie was lying on her back with several pillows propped under her knees. She'd been awake since around four with a backache and hadn't been able to get comfortable. "I thought maybe you'd want to tag along with Grandpa and Grandma when they take Martha to the parade this morning. Have a little fun on the Fourth."

"Very funny," Jerry chuckled, turning

around and placing his hand on her stomach. "I suppose Blue might be willing to drive you to the hospital if you go into labor. Or I could have Charlie saddled up, and you could just ride into town."

"It was just a thought," Marjie said. "I hate to keep you so tied down here. Talk about boring."

"Boring is milking the cows at five in the morning, and if I don't get out there soon, one small cow dog's going to be barking at the door," replied Jerry, standing up and reaching for his work pants. "I'm going to ask you this one more time, though. I really wish I could wait outside the delivery room when the baby comes. It just don't seem right for me to be in there. Men don't do this stuff."

"You're wasting your breath, Farmer Macmillan," Marjie said. "I don't care what anyone else thinks about this. You cannot imagine what you missed seeing when Martha was born, and I *will not* let you miss the second show. I want you there."

Jerry was silent as he buttoned his shirt and sat back down on the edge of the bed to pull on his socks. "What if I faint or do something stupid?" he finally asked.

"A big farm boy like you?" Marjie teased.

"Who knows what I'll do?" Jerry replied seriously.

"And who knows what I'll do?" Marjie answered. "If they give me a shot of that gas again, I just might get up and start dancing with Clark Gable. Don't worry about it."

"Well, those nurses better keep the bargain and keep a lid on this," said Jerry. He stood up and walked to the bedroom door. "People better not find out."

Marjie lay in bed laughing to herself as she listened to Jerry's footsteps on the stairway and then the creaking of the floor as he headed to the back porch to put on his work boots. She had thought that he'd get used to the idea of going into the delivery room with her, but if anything he had grown more reluctant as the time drew nearer.

The back door slapped shut as Jerry headed for the barn. And then the first pain hit. Surprised by its intensity, she held her breath and clenched her teeth to hold back a yell. But when the pain did not subside, she took several short breaths, followed by muffled groans. "Goodness, goodness, goodness," she gasped when it finally let up, then she took a deep breath. "How can the first one be so blasted long and hard?"

Lying perfectly still for the next few minutes, Marjie stared at the dull ceiling and hoped she had the strength to face what was coming. "Well, this is it, finally," she whispered to herself and the baby. "The Fourth of July, nineteen forty-four. What a way to celebrate." Then she muttered to herself, "Maybe I'd better go downstairs. No point in waking Martha if I don't have to."

Climbing carefully out of bed, she put on her bathrobe and gathered her pillows and a blanket. Then she made her way slowly down the stairway and arranged a temporary bed on the davenport, then crossed the room to turn on the radio. She had just made it back to the davenport when a second contraction hit with a burst of fury that seemed to go on and on and on. "Enough!" she finally moaned, but the pain lasted for at least another fifteen seconds. "Wow!" she panted. "I can't do this. Oh my."

Marjie shut her eyes and breathed deeply. From the radio across the room she could hear the nasal-toned voice of one of the war correspondents. "Nearly a million Allied troops have reached France," he said. "While the Americans have captured the badly needed port of Cherbourg, British and Canadian soldiers continue to fight their way to Caen.

"In the Pacific," he continued, "American forces are on the move in the Mariana Islands. Having already captured Saipan and devastated the Japanese navy and airpower at

Philippine Sea, American forces are now focusing their efforts on the island of Guam. Occupation of the Marianas will bring Admiral Nimitz's forces within bombing distance of Japan."

"Thank God," Marjie whispered, but when the war report continued with the details of Allied losses in France, she got up and shut off the radio. "No more today, mister. I got my own battle to fight."

Marjie lay back down on the davenport and propped her knees up with the pillows, waiting. In the early morning quiet, mixed between the robins' singing and the occasional clinking of the metal feeders in the pigpen, she could hear the sound of Jerry singing while he did the morning chores. "It is well, it is well with my soul. . . ."

With all the barn windows open, his clear baritone voice carried easily across the farmyard. Marjie began to hum along, but another contraction took away her breath. *It may be well with his soul,* she thought after the agony subsided, *but it's not so great inside this body.*

With that contraction, Marjie began to watch the time. She guessed that the first few were less than ten minutes apart, but once she had been on the davenport for a while, they jumped down to every five minutes.

Should I call Ma? she wondered. *Doc Sterling said this baby might come faster than Martha did. But it couldn't be this much faster. I can wait a little bit.*

But the contractions did not slow down. If anything, they seemed to get longer and harder. By seven o'clock, Marjie knew the doctor's warning was right, but she was afraid that he might be too right. She waited for another contraction to stop, then got up as quickly as she could and went to the phone. Ringing her mother's number, she waited, but not for long.

"Ma, it's me," she spoke fast into the mouthpiece. "I've been in labor for two hours, and you better come right away. It's going too fast, and I'm heading out to the barn to get Jerry. Martha's sleeping. If we're gone when you get here, you know what to do."

She hung up the receiver and felt another contraction building, but all she could do was hang onto the big wooden phone box and wait it out. Leaning there against the wall, she wondered for the first time whether she could make it to town in time. She wondered if she should call the hospital and ask them to send the doctor out, but when the pain subsided, she thought she'd be all right.

Pushing the front screen door open, Marjie

took a deep breath and headed down the sidewalk for the barn. "Oh good, he's done milking," she whispered, seeing the Holsteins parading out the south door of the barn. Then she muttered, "Who moved the barn back so far?" Every step seemed a mile long.

"Oh no!" she gasped as another contraction caught her one step into the milk room. Jerry was not in there, and the pain forced her down to her knees on the hard concrete floor. "Jerry!" she cried, but then all she could do was wait for it to subside. What was different this time was the sudden intense urge to push, and the fact that her water finally broke. "This baby's coming now!" she exclaimed.

Marjie slowly got back up on her feet and pushed open the door into the milking parlor. All the stanchions for the cows were empty, and Jerry was nowhere in sight. Then she noticed that the door that led outside to Charlie's pen was open.

"Jerry!" she cried again as loud as she could yell. Then she sat down on a big pile of clean straw by one of the calf pens, feeling like she would collapse if she took one more step.

The next minute, Blue came racing back through Charlie's door and leapt over the wooden gate. Jerry was close behind.

"What's wrong?" Jerry called out as the dog jumped up on the straw pile and started licking Marjie's face.

"Get out of here, Blue!" Marjie scolded, pushing him away.

"Go on, Blue!" Jerry added, racing down the aisle. The little Australian cow dog backed off and lay down by his water bowl, putting his head on his paws.

"The baby's on its way?" asked Jerry as he knelt down beside Marjie, who had her hand on her forehead. "Here, I'll help you to the car, and then I'll go get your bag."

"No," Marjie said, looking up at his frantic expression. "It's come too fast. I'm not going to make it to the hospital."

"Of course you're gonna make it!" Jerry urged, taking her arm. "Now come on. Did you call your mother?"

"Yes," Marjie said, ignoring Jerry's tugging. "She's on her way. But I should've called the doctor and gotten him out here. Jerry, I am not going to make it into town in time. I waited too long."

"He told you it was going to be faster this time!" Jerry sputtered. "Come on. We've gotta try to get there. I can carry you to the car."

"There's no time!" Marjie repeated, feeling another contraction. "Go call the doc, then bring some clean sheets out here. We're going to have to do this ourselves."

Jerry's protest ended quickly as he saw the look on Marjie's face from the onrushing labor pain. She had such a desire to push that she had to puff out air to help resist the urge, and the contorted face she made even had Blue looking up in wonder. Jerry tore out of the barn and dashed for the house.

"Oh boy . . ." Marjie sighed when the contraction subsided, bringing Blue to his feet and up on the straw pile to her side again. She saw the funny look on his face and had to laugh. "No one's gonna believe it, Blue Boy. Where do you suggest we do this? Guess this is about the best spot in the house."

Marjie pulled herself up on the wooden gate and grabbed a three-pronged hayfork. As best she could, she spread the straw around in the aisle, trying to get it as even as possible. "At least it's clean," she whispered, dropping down to her knees on the straw as another contraction swept over her. Blue moved in beside her and began to lick her face again, but she was too preoccupied to protest.

This time Marjie stayed down after the pain finally ended. She was sure, if she so much as wiggled, that she'd have the baby right on the spot. "Come on, Jerry," she whispered. "Please, God, give me five more minutes."

One more long contraction followed, and then Marjie heard Jerry's racing footsteps and the slapping open of the door to the milk parlor. He dropped the white sheets down on the straw, then helped Marjie move to the side. Spreading a sheet out over the straw and then spinning around, Jerry tucked Marjie into his arms and laid her in the center of the makeshift bed.

"I liked that," Marjie said, lying flat on her back with Jerry's arms still under her. "You're better than the nurses were last time. I hope you can hold your own as the doctor."

"Cottonpicker! What do I do now?" Jerry asked as he gently let her go.

"Take another one of those sheets," Marjie said. "Then unfold it and get it ready to wrap the baby with."

"Oh my goodness!" cried Jerry, grabbing the sheet and pulling it open. "This is too fast. What am I gonna do?"

"You are going help me, that's what," Marjie replied, propping herself up on her elbows and pulling up her knees. "There we go. Pretend you're helping the vet birth a calf. Are you ready?"

"As ready as I'm ever gonna be!" Jerry exclaimed, kneeling down by her knees. "I think

I can do this. Tell me when."

"Ohhhh! Here it comes!" Marjie cried, feeling a huge wave of energy, then she pushed with all of her strength.

"There's the head!" Jerry nearly shouted, holding out his hands. "There's the head, Marjie! Push!"

"I am!" Marjie screamed, and out shot the baby, slippery and wiggling, into Jerry's hands. A second's silence, then Marjie heard an energetic wail. Blue was so excited that he took off on several laps around the inside of the barn, barking and jumping.

"It's a boy!" Jerry called out, tears spilling down his face. "Marjie, we've got ourselves a boy!"

Chapter Twenty-two

All's Well

"What do you think, Doc?" Marjie asked, lying on the bed in the bedroom off the living room with the newborn boy sleeping soundly beside her. "Are we going to pull through?"

Doctor Sterling was putting some of the medical instruments he had used while examining the mother and child back into his black leather bag. He looked up, his lean, creased face breaking into a rare smile, and said, "You two or your husband? You and young Robert couldn't be better, but Jerry looks like he could use a few days of bed rest."

"He went a little crazy when he got that chunky little boy in his hands," Marjie said with a laugh. "What did you say he weighs?"

"I'm putting down nine pounds four ounces on the birth certificate," the doctor replied, surveying the official-looking document that he had filled out. "But you don't have an accurate scale here, so his weight is my guess based on the delivery of hundreds of children. Are you sure you don't want to come down and stay in the hospital for a few days? Just to be safe?"

Marjie threw him one of her patented smirks. "Because you think we should, or because it's policy, or is it the smell of money?"

"I wouldn't tell you if it was the latter," he responded with a smile. "But you know from your first baby that we like to keep mothers in for several days."

"Are you saying we *should* come to the hospital?" asked Marjie. "Is there any medical reason why we shouldn't stay home?"

"No. But don't you dare say that I said that. You realize the hospital budget would get mighty lean if all the new mothers started going home right away," Doc Sterling replied, standing up straight and taking his bag in hand. "But now, as long as your mother's here to help you, you should be fine. Your body was designed for easy deliveries, and I think you're going to find your recovery much faster this time than with your first delivery."

"Sounds good to me," Marjie sighed. "Guess Jerry and I should have lots more kids."

"That's up to you," the doctor answered. "But I'm going to tell you one more time. If you get pregnant again, you are to come immediately into the hospital when you feel the first hint of a contraction. That's an order. Unless, of course, you want to shave off a couple more years from your husband's life."

"You don't write life insurance policies, do you, Doc?" Jerry asked, poking his head in the door from the living room and laughing. "I might be needing one, the way she's treating me."

Doc Sterling turned toward Jerry. "Not a bad idea, I'd say. Twenty-two years I've been making house calls, and I've never seen a wife ask her husband to deliver their baby by himself in the barn with one dog to assist."

They all burst out laughing, including Sarah, who was standing next to Jerry and holding a sleepy-eyed Martha. Sarah had arrived before the doctor and had helped Jerry get Marjie and the baby from the barn to the house as well as get them cleaned up.

"I simply did what she told me," Jerry said proudly, looking down at his tiny son. "If you ask me, I think little Robert Benjamin's going to be a pilot, the way he flew out of there. He was airborne. I should have had a catcher's mitt."

"If there's a next time around, and you try your barn delivery tricks again," the doctor said after he stopped laughing, "you'd better get that mitt out and keep it ready. I'm guessing the delivery time will be less than an hour for your third child. You did wonderfully without me this time, but I don't recommend it as a rule."

"Don't worry," Jerry said as the doctor moved toward the bedroom door. "Once was enough in this lifetime for me."

"Well, congratulations to you all again," Doctor Sterling said, turning around to Marjie. "I'll have one of the nurses give you a call later to see how it's going. I want you to take it easy and let your mother help here. Even if you feel perkier this time around, you need to rest."

"She will," Sarah said firmly from the living room. "For the next three days or so, I'm the boss. Period."

"Good," the doctor said as he walked out

into the living room and headed for the front door of the farmhouse. "If she won't rest, I suggest you strap her down."

"We will," Jerry said, following him to the door. "What do we owe you, Doc?"

The doctor stopped and turned as he stepped out the door. "You'll get the bill in the mail. I hate doing house calls, so tell Marjie she may not have saved as much money as she thought."

Jerry laughed and waved goodbye as the doctor closed the door. Just then Blue started to bark and ran up the driveway as a car approached. Jerry waited at the screen door as Benjamin's car turned the corner and approached the old white farmhouse, beeping his horn several times as he rolled down the driveway.

"For crying out loud!" Benjamin shouted as he jumped out of his car. He took no notice of Blue's repeated attempts for some attention. "Sarah called and told me you had the baby in the barn! What in the world are you people doing?"

"We're pretending to be pioneers," Jerry answered, laughing as his father raced red-faced up the sidewalk. "You can slow down, though. All's well. You have a nine-pound, four-ounce grandson inside."

"Congratulations, son!" Benjamin cried,

hugging Jerry and patting him on the back. "And you delivered the baby yourself . . . in the barn?"

Jerry nodded and hugged his father back. "Didn't have a choice. It was either me or Blue, and he chickened out."

"Come on in and see your grandson," Sarah spoke from the doorway. "He's a big strapper."

"A boy!" Benjamin exclaimed as he greeted Sarah with a kiss on the cheek at the screen door. "Can you believe it?"

"Yes, as a matter of fact I can," she replied, pointing into the first-floor bedroom. "He's waiting for you, and his sister's there as well."

"Boy, this beats the hospital hands down. Nobody to keep kicking you out of the room," Benjamin said, marching toward the bedroom. Stopping at the door, he peeked around the corner.

"Come on in, Gramps," Marjie called out.

"Look at that rascal," Benjamin announced with a beaming smile, stepping into the room and taking Marjie's hand. The baby was lying to her left, and Martha snuggled up on her right, thumb in mouth. "Gapa," she said in greeting.

"Hi, sweetie," he said, leaning over to kiss the little girl before inspecting the newcomer. "My goodness. He looks just like Jerry did when he was born. Not a hair on his head. How can that be? Martha had all that silky dark hair."

"Must be the Macmillan side," Marjie teased, with a pointed glance at Benjamin's bald head. "He's ours, though, that I know. Nobody switched babies in the nursery."

Benjamin ran a large calloused finger along the baby's pudgy cheek. "Little Robert, I'm Grandpa Benjamin. You got your other name from your other grandpa. We're gonna have ourselves a lot of fun together. Just like your sister and me. You two are gonna come and stay at my house for days on end, and we'll—"

A sudden cry from the newborn interrupted Benjamin, and Marjie said, "It may be a couple of days before they can come to your house. I think this little guy is hungry. So, if you all don't mind stepping out for a bit, I'm going to attempt feeding him. Unless you care to watch."

"No, thank you!" Benjamin sputtered, standing up straight. "You want to come with Grandpa?" he asked Martha. But she shook her head no.

"I think she wants to get to know her brother," Sarah said, taking Benjamin by the arm. "Let's go get some coffee."

Jerry closed the bedroom door as he and

Sarah and Benjamin exited the room. "You go ahead and get some coffee," he said. "I've got some sheets and towels to wash. That was not the prettiest of sights out there."

"Don't you even think about doing wash," Sarah said, spinning around. "That's my job, and I told you I'm the boss now. I'll take care of that mess later. I'll bet you got some field work that you could use Ben's help with today."

"Yeah, if that's an offer," Jerry said. "I got some hay drying that I was hoping to get up today. It's been on the ground too long already."

"That wasn't an offer," Benjamin replied with a smile. "That was an order. And I think it's a hint that somebody would like the two of us out of the house today."

"You're brilliant, Ben," Sarah said, heading to the kitchen. "That's one of the reasons I married you. You haven't eaten yet, have you, Jerry?" she asked, looking around the undisturbed kitchen. "No coffee or nothing?"

"No, I tried to sneak away and get a bite to eat, but the baby just wouldn't wait," Jerry teased, shrugging his shoulders. "I hate it when that happens. Fella could starve to death."

"I didn't get anything either," Benjamin spoke up, laughing at Jerry. "Did you eat,

Sarah?"

Sarah stopped and had to think about it for a moment. "By golly, I didn't," she said and chuckled. "Guess I'd better make something for Marjie as well. She's going to be hungry. I'll get you boys some coffee first."

Jerry and Benjamin plopped down in their chairs at the dining room table, and Jerry stretched and yawned. "This is the wildest Fourth of July I've ever seen," he said to his father, rubbing his cheeks, "and it's barely even started. Can you imagine that I was embarrassed by the thought of going into the delivery room with Marjie, and I ended up having to do it by myself!"

Benjamin laughed and shook his head. "It's always surprising what a person can do when he has to," he said. "Driving Marjie to the hospital when Martha was delivered was scary enough for me. I've never driven that fast in my life. My legs were shaking afterward. We didn't make it by much that time around, either."

"Marjie does everything with a certain flair, doesn't she?" Jerry commented.

"Never a dull moment, I always said," Sarah added in, coming around the counter. "Jerry, where's the eggs?"

"Oh, there on the table in the back entry," Jerry responded. "Marjie didn't bring them in yet. I'll get—"

"Sit still," said Sarah, about to turn around when Blue started to bark. "Who's that, now?"

Jerry stood up and went to the dining room picture window as a car turned into the driveway. "It's Ed Bentley!" Jerry exclaimed, shaking his head. "You don't suppose—"

"Somebody called him," Benjamin filled in Jerry's sentence. "And he smells another story."

"That stupid party line," Jerry groused, stepping to the front screen door. "When I called the hospital, somebody was listening in again."

"What's going on?" Marjie's muffled voice called from the bedroom.

"It's Ed Bentley," Jerry called back. "I'll try to get rid of him."

Jerry went out onto the sidewalk as Bentley jumped out of his car and grabbed his camera. Shutting the car door, the wiry, middle-aged reporter from the *Preston Republican* saw Jerry waiting and called out, "Jerry, how you doing? Somebody down at the paper heard that Marjie delivered a baby out in the barn this morning. That true?"

"Aren't you busy today?" Jerry asked, crossing his arms as the reporter came up the sidewalk. "Lots of Fourth of July stories to cover?"

Ed Bentley stopped and pushed his wire-rimmed glasses back up on his nose. "I got about two hours before I have to be at the parade. If what I heard is true, you have a better story here than I can scratch up going around to the parades. You actually delivered the baby yourself?"

"Who told you that?"

"I . . . ah . . . met the doc heading back to Preston and flagged him down," Ed replied with a crooked smile. "He was pretty amazed. Nine pounds four ounces, I believe."

Jerry shook his head and rubbed his forehead. "This is a family affair, Ed. Marjie's just had the baby. Can't we talk it over and give you a call in a couple days?"

"By then it'll be old news," the reporter said. "If I can get it in today, it's a front-page story. I've never heard of anyone being born in a barn."

"I can think of one at least," Jerry replied, raising his eyebrows and smiling.

"Oh yeah," Bentley said, chuckling and straightening his black bow tie. "But how about it?"

"No," Jerry answered. "I can't bother Marjie and—"

"Jerry!" Sarah called, stepping out onto the

front steps. "Marjie says she's willing to make a deal with Ed."

"Oh no," Bentley growled, squeezing his eyes shut. "What now?"

"Do you really want the story?" Sarah asked.

"Yes," the reporter said, nodding and opening his eyes. "But what's the trade this time? Let me guess. Photos and papers."

"You're very good, Mr. Bentley," Sarah replied. "Marjie'll give you the story if you'll give her twelve prints of the newborn with Marjie and Jerry and Martha together."

"How many newspapers?" Bentley asked.

"One bundle," said Sarah.

"A bundle!" Ed cried. "What's she going to do with a whole bundle of newspapers?"

"Is it a deal?" Sarah asked pointedly. "I suppose a photo of the World War One veterans marching in the Fourth of July parade will sell more papers? I always love those, don't you?"

"I surrender," Bentley replied, walking past Jerry and up the steps. "Where does she want the picture taken, anyway?"

Chapter Twenty-three

Moving Day

"I thought that Dorothy would probably be here by now," Sarah said, glancing up from her needlework and checking the time on the wooden mantel clock in the living room. Then she turned to Marjie, who was lying on the davenport. "Jerry and Ben had that moving truck loaded before ten o'clock this morning. I suppose she's trying to get the place spic and span before she leaves."

"Knowing her, the parsonage will be spotless for whoever moves in next," Marjie replied. "What's Benjamin got to say about the search for a new pastor? Have they found any candidates yet?"

Sarah set the pillowcase she'd been embroidering on the table beside her chair and took a deep breath. "I haven't heard much yet, even though Ben's on the committee. They've talked about a couple of pastors who seem to be possible candidates, and Ben and some of the others on the committee are going to drive down to Des Moines to hear one of them next Sunday."

"You're not going?" Marjie asked her mother.

"No," Sarah replied, shaking her head.

"They've got a full car, which is a good excuse for me to stay home. But I don't think I'd go even if there was room. It's just too hard for me to think about finding a new pastor."

"I hate the thought of it, too," Marjie said, turning on her side toward Sarah. "How do you replace someone you've come to love like we did Fitch? And I hate the process as well. It just doesn't seem right to be sending out church members to see if someone who's already the pastor of another church might be a candidate to pastor our church. 'Church spies'—that says it all."

"I don't like it much, either," said Sarah, "but Ben says we have to work with the system, even if we think it's a flawed system. To tell the truth, I have trouble with the notion of professional pastors who move from church to church over a long career. Seems like pastors were meant to come from within a church, so they're really a part of things. Too bad Chester didn't stay around."

"Without the academic credentials, Chester wouldn't have had a chance," Marjie observed. "He has the heart of a pastor, he is a wonderful teacher, and everyone loved and respected him, but it would take seven years of school and a pile of money for him to qualify for the position. Makes you wonder how many are held back from being pastors because they could never afford it."

"That was a wonderful letter from Margaret," Sarah said, standing up and going to the living room window. "With the huge build-up before D-Day, it sounds like they arrived in Scotland at just the right time."

"Twenty-seven hundred ships," Marjie mused. "You can imagine the throngs of sailors and soldiers in Glasgow. I can just see Chester out in the streets handing out invitations to come for a free meal at the church. Sounded like hundreds of men have been coming to faith through Margaret's father's preaching."

"I'm sure that Chester's doing his share of preaching, too," Sarah reflected. "And what a place for Margaret as well. Makes me wish I could pack up and go join them."

Marjie stared at her mother as she stood in the window's bright summer sunshine, a hot July wind lightly chasing some loose strands of gray hair that had fallen across her forehead. Nothing about the woman Marjie called mother had changed physically, but everything else was so new and different that Marjie found herself caught at times in wonderment. "Too bad you and Ben are needed so badly here," she said. "You'd be perfect for that kind of work as well."

Sarah chuckled and turned back toward Marjie. "If Ben and I were young again, we might do more than dream about it," she said. "I am so glad, though, that we've been able to send some money over to help support Chester and Margaret. Do you know this is the first time in my life that I could afford to do something special like this? I can't tell you what it feels like for me. Even if I would have wanted to before—and I never did—there wasn't an extra penny."

"Jerry thinks it's fun." Marjie laughed, sitting up and stretching her legs. "Can you imagine someone milking extra cows—every day, twice a day—just so he can have the thrill of tucking twenty bucks into an occasional letter? What's happened to us, Ma?"

Laughing richly, Sarah said, "We've either lost our marbles, or else something very good has come over us—something divine, I hope. Your father would have said it was 'amazing grace.' And I didn't understand a word Robert was saying. I'm sure he'd be thrilled."

"I wonder if he and Pastor Fitchen have gotten together yet?" Marjie said, the thought suddenly springing into her head. "Do you suppose?"

"Why not?" Sarah replied, turning and looking out the window again. "That's one conversation I'd like to listen in on. Your father loved to dance, and I'll bet he's been doing some jigs around the throne. Someday I'd—"

Sarah's reverie was cut short by the sound of tires on crushed rock as Dorothy Fitchen's car pulled into the driveway and slowly approached the farmhouse.

Marjie stood up and walked to the front screen door and waved. "I wonder if anyone ever told Dorothy that her car has three gears," she said to Sarah. "She's the slowest granny I've ever seen on the road."

"It's amazing she drives at all," Sarah replied, joining Marjie as she stepped out the front door onto the porch. "Most women her age never even thought about learning how to drive. If your father hadn't gotten sick, you wouldn't see me driving."

"I thought that Grandpa would be back with Martha by now," Marjie said, looking down the empty driveway toward the mailbox. "He doesn't want to miss saying goodbye, does he?"

"No, he'll be here soon," replied Sarah. "I'll bet he stopped at the store in Greenleafton to treat Martha to a malt."

Dorothy Fitchen looked thinner and more exhausted than Marjie could remember, even during the time when her husband had been recovering from the mild stroke. Her straight white bangs weren't so straight, but her friendly brown eyes still managed to smile as she looked up at her friends.

"Well, it's done," Dorothy said wearily, giving Sarah, then Marjie, a hug. "All of my earthly belongings that I didn't either sell or burn are on the road for Illinois, and the big old parsonage is clean as a whistle. One thing I won't miss—cleaning that place. It was three times bigger than what we needed."

Sarah and Marjie laughed, and Sarah opened the screen door. "I sure wish you would have let me come up to help," she said as Dorothy stepped into the house and walked to the dining room table.

"You packed half of the stuff that I shipped," Dorothy protested, sitting down quickly into one of the chairs. "You deserved a rest. Plus, it seemed like a good idea to let some of the other ladies help. Everybody's been so kind. Boy, it feels good to sit again."

Marjie sat down next to Dorothy while Sarah went into the kitchen to get the coffee and something to snack on.

"What'll it be?" Sarah called out, looking over a counter crowded with foods that neighbors and friends had dropped off when they heard Marjie had had the baby. "Apple pie, pumpkin pie, chocolate cake, brownies, apple crisp, cinnamon rolls, or . . . my personal favorite and the one we have to eat quickly before it spoils . . . banana cream pie?"

Dorothy was laughing before Sarah finished her list. "I'll take a double on the banana cream. I didn't think about lunch, and I am starving. Looks like I came to the right place."

"You did," said Marjie. "We've been given so much food that I've been sending Jerry around to some families who we thought could use it. We couldn't possibly eat it all."

"That's the way it was the first week after Fitch died," Dorothy said. "I didn't have the appetite of a mouse, and my kitchen looked like a bakery. I felt like Robin Hood, driving around the country passing out goodies. At the time, it was a lot more fun giving it away than eating it."

"I remember what that was like," Sarah said, setting a cup of coffee and the huge piece of pie in front of Dorothy. "What would you like, Marjie?"

"Give me about half of that," she replied. "I just sit around all day and don't burn off an ounce of what I eat."

"That was a wonderful picture and story in the paper," Dorothy said after she swallowed her first bite of pie. "I still can't believe you and Jerry pulled that one off. I was in labor with my babies for so long that even my husband could never convince me that there is no purgatory. I experienced it firsthand, and it lasted just short of eternity."

All three women laughed, and Sarah sat down on the other side of Dorothy after she'd handed Marjie a piece of pie and a steaming cup of coffee.

"It doesn't seem fair, does it," Marjie said, shaking her head. "Like so many other things."

Dorothy swallowed another bite of pie and looked into Marjie's face. She nodded and said, "Such as my moving away?"

Marjie smiled and sighed, pushing down on her piece of pie with her fork. Then she said, "Yeah, I've been dreading this since the funeral. I think it's wonderful that you can be close to your daughter and her family, and I know it's something you planned a long time ago. I just think it's a rotten deal that when the pastor dies, his widow needs to move on so the next family can move in. You're as much a part of our lives as Fitch was."

Closing her eyes and taking a deep breath, Dorothy laid her fork down and sat still for a few moments. "You could have at least waited for me to finish my pie before you started in," she said, smiling and opening her glistening brown eyes. "It does look like a rotten deal, and . . . there have been plenty of times over the past few weeks when it's felt like a rotten deal, but I could choose to settle in the area if I wanted to."

"I'd think the worst part is having to move so quickly," Sarah said. "When Robert died, it took me at least a year before I felt like I was making good decisions. I would have hated to make a move during that time."

Dorothy nodded and rubbed her forehead. "You know, for years I've been looking forward to retiring close to my family. I honestly didn't think it would be hard to leave, although Fitch and I both liked it here. And then you two Macmillan families have to come traipsing into our lives and wreck it all."

She shut her eyes again, and Marjie didn't know whether Dorothy was laughing or crying or both. But her mouth was scrunched up funny and her shoulders were bouncing up and down. Sarah reached over and put her hand on Dorothy's arm, then they waited for Dorothy.

"Do you know," Dorothy said finally with her eyes still closed, reaching around and massaging the back of her neck, "in all of his years of ministry, Fitch never had a friend like Benjamin. There was always this fine line of being friendly but not getting too close. And I . . . did the same thing . . . until you two came along. I'm not even sure how you jumped over the line, but I feel like I'm saying goodbye to my best friend and another daughter. It's terrible."

"We love you, too," Sarah whispered as the tears began to pour down from the corners of her eyes. She reached her arm around Dorothy and hugged her friend. "We couldn't help it, though. You were too nice to us. I hate to think I can't stop in to see you."

Marjie wept as well, quietly and to herself. She knew she would miss Dorothy Fitchen as she already did the good woman's husband. They had been there for her at every major step she had taken as a believer, and the hole of her absence would not be quickly filled.

Chapter Twenty-four

Childhood Fears

"Why didn't you tell us sooner!" Marjie complained to Ruth. "I suppose we're the last ones to find out."

Ruth Wilson was standing at the screen door, laughing at Marjie while watching Billy and Jerry play in the front yard of the farmhouse with Martha, Ellie, and Timmy. "No, you're about the first ones we've told," she said, turning toward Marjie, who was setting out a light meal for their Sunday lunch. "But it all happened so quickly that we hardly had time to talk it over ourselves. Billy overheard Mr. Stockdale tell someone at the bank that the McDuff house in Greenleafton was going to be put up for sale this week. It was such a good price that he called them before it went on the market, and we signed the papers on Friday night."

"I just can't believe it, Ruthie," Marjie said, setting out the hot dog buns and ketchup on the dining room table. "You and Billy are going to be so close. When will you move?"

"Not till the end of August," Ruth replied. "McDuff's daughter is moving back to Minneapolis then. It can't happen soon enough. Our apartment was fine for just Billy and me, but we really need something bigger with the kids and all. We were looking around Preston, but I'm thrilled this little house opened up in Greenleafton. Except for Billy's job, it's closer to everything we're involved with. The house is in pretty bad shape, though. You still looking for roofing work?"

Marjie laughed and nodded. "I'm a little rusty since finishing our garage, but it's a pretty small roof on that house. What are you willing to pay?"

"I'll trade you some babysitting hours," Ruth answered. "This mothering business is more than I bargained for."

"It's around the clock, isn't it?" Marjie commented. "How are they doing? You still feel good about trying to adopt?"

"Timmy's doing really well, but he keeps asking about his goats," Ruth said with a smile. "Did I tell you that one afternoon Ellie told me her mother had let those goats come and go in the house? We had a hard time finding any of their clothes that were worth trying to save. I think something must have been wrong with Lily long before her appendix got infected."

"You could tell me almost anything strange about that house, and I'd believe it," said Marjie, untying her apron and setting it on the counter. "Let's go sit in the living room until those guys are ready for lunch."

Marjie followed Ruth into the living room, and they both sat down on the davenport.

"So how's Ellie?" Marjie asked.

"She's exceptional with her schoolwork," Ruth replied. "Ellie's very bright, and I think she'll be ready for school come September. But she misses a lot more than Timmy's beloved goats, that's for sure. She knows that her mother's gone, but she keeps thinking her father's coming back. And she's so afraid that someone's going to take her from me or that I'm going to leave her. It just takes a lot of time with her."

"She's like a scared little puppy," said Marjie. "That's probably the way it will be for a long time. She needs to know that nothing's going to happen to you or Billy."

Ruth's dark eyes flashed, and she said, "That reminds me of something good that happened to Billy this week that we haven't told you about. Mr. Stockdale promoted him to manager of all farm loans at the bank."

"Are you kidding?" Marjie sputtered. "That's a powerful job. Wasn't Stockdale doing that himself?"

"He was," answered Ruth. "But he's been letting Billy handle some of the new loan applications as well as review and make recommendations on the loans that are out there, and he's been impressed with what Billy does. Stockdale also thinks that when the war ends there's going to be a flood of farm loan applications, and I think he'd rather not handle all that work."

"And Billy got a nice fat raise, I hope," Marjie said with a smile.

"Compared to what he had been getting, it was . . . nice and fat," Ruth replied with a laugh. "With the work we need to do on the house, and me not teaching this fall, we *really* needed it. Talk about timing, eh?"

"It's perfect," Marjie replied. "Maybe Billy

can use all that power he's got now to put the squeeze on the creamery to jump the price of milk up. Then we might be able to afford to take a vacation once. Remember the old tourist slogan? 'Come point your car to Minnesota's cool north woods. Let the tall pines be your roof, the star your night lamp, the spicy air your tonic.' "

"I do remember that one," Ruth said. "But except for visiting relatives, our family never took a vacation. Wouldn't that cool north woods feel good today?"

"You said it," Marjie answered. "We never took a vacation either. We did drive up to Minneapolis for the state fair once when I was little. That was like a dream for us kids. I always wondered where the folks dug up the money for that trip."

"They probably did the same thing my folks did—sacrificed something they needed so that us kids would have something special," said Ruth. "I think my dad wore the same old suit until the coat fell off his back one Sunday morning."

Marjie laughed, then she got up from the davenport and stepped over to the window. "The kids look like they're still having a ball," she said, "including those kids we call our husbands. Do you think I should put the water back on for the hot dogs?"

"No, let them play," Ruth said. "It won't take long to get the water boiling again. We have to take advantage of every free minute we get to talk. Here I've been blabbing about me all the time. What's new out here?"

"On the farm—something new?" Marjie joked and laughed. "With the baby, I've got about all the 'new' I can handle right now. But I have been thinking a lot about Lily the past few days, and it's really been bothering me."

"Why? You didn't even know her, did you?" asked Ruth.

"That's exactly what's been bothering me," Marjie said, sitting back down on the davenport. "Here there's a woman who lives less than half a mile away, and I never even knew her name before she died. I met her husband once when he hit Blue with his car, but I hardly even knew that Ellie or Timmy existed. And they were just down the hill from us, Ruthie. That's not right."

"Well, I wouldn't torment myself too much," Ruth offered. She leaned closer to Marjie. "They were strange birds, Tom and Lily. As far as I can tell, no one really *knew* them, and they apparently didn't want to have a thing to do with anyone. Not much you can do with people who want to live as recluses."

Marjie shrugged her shoulders. "I realize that. Actually, I'm not feeling guilty about them. I still feel like I'm a newcomer to the area, and there are a lot of families I haven't met yet. But it bothers me that the Metcalfes could have lived as long as they did within two miles of our church and no one from the church seemed to notice they were alive. I didn't hear one person say that they'd ever invited the Metcalfes to church, let alone tried to befriend them."

"I suppose most people figured the Metcalfes were so odd it wasn't worth trying," said Ruth.

"And yet they're human beings like us, however eccentric they were," said Marjie. "And they had two wonderful children. It just seems beyond reason that years could go by and no one sought them out. Mr. Biden traveled halfway around the world to reach people who have never had a chance to know Jesus, and yet we have a family within a stone's throw of our house and we have no idea where they stood with God. Now Lily's gone. No one has a chance to knock on her door now."

Ruth nodded and sat quietly for a few moments. "You're right, Marjie," she said finally. "It's a rotten shame about Lily. As sweet as Ellie is, she must have gotten some of it from her mother. Maybe she wasn't as strange as people thought."

"And maybe she was the strangest person in the world. But we'll never know for sure," said Marjie. "I just don't want it to happen again."

"So, what's the catch?" asked Ruth. "You're cooking on an idea, aren't you?"

Marjie laughed and said, "Not much of one, probably, but Jerry and I have talked about what we might try to do if there was someone in the area who seemed isolated or new to the community. It's not just the extreme cases like the Metcalfes. There are others who, for whatever reasons, don't mix much with their neighbors and don't seem to have a church. Think of Chester's parents. It sounded to me like the Mormons and the Jehovah's Witnesses were a lot more interested in them than any of our church people."

"And I take it that you'd like to know if Billy and I might be interested in joining you and Jerry in trying to do something for these type of people?" said Ruth with a pinched smile.

"Exactly," replied Marjie, returning the smile with a nod. "But not like a church program or something we have to do. I'm only thinking that we'd keep each other aware of the people around us who are needy like this, and perhaps put our heads together occasionally to see if we can do something good for them or pay them a visit or just call them on the phone. I don't know, but I feel like it's worth a try."

"I think it's a great idea," said Ruth. "I'm sure Billy's going to be interested in it, too. I wonder if he and Jerry could find a way to get to know that old bachelor who lives back in the woods by the Abeler farm. What's his name? Phil . . ."

"Rogers, I think," Marjie added. "No car, no tractor, no electricity. He's got that dog that looks like a wolf and always runs alongside his team of horses and the wagon. Jerry told me that all you kids in the country school used to believe the old man was a horrible troll who had a pile of money stashed away in the walls and floors of his creepy house. And you think he's a good candidate for Jerry and Billy to start on?"

Marjie and Ruth both laughed, and Ruth said, "It's probably a tad aggressive, but like you said, you never know until you try—and I'll bet nobody's ever tried. He must be about a hundred and twenty years old. Maybe we could offer to help him cut wood for the winter or something."

"Or just offer to drive him to church once," said Marjie. "Even in Greenleafton, I think there are a couple of families who seem to have nothing to do with anyone around here. Maybe there's a way to step into their lives and make a difference."

Ruth nodded. "There is one other thing I'm going to do, and that's to help strengthen our church. With Dorothy leaving, there's no one in charge of the Sunday school program for children. She's been running that program since forever—it was sort of her understood job as the pastor's wife—and the last few years it's really needed a boost. I'd like to take the program over and see what I can do with it."

"That's—" exclaimed Marjie, but anything else she was going to say was cut short as Billy Wilson pulled open the front screen door and stepped into the farmhouse. He was sweating up a storm and panting.

"What are you ladies doing in here?" Billy asked, looking into the dining room at the half-prepared meal. "Where are the hot dogs and beans? And I need a drink!"

"You know where the glasses are, don't you? There's plenty of water if you turn that faucet at the sink," Marjie teased. "We're on strike for higher wages now that you got your big raise."

Billy smiled and laughed. "It's not that big, and the kids are coming in, Missy Witty, so I suggest you get the dogs cooking."

"Yessir, Pa," Marjie replied, jumping up from the davenport and walking toward Billy. "How are your legs doing these days?"

"Same as always—rotten," answered Billy, mopping some sweat from his forehead with his T-shirt. "Why?"

"Well," Marjie answered, "Ruthie tells me that you and the ancient troll, Phil Rogers, are old buddies, and she said you might be going down to help him cut up some wood for winter. I just thought it might be hard on your legs."

"What are you talking about?" Billy protested. "I've never talked to him in my life. I've always been scared of him and his monster dog. Jerry and I always thought the woods around his shack were haunted."

"You better speak with your wife then," Marjie teased, walking past Billy and giving him a playful shove. "We think it's time for you to face some of your childhood fears."

Chapter Twenty-five

A Country Boy

"It's too hot in that kitchen for me," Sarah Macmillan called out to Marjie, letting the screen door slap behind her as she and her dog Tinker came out of the farmhouse. She walked across the lawn to where Marjie was rocking in the wooden glider in the shade under one of the tall elm trees in the side yard. Baby Robert lay sleeping in Marjie's lap with one pudgy fist in his mouth. "I should have made something cool like chicken salad instead of baked chicken and dressing."

"Trying to impress the preacher and his wife?" Marjie teased as she stopped the glider and let her mother take the seat across from her. Tinker flopped down in the grass alongside the glider with a protracted groan. "What did you think of Mr. Holmes?"

Sarah's hair was tied back loosely, and a late-August breeze gently tugged at the loose gray tendrils. "I liked him a lot, and his wife and children," she said, relaxing back in the seat of the glider. "He's not flashy, that's for sure. Seemed almost dull compared to the other young man we had two weeks ago. But he kept his message simple, and I liked it that I could understand what he was saying. Reminded me a little bit of Pastor Fitchen, I guess."

"Talk about your contrast between two candidates," Marjie said. "That first guy—Richard Felding—is fresh out of seminary, handsome, dressed to kill, fast-talking, smart, enthusiastic. He acted like some of the high-powered businessmen that used to come into the restaurant when I worked in Rochester. But Edward Holmes is low-key and slow; his suit is worn, and his tie was crooked. Not exactly a model for Sears and Roebuck."

"He seems like one of us, doesn't he? Just an ordinary Joe," Sarah commented casually. "Same with his wife and three children—sorta plain and simple. What was her name? Helen. She can't hold a candle to that Richard Felding's wife in the looks department. Talk about looking like a model. And I think she knew it."

Marjie laughed and said, "I think so, too. She was turning the men's heads, and her husband had the women sneaking peeks. If looks count, I can tell you who's going to get the church's invitation."

"No question," replied Sarah with a nod. "I hope that's not all we go by, though. Did you understand what Felding's sermon was about?"

" 'Five Links in the Golden Doctrinal Chain,' " Marjie repeated, raising her eyebrows and pressing her lips together. "No, I didn't get much out of that message. Every other word was some theological something-or-other expression that I've never heard before. But Richard Felding certainly seemed to think it was important."

"What did Jerry think?"

"Jerry thought the guy's wife was a knockout."

"No. What did he think of the sermon?"

Marjie laughed and stroked her little son's back. "What do you think he thought? Jerry couldn't understand a word the guy said. Analyzing the Greek text when you don't even know what word he's talking about in the English isn't exactly up Jerry's alley."

"Or mine. So why are people buzzing about Felding?" asked Sarah. "If what we see is what we get, I don't like it."

"Six feet tall, college football star, summa cum laude, pitch black hair, strong jawline, beauty-queen wife. What do you want?" asked Marjie, half seriously. "The man's a winner, and we all like winners. He's going to do something big somewhere, and I suppose people figure that we're lucky to even have a shot at getting him here. And his preaching's probably going to get better. Nobody can talk to himself like that forever."

"Don't bet on it," Sarah sputtered. "You think we should try to get Felding?"

"No," Marjie replied, shaking her head. "I think we should try to get Chester and Margaret back and forget about calling anyone. I'm just saying that I understand the buzz about Felding. Mr. Holmes didn't give anyone much to jump up and down about this morning."

"Maybe slow and steady is what our congregation needs," Sarah said, shrugging her shoulders. "I just wish the wind was from the north. Nothing like a hot southeast breeze cutting past the hog barn, is there? It'll be interesting to see how this preacher and his family react."

"It's a rich, sweet, well-brewed aroma today," Marjie said and grinned. "You could almost cut it with a knife. I'd like to see Richard Felding and his wife take a whiff. I bet their toes would curl."

"I doubt they've ever seen the inside of a barn," Sarah added, turning to look down the road as a car approached. "Well, there's Jerry and Ben. I figured the preacher's car would be following them."

Tinker jumped up from her resting spot and trotted out to the farmyard to meet the car, but she didn't bark.

"I don't see Martha in there with them," Marjie said, scanning the windows as the old black Ford came up the driveway and into the farmyard. "Wonder if she's lying on the seat sleeping?"

"Must be," Sarah replied. She waved to Benjamin as the car stopped.

Benjamin and Jerry jumped out of the car

and slammed their doors shut as Tinker jumped up and down for some attention from Jerry.

"Aren't you forgetting something?" Sarah called out to the men. "Where've you got my granddaughter?"

"She's . . . ah . . . riding with the Holmes," Jerry called back, bending over to scratch the dog's ears.

"What?" cried Marjie. "You left her with them?"

Jerry looked up and nodded nonchalantly. "Yeah. Their kids fell in love with her and begged to let her ride with them. They'll be here pretty quick."

"We don't even know them!" Marjie protested. "You shouldn't have done that."

"Martha's fine," Jerry assured her, walking up to the wooden glider. "Those kids are really nice. The oldest girl is fourteen."

"Well, I still don't like it," Marjie grumped. "Where are they?"

"Oh, they just stopped back at the corner," Benjamin replied. "The kids wanted to pick some of those wild daisies that are down in that ditch. Here they come now."

An old black Ford like Jerry's came rolling down the gravel road and turned into the driveway. One of the children who was sitting in the backseat was holding Martha and helping her wave through the open window.

"See," Jerry said confidently. "She's in good hands."

"Those good hands better keep a good grip on her," Marjie warned. "She could jump right out."

The car pulled up next to Jerry's car and stopped. The doors quickly opened and the three Holmes children, along with Martha, piled out and headed straight for the pig barn with Tinker right on their heels.

"Do you mind if they look around?" Edward Holmes called out apologetically as he shut his car door. "They love being on a farm, and I'm afraid we're not going to have much luck with keeping them inside."

"No, as long as they stay out of the pens," Benjamin called back. "Sometimes the sows are in a bad mood, and they can hurt you in a hurry, especially a kid."

"Stay out of the pens!" Mr. Holmes called out to his children, who had already reached the fence and were reaching in to feel the hairy, tough skin on the backs of the pigs lying along the fence.

Helen Holmes was shaking her head as she approached the gathering of Macmillans by the wooden glider. "Nothing like a farm to bring out the wild side of my kids. They think this is heaven, with all the critters to play with. I brought along some old clothes for after lunch, but it looks like I may be too late."

"They don't mind the smell?" Marjie asked, tapping her mother on the foot with her shoe.

"Not at all," Helen replied with a hearty laugh. Her husband laughed behind her as well. "Nothing like a hot summer breeze through the pig yard, is there? Makes me feel like I'm home again. We send our kids out to my folks' farm for a couple of weeks every summer. Then we have to try to drag them back to town afterward. They get bored stiff in the city."

Sarah tapped Marjie back on the shoe and winked. "So, are you folks both from the farm?"

"Born and raised," Edward answered with a disarming nod. "And mighty proud of it. If I wasn't so sure I've been called to be a minister, I'd pitch this old suit tomorrow. I drive by these wonderful farms out here, and I have to fight with some severe jealousy."

The Macmillans all laughed, and Marjie immediately was struck with how relaxed and comfortable it felt to be with the Holmes. "I imagine a big city like Des Moines was quite a change of pace for you?"

Edward smiled and leaned up against the tall elm tree. "In more ways than one," he said, glancing over at his wife. "We got married right after college, and then I did seminary, so we've learned to live in the city, even if we don't care for it that much. But it's another story, for me at least, to try to pastor a city church when I'm really a country boy at heart. At times I think it's not such a good match. I don't think I'll ever quite measure up to what they're looking for in me."

"That's why we're here," Helen continued, reaching up to straighten the collar of her light blue cotton dress, which had flipped up in the breeze. "Edward would really like the opportunity to pastor a country church. I keep telling him that he needs to find a place where he can get out and shovel manure every once in a while. Get some dirt back underneath his fingernails."

"Boy have you came to the right place," Jerry declared with a smile. "I can't imagine living in town, let alone trying to pastor a church of city slickers. They'd probably run me out of town on a rail after a week of putting up with me."

Edward Holmes laughed and wrapped one of his long arms around his wife. "It's never been quite that bad," he said. "And the Lord has really taught us a lot the last few years about loving people who are different from us. But I do think there's some advantage in having a country church pastored by someone who grew up on a farm. You're just more familiar . . . but then I guess that sounds a little too much like . . ." His voice trailed off, and he changed the subject, looking around behind him and asking, "Jerry, do you mind showing me around the farm? Or will we be eating first?"

"No, go ahead and look around," Sarah said, getting up from her seat on the glider. "I'll check on the chicken, but there's no rush. Helen, why don't you sit here by Marjie?"

"Thank you," Helen responded, stepping onto the glider and sitting down across from Marjie. "It's so nice and cool in the shade."

Handing Helen his suit coat, Edward turned to follow Jerry and Benjamin toward the barn. "Say, I hate to even ask, but I see that John Deere in the shed. I'd pay you money if you'd let me start it up and drive around the yard. Any chance I could do that?"

"Oh brother, this is embarrassing," Helen groaned to Marjie, looking over at the pig barn. Her dark green eyes were smiling along with the look of delight on her face. "Edward's a nut for John Deeres. I think he'd prefer a tractor to a car any day. My kids look like they're getting set to jump the fence and try riding the pigs bareback. Marjie, I'm afraid you're getting to see us the way we really are, which is kind of scary."

"Oh, I don't know," Marjie said. "I think I like what I see. Did you ever ride a pig?"

Helen laughed and said, "I had four older brothers, and I tried everything they did, but a pig's not half as much fun to ride as a calf. They can get up just like a bucking bronco. Just don't tell my kids that I did it."

"Do you like horses?" Marjie asked.

Helen shut her eyes and sighed. "When I was teenager, I would have gladly traded any or all of my brothers for one horse. But we could never afford one. Do you have a horse?"

Marjie nodded and smiled. "Do you have a fourteen-year-old who is a wonderful babysitter?"

"It's a deal!" exclaimed Helen.

Chapter Twenty-six

The Big Fizzle

"When do we have to leave for the meeting?" Marjie asked, sitting down at the dining room table next to Jerry. Sarah and Benjamin were already on their second cups of coffee.

"We should probably get out of here in ten

minutes or so," Jerry replied after checking the time on his watch. "We always seem to get there so late that we end up hunting for a decent seat."

"Marjie, what do you think's going to happen tonight?" Sarah asked. "Have you heard much?"

"I've heard enough to know that Richard Felding turned a lot more heads than Mr. Holmes did," answered Marjie. "At least that was the impression I got after prayer meeting last Thursday night. People are really excited about what's going on in Europe, and they talked up a storm after we got done praying. Most of them were very impressed with Felding."

"With the liberation of Paris and Antwerp, there's a lot to be excited about," Jerry said, stirring a spoonful of sugar into his cup of coffee. "Patton is driving the Germans back to the Rhine, and Montgomery's already in Belgium. The Russians have pushed into Romania and Bulgaria. Everyone thinks the Germans have had it."

"Tell that to the Poles," Benjamin said. "That Stalin just sat back and let the Germans wipe out the Polish Home Army, even though he had Russian troops on the outskirts of Warsaw. He's as ruthless as Hitler."

"He may be worse, for all we know," Jerry

replied. “But the Germans aren’t going to roll over and throw up the white flag. Hitler will never let them do that.”

“Still, there’s a lot to be thankful for,” Marjie said. “And I have a feeling that it’s influencing people in how they look at the two pastors. Look at it, Jerry. Felding is young and daring and exciting—and folks are ready to roll forward. Edward Holmes . . . what do you say about him?”

“I have several things to say about him, but you’re right,” Benjamin commented. “Richard Felding has a lot going for him. He’s going to get overwhelming support.”

“At least you don’t have to fight with Orville Manning tonight,” Sarah said. “Since he left the church, the meetings have at least been civil. You can bet who he’d be for if he was here.”

“I wouldn’t bother to go if he were in charge,” said Benjamin. “And he’d be in charge. I wonder if it bugs him that the church has somehow survived without his money?”

“He’s not the kind to look back at anything he says or does,” Marjie said. “Isn’t it funny how a guy like that could bully the church around for decades, and everyone knew he was doing it with his financial clout, but when Manning finally said out loud what he was doing, everyone was offended. Surprise, surprise. Like no one had noticed before."

"And then they reached in their pockets and have been giving so much more that Manning's contributions haven't actually been a loss," Jerry observed. "It don't figure, does it?"

"Nope," Benjamin said. "Like a lot of things. We better get going, though. Sarah did tell you that Jack and Doris are coming in late October, didn't she?"

"Yeah, I can't believe it," said Jerry. "Driving through the mountains from Seattle this late in the year. I wouldn't dare do it. But big brother was always more daring than I was."

"What did you say it had been?" asked Marjie, getting up and pulling on her black sweater. "Eight years since he's been out here? He won't even recognize you two birds. Or your lady friends."

Benjamin laughed and rubbed his freshly shaven neck, looking at Jerry. "It's been way too long, and there are a lot of things that have changed. When he left, he was none too happy with me, and I was hard on him back then. I've written and tried to make amends, but he hasn't responded. Doris writes occasionally, but she mostly talks about what Jack is doing. I'm not even sure how he did it, but he's made a pile of money out there as a contractor. Could be an interesting time."

"I think it will be," Jerry said, taking a deep breath. "Like tonight will be."

Arriving at the church and going straight down the basement stairway, Benjamin took his place at a large wooden table in the front with the other members of the pastoral search committee while Marjie and Jerry found chairs next to Billy and Ruth Wilson. It was a large gathering, and despite their intentions to get there early, the meeting was about to begin.

"Who's watching Ellie and Timmy?" Marjie asked Ruth as she sat down by Ruth.

"My dad is, if you can believe that," Ruth said and smiled. "He just loves the kids, and he figures Richard Felding's got it by a landslide here tonight. Plus, he doesn't have to drive all the way into Preston, so it's pretty easy. Grandma's with yours?"

"Of course," replied Marjie. "So your dad thinks there's no contest?"

"Are you kidding?" Ruth whispered. "This will be over in about ten minutes. Felding's the talk of the town. Now that I'm a Greenleaftonite, I get in on all the news."

"You and Billy better speak up then," Marjie urged her. "We have to try."

Ruth ran her fingers through her black hair and shrugged her shoulders. "What are we supposed to say? That there was something about the man we don't trust? That everything about him was just too smooth? Marjie, we have nothing to go on but our feelings, and that's not a fair deal to Felding. How can you start to question his character without knowing the facts?"

"Yeah, I know. I've been thinking about this for weeks," Marjie said, leaning close to Ruth. "But we don't have to call Felding's character in question just to say we feel very good about Mr. Holmes."

"True," Ruth acknowledged, "and I've been doing that in conversations I've been having around town. But people don't seem to give a hoot what I think. They like what they saw. And we have to remember that whatever we say about Richard Felding, he'll probably be our pastor within a month. We have to live with what we say."

"Yeah," said Marjie solemnly, taking a deep breath of air as Lou Billingsley stood up from his seat next to Benjamin and walked to the wooden lectern.

"Thank you all for coming," Billingsley called out, quieting the chatter in the crowded basement. "Our search committee, with recommendations from our regional denominational director, has interviewed a number of pastoral candidates and narrowed the field to two men, Edward Holmes and Richard Felding. During the month of August, both have preached in our pulpit, and many of you have had the chance to meet them personally.

"Tonight's meeting is to discuss how we feel about the two men," he continued, "and then we're going to have a ballot vote. It's already mid-September, and we feel like our pulpit has been vacant too long already. I've asked a couple of the members of our search committee to bring their views first before we open it up to the floor. Audrey, why don't you go first, and then Benjamin."

Lou Billingsley's attractive wife smiled and stood up to address the crowd. "Over the past weeks, I've talked with many of you about how I feel, so I'll try to keep this brief. Mr. Holmes seemed like a very nice man with a fine family. I don't think anyone can find a fault with the man. But I think we have to consider the future of our church and whether we want to stay about the size we are and the way we are. If we're content with the way things are, Edward Holmes is a good candidate."

Pausing to take a deep breath, Audrey Billingsley continued. "But if we want to grow as a church, if we want to draw our young people back into the membership and add some excitement to our programs, Lou and I feel that Richard Felding is where our future lies. He's dynamic, he's personable, he's very intelligent, and he's young. We're an older congregation, and many of us feel we need a bold new push. I think we're fortunate to have the opportunity to get such an outstanding young leader, and I think his wife will be a wonderful addition."

As Mrs. Billingsley sat back down in her chair, Marjie was surprised by the applause. "I didn't realize we were voting already," she whispered to Ruth.

"I think we already did," Ruth returned as Benjamin stood up and waited for the clapping to cease.

"It's fairly obvious how most of you feel," Benjamin said loudly with a smile. "And I can understand that. Richard Felding is going to go a long way in our denomination. So while I don't expect my question to be a popular one, I still think we have to ask ourselves which man is the right fit for our congregation."

A mild murmur broke out among the church members, and Benjamin again waited until it was quiet. "There is no question that Edward Holmes does not bring the excitement of Mr. Felding. But as a member of a rural community church and as a simple farmer myself, what I hope to find in my pastor is someone who really understands me and the things that I'm facing. Having spent time with Mr. Holmes and his wife, who both grew up on farms and loved it, I really believe that he could become my pastor. Having been such a good friend of Pastor Fitchen, I didn't think I would be able say that about any candidate, but I was very impressed with Edward Holmes. I believe God has put it in his heart to pastor a country church. I leave it with you to consider whether the same is true of Richard Felding."

There was no applause as Benjamin Macmillan sat back down, but Marjie had the impression from the hush that he'd at least gotten the members to think. Even the whispers were subdued.

Lou Billingsley looked out over the crowd from behind the lectern and said, "I think those two opinions probably represent most of us in this room. Anyone else like to add in their thoughts?"

Betty Trent, who had been in Billy Wilson's youth group and had recently turned eighteen, was the first one to stand up. "I thought that both of the men were good, but after having an older pastor for so many years, I'd love to see us choose Mr. Felding. He and his wife were wonderful."

Several heads nodded and a ripple of chatter started up again. Then a sour-faced woman near the back stood up.

"It's your old friend Edna Miller," Marjie whispered to Ruth.

"Oh no!" Ruth gasped, leaning against Marjie. "What's she cooked up now?"

"I wonder why no one has mentioned the fact that the wife of Edward Holmes plans to continue teaching in a public school if her husband is offered this pastorate." Edna gave the crowd a questioning look.

Lou Billingsley stood up a bit straighter behind the lectern and said, "Why is that important?"

"Why?" Edna asked, putting her hands on her hips. "Because we expect that the pastor's wife is going to serve alongside of her husband. We pay our pastor a salary that should amply care for his family. I think it should be a rule that the pastor's wife doesn't work. Times may have changed, but we've never had a pastor whose wife went to a job every day. Richard Felding's wife told me that she has no intention of getting a job. 'My place is beside my husband,' she said. And she's right."

Marjie groaned and had all she could do to

keep from jumping up, but she knew that many of the people in the crowded basement agreed with Edna, despite the offensive way she said it.

Shaking his head, Billingsley replied, "We've never considered that as a pastoral requirement, and while we may prefer that the pastor's wife doesn't have a job, we really don't have any right to make that call. If we call Mr. Holmes as our pastor and his wife wants to continue her career, that has to remain as their business, not ours."

"Well, we should make it our business," Edna declared as she sat down.

Marjie glanced over at Ruth and could see that her black eyes were flashing and her face was red. Then she looked down and saw the same look on Jerry's and Billy's faces. Marjie felt Ruth coming up out of her chair, but another voice rose from the back before Ruth could speak.

"I should have probably spoken to the search committee first, but I really didn't have time," Everett Cunningham spoke out. Marjie knew him as a quiet farmer who came regularly to her prayer meeting but seldom made his presence known. "Some of you know that my boy went to college with Richard Felding and that they are still good friends. Well, Bud called me yesterday and said that Richard told him he really wasn't all that interested in our church; he was looking at it as a stepping-stone to a larger church. Matter of fact, he said Richard is checking into a church in Minneapolis that might have an opening."

"Wow!" Marjie exclaimed to herself as the entire gathering of church members gasped collectively.

"Hold on, Everett!" Billingsley called out, trying to calm the crowd by holding up his hands. "This really isn't fair to Mr. Felding. You should have called one of us on the committee so we could talk with him."

"I already done talked with him," Everett replied, hushing the crowd. "I thought it was only fair to hear what Richard had to say, so I tried to call him several times, but I couldn't get ahold of him until after chores tonight. I didn't have time to get ahold of you."

"Well, what did he say?" Billingsley asked.

"Pretty much what he'd told Bud," Everett announced. "Richard said that he liked the welcome he received from our congregation and he thought it would be a good starter church for him, but he's really hoping to find a bigger city church, whether something opens up now or later. And he said it was okay if I said this in our meeting tonight."

With every word Everett Cunningham

spoke, Marjie thought she also heard the fizzle of a big firecracker that refuses to blow. By the time he had finished and sat down, every grand vision of brighter days ahead under the leadership of Richard Felding lay smoldering in ashes on the basement floor. And the simple country boy, Edward Holmes, looked like a rising star.

Chapter Twenty-seven

Steamed Salmon

"That's the last of it!" Jerry called out to Marjie as he wheeled the small Ford tractor into the farmyard with a wagon full of picked corn and stopped by the corn crib. Shutting off the engine and jumping down from the tractor, he said, "They're not here yet?"

"Not unless your brother and his wife are hiding in the big pines or down the hill somewhere," Marjie said, reaching down and wiping Martha's running nose with her handkerchief. "Must feel good to have all the corn out of the fields by the end of October."

"It feels great!" exclaimed Jerry, walking across the yard toward them with Blue on his heels. "Now it can snow whenever it wants, and I'm ready for it. Getting the corn out of Tom Metcalfe's field was the worst mess I think I've ever tackled. The weeds were like a jungle down there. I guess it really wasn't worth trying to plant his crop if we didn't have time to keep it cultivated."

"So you're going to sell his corn and use the money to pay off his debt at the mill?" Marjie asked.

"Yeah, I thought we'd covered most of Tom's bills with the money we got when we sold the livestock off," Jerry said, opening the front gate and giving Marjie a hug, then scooping up Martha and planting her on his shoulders, where she giggled and waved her arms. "I should have thought of Bernard. You know how he extends credit at the garage and mill and doesn't make a fuss about it. Except for the gas Tom bought at the pump, he must not have paid Bernard for all the garage and mill work he had done in the last couple years. And Bernard never said a word to me when I was telling him how we paid off the bill at the store and the feed company."

"You wonder how Bernard ever pays his own bills," said Marjie. "The guy is so good-hearted that half the township takes advantage of him. It's a shame, really."

"It is, but it's the way he's always operated, and he seems to keep the business floating," Jerry replied.

"So is there anything else down at the Metcalfe farm that's going to be sold other than the land?" Marjie asked as she reached down to scratch Blue in his favorite spot behind his ears.

"There's nothing of any value left," Jerry answered. "Whoever buys the property is going to be stuck with getting rid of all that old rusty equipment. The house, the barn, and the other buildings are in such bad shape that I can't imagine anyone living back in there again or even trying to use the barn—a good wind could topple it in a hurry. The bank's not going to get much for the property."

"I never asked you if you were interested in the land," said Marjie. "Maybe we could get our friend Billy to get us a good deal on it."

"Shoot, no!" exclaimed Jerry with a laugh, bouncing up and down a little to give Martha a better ride. "I got plenty to handle here on my own. Most of that land is woods and pasture. He only had about fifteen good acres, and those were down on the bottom flats where it stays wet so long in the spring. I don't need those headaches, believe me."

"You coming in for some coffee or what?" Marjie asked. "It's a bit early in the afternoon for you. I don't want you to get thrown off your schedule."

Jerry laughed and said, "Might as well

while I'm up here. I have to unload the corn from that wagon, but it looks pretty good right where it's sitting at this moment. I've shoveled about as much corn as I care to today. What are you two doing out here? Little cool for playing outside, isn't it?"

"Just a little," Marjie said, turning and walking up the sidewalk toward the farmhouse. "She needs to take a nap, but she was so full of energy. I thought if she ran around out here for a while, that would tire her out. But Blue followed you out to the field, so I ended up having to run around with her. Guess who tired out first?"

"Boo," Martha stated, pointing to the cow dog as if continuing her mother's explanation. Then she commanded, "Down."

"Down, *please*," Marjie prompted.

"Peese," she was repeating when the blare of a car horn from somewhere down the county road grabbed their attention. Blue jumped the iron fence and raced up the driveway, stopping by the mailbox for the oncoming car, but it was still out of view to Marjie and Jerry.

"That has to be Jack!" Jerry exclaimed, lowering Martha to the ground as the sound of the horn and tires on gravel got closer. "When he drove out of here eight years ago, he must have held his horn down until he got all the way through Greenleafton."

"Wow!" Marjie exclaimed as a dark blue 1937 Packard Victoria convertible rolled around the corner with the top down and the horn still blasting. With the big chrome grill shimmering in the afternoon sunlight, the sleek design of the front fender and spare wheel covering and the powerful rumble of the motor accentuated the car's luxurious beauty, especially when it pulled to a stop alongside Jerry's old black Ford.

"Tell him that's our second car," Jerry muttered to Marjie as the convertible's engine and horn went silent at the same moment. Martha had been holding her mittened hands over her ears as the car went by and finally put her hands down. "Jack likes to compare."

Marjie glanced at Jerry's serious smile as he waved at Jack and headed toward the garage to greet them. She had never met Jerry's brother; about all she knew was that he was thirty-two years old and very successful. As she followed Jerry, Marjie thought it was strange that neither he nor Benjamin had ever talked much about Jack—not even since they'd heard that Jack and his wife Doris were coming to visit. Both men had included Jack in many of their stories from around the farm, of course, but what he was like remained a mystery to her. The thing she recalled most was that Jack seemed to have enjoyed beating and bullying Jerry whenever their father and mother weren't looking.

The man who jumped out of the car and strode toward them looked incredibly like Jerry. Although Jack was an inch taller and considerably broader, he had the same boyish good looks, short blond hair, and smooth athletic movement. Probably the biggest difference was his hazel eyes and the beginnings of crow's-feet at the corners of his eyes when he smiled. And of course his clothes were different. In a tight green sweater, khaki slacks, and white dress shoes, Jack reminded Marjie of a professional golfer, while Jerry's worn dungarees clearly showed him to be the hardworking farmer that he was.

Doris Macmillan had stepped slowly out of the car and stood stretching her arms while Blue leapt and cavorted around her. Marjie had seen Doris in their wedding photos and Jerry had mentioned that his sister-in-law was very attractive, but she hadn't anticipated a Lana Turner look-alike. Doris pulled off her white silk scarf to let wavy honey-colored hair fall free over her shoulders, and blue eyes flashed a smile at Marjie. She wore a sleek white dress with a dazzling gold brooch.

"Why is this dame so decked out?" Marjie grumped to herself, glancing quickly down at her plain white blouse, worn slacks, and old shoes. *I look like Old Mother Hubbard!* she thought.

"Blue!" Marjie called out as the cow dog made another high leap beside the lovely newcomer, "Get down!" Walking up to Doris, she said, "My apologies. That dog thinks he owns this place and pesters everyone who drives in here. You must be Doris."

Doris smiled and replied, "And of course you're Marjie. I'm so pleased to meet you." Then she surprised Marjie with a warm hug. "What a beautiful farm you have! You must love to look down into the valley."

"I do," Marjie replied, stepping back with a big grin. "The view from the dining room is so pretty I could stand there all day. You don't look much like a farm girl, though."

Breaking into a laugh, Doris looked over at Jack, who was still preoccupied with Jerry and Martha, then she leaned close to Marjie. "I grew up on a farm that's just north of Preston, and I could slop pigs with the best of 'em. Jack wanted me to wear this dress. He thinks that first impressions are important."

"I'm impressed," Marjie said with a smile.

"Good," Doris replied under her breath as the men came around the car. "That means I can go into the house and change later."

"Jack, this is my wife Marjie," Jerry said

proudly, nodding toward Marjie and then stepping to greet Doris as well.

"And the lovely mother of my beautiful little niece," Jack added with a charming smile, greeting Marjie with a strong hug and a kiss to the cheek. "I'm delighted to finally meet you. You're even prettier than those famous photos I saw in the newspapers Dad sent."

"Thank you, and I'm pleased to meet you as well," Marjie replied, looking over as Doris squatted down and spoke solemnly to Martha, then picked her up and cuddled her close. "If I didn't know better, I'd say you and Jerry look so much alike that you must be brothers."

Jack laughed, and the wrinkles around his eyes multiplied. "You must have charmed my little brother right off his feet. He was the shyest kid I think I've ever seen. I used to get so mad at him when he wouldn't talk in school. What did you do? Give him a pill or something?"

"Something, I guess," Marjie said, slipping her arm around Jerry and snuggling up close. "I thought I was going to end up an old maid before he got the nerve to propose."

"It was Pearl Harbor that did it," Jerry said. "There were too many good-looking fellas knocking on her door to risk going to war without marrying her first."

"I can see why," Jack said, leaning back on the dark blue Packard. "I can't believe you waited so long, Goofus Laroo. Say, where are you hiding that nephew of mine that was born in the barn? Talk about cutting costs. I like that."

"Robert's doing what he does best right now, and that's snoozing," replied Marjie, reaching over and touching Martha's cheek, which was pressed tightly against Doris's shoulder. "Which is exactly what this little girl should be doing. She should have had her nap an hour ago. She'll disappoint Grandpa if she conks out too early tonight after dinner."

"Maybe you want to take her to the house?" Doris asked. "I'd like to freshen up a bit. But I'll need to get my bag."

"Sure," Marjie said. "That would be good." She took Martha into her arms and waited as Doris opened the car door and reached in for a black leather travel bag.

"What do you think of my wheels, Jerry boy?" crowed Jack with a satisfied smile. "Ain't she somethin'?"

"She's a beauty," replied Jerry, scanning the expensive automobile as Doris pulled out her bag. "I saw one just like it up in Minneapolis, but there's nobody around here with a car like that. What's it worth?"

"More than you want to know," said Jack. He ran his hand affectionately down the silky front fender. "This is my work car. You should see what I bought Doris to drive—a '37 Cord Sportsman that matches her hair. That sucker is one incredible machine. You ever seen one?"

"I saw one down by the shipyard in Norfolk," said Jerry. "It purred like a kitten and was fast as lightning. Not the kind of car you'd want for driving around on these country roads."

"Are you boys coming in with us, or are you more interested in jabbering about cars?" asked Doris.

"Tell you what," said Jack, looking at Jerry. "I'd like to walk around the farm and just look over the old place. Care to come along?"

"Sure," said Jerry. "Nothing much has changed, though."

"I've gotten older," Jack replied, raising his eyebrows and stepping out around the front of the car. "Let's head down through the woods and check out the creek. We'll see you ladies later. Fresh steamed salmon for dinner, I hope."

"Hope again," Marjie called out as she and Doris headed for the farmhouse. "I do have some old canned salmon, but I suspect that isn't what he means."

"Not quite," Doris answered. "Jack loves to eat seafood, and he claims that his mother fed them so much pork that he won't let me buy it—ever."

"Guess who's having pork chops tonight?" Marjie said with a wry smirk. "I thought it might be something he liked."

"Too bad for him," Doris said with a shrug of her shoulders. "I love pork chops."

"Good, because that's all I've got ready to go," Marjie replied. She reached the front door and opened it for Doris. "Tell me something. Isn't it a little on the cold side to be driving the car with the top down? I would have thought you'd be freezing."

Doris burst out laughing as she stepped into the house, then went to the dining room table to set her bag down. "Jack stopped about a half a mile back down the road and said we had to put the top down so you'd be impressed. He loves to wow people wherever he goes, especially with his cars. I put my scarf on so my hair wouldn't get tangled, but there's no way I ride around in cold weather with the top down."

"I'll bet your house is 'wow' as well," Marjie said, noticing how old and tired the oak dining room table and chairs suddenly looked with Doris standing beside them. "Not quite like this old place."

Doris rested her hand on the table. "I love our house," she said with a smile. "It's far grander than anything a farm girl from north of Preston would have ever dreamed of owning. But . . . not every house is really a home, and we sometimes confuse the two."

She looked wistfully around her at the faded walls and the worn furniture, at the sun streaming in through the dining room windows. "An old farmhouse that's a home beats a mansion that's only a house any day."

Chapter Twenty-eight

Fast Bucks

"Benjamin was quieter tonight than I've ever seen him," Marjie said to Jerry as she sat at the bedroom dresser brushing her wavy brown hair. Setting her brush down in her lap, she turned toward him. "What's the problem between him and Jack? Do you know?"

Jerry doubled his pillow over and propped his head up so he could see her better as he lay in the bed. "I really don't know," he said. "Jack and Dad had a lot of arguments, and Dad wasn't afraid to tell either of us boys when he didn't like something we were doing. But Jack would get into it with Dad, and sometimes I thought he would taunt him just to get him riled up. After Mother died, Dad was a bear to get along with, and Jack would never back off. Sometimes I'd just leave the house and go for a long walk."

"And instead of arguing with your pa, you just stopped talking to him altogether," Marjie observed. "It's been eight years, though, and Jack was married and on his own when he and Doris moved to Seattle. Did something happen then?"

"I don't know. I thought it was just a lot of hot air that neither one of them meant at the time," replied Jerry as Marjie picked up her brush and began to run it through her hair again. "Dad told Jack that he thought he should stick with his job at the lumberyard in Preston. Jack had taken over the daily management of the business in no time flat, and he was pulling in what we thought was a good salary. But Jack wanted more, and he said he wasn't going to get dead-ended in some dinky little town like Preston. Jack and Dad argued about it, and Jack ended up telling Dad to keep his nose out of affairs he had no say in."

Marjie laid her brush down on the dresser and stared absently into the mirror at her heart-shaped face. "No wonder Benjamin's so quiet," she said, shaking her head.

"Sounds like they both made their share of mistakes. I'll bet Benjamin's trying to figure out how to make up for some of the things he probably regrets saying. It doesn't seem to be bothering Jack much, though. *He* talked all night."

Jerry laughed and rolled over on his back. "Are you going to shut that light off and come to bed?" he asked. "Or are you working on a new hairdo to match Doris's?"

"Right," Marjie sputtered, running her fingers along her cheek. "She probably changes her hairdo every other week. And she's so beautiful that she could wear her hair any way she likes, and she'd still look great. I feel like such a country bumpkin next to her. But she really is very sweet, Jerry. I wonder how she and Jack really get along."

Shutting off the light, Marjie crawled into bed and snuggled up against her husband. "You're so warm and cozy," Marjie said as he wrapped his arm around her. Then she sighed. "I got the strangest sense that Doris is a very sad person. Or lonely. Did you?"

Jerry shrugged his shoulders and replied, "I was so busy listening to Jack talk that I guess I hardly noticed. She was pretty quiet, but he doesn't give anyone much of a chance to get a word in."

"He has to be in charge of everything,

doesn't he?" Marjie said. "I noticed that even when you guys went for a walk this afternoon, he had to march ahead. Makes me tired just to watch him."

"That's my big brother Jack," said Jerry. "He always had to win, no matter what was going on. Just watch him tomorrow. He studies what's going on around him, always stays a step ahead of the game. And he only plays where he's convinced he can win."

"You make him sound sort of ruthless," Marjie said.

"It's more like he gets so focused on doing one thing well that nothing else seems to matter."

"Well, I'm just glad I've got you instead of him," Marjie said, kissing Jerry on the lips. "He and I would lock horns, I'm afraid."

"I'm absolutely certain you would," Jerry agreed with a chuckle. "And I have a feeling that old Jack might not walk away unscratched."

"You might be right," Marjie said with a satisfied smirk. "Right before we had pie, what did he say to you and Benjamin about the farm? I could have sworn that Benjamin flinched."

Jerry was silent for a moment, then he took a deep breath. "Oh, I hate to even repeat it. He said the same thing to me a couple of times when we were out walking. Jack wonders what it is about this stony old place that kept Dad here all these years and what it is that keeps me here now. He can't imagine working so hard to earn so little, especially when he sees so many opportunities to make a killing financially."

"From what Doris was telling me, Jack knows how to make an honest buck," Marjie said.

"Bucks," Jerry corrected her. "Fast bucks, and lots of bucks. Listening to him talk about what he's got his money into, I start to wonder what I'm doing. Seven days a week I drag my body out to milk the cows before the sun even thinks about coming up, and I drag the same old body back to the house after the sun has set. Seems sort of stupid, don't it?"

"Only when you think too hard about it," Marjie teased. "Maybe we should invest all of our life savings in stocks and bonds. I've heard that plastics are what you want to be in."

"Just don't put all ten dollars in the same company," Jerry added with a laugh. "But seriously, there are times when I wonder if it's worth all the hard work. I can't believe how much money Jack has made building houses in Seattle during the war. He was in the right place when Boeing went into high gear building planes for the war. But he claims that's nothing compared to what's coming."

"What do you mean?" asked Marjie.

"He says that when the war is over and all the young men come pouring back, most of them are going to be looking for houses to buy," Jerry said. "I'm sure he's right, Marjie, and I'm sure he's going to make a killing off it. He's already bought up a lot of prime property, and he's already starting to develop it. Jack's going to be a millionaire if it does half as well as he predicts."

"Always a step ahead of the game." Marjie shook her head. "He is a sharp cookie. So what happened to you anyway?"

Jerry shook his head. "I wonder about that myself. But I better get some sleep. Those stupid cows will be waiting for me in the morning with their big black eyes staring down the row at me, wondering why I'm late, upset that I've kept them. I can't afford to have my ladies get feisty with me."

"How about a few kisses to keep this lady happy?" Marjie asked. "Then you can go to sleep."

"Do you really want to come along to the prayer meeting tonight?" Marjie asked Doris, who was sitting in the rocking chair feeding the baby a bottle of milk. "I don't want you to feel like you're stuck with me just because Jack's gone bowling with Jerry and Billy Wilson."

Doris looked up and smiled. "I wouldn't have asked if I didn't want to come," she said. "It just sounds like such a great idea that I have to see it while I'm here. Our church doesn't have anything like it, and I'm not even aware of any church in Seattle that's doing what you're doing. How did you ever come up with the idea?"

Marjie chuckled. "You'd think it would have been because of what I went through while Jerry was in the navy and my brother overseas and all. But what actually triggered it was talking with a young woman in our church whose husband had been killed in the South Pacific. You might meet her there tonight; her name is Betty. Anyway, nobody knew what to say to her, so we just sort of tiptoed around her month after month when we should have been there to surround her with love and care. Then she and I got to talking and . . . well, it just seemed like something that needed to happen."

"And you had only recently become a believer, isn't that right?" Doris asked. "You were very brave to take on this prayer meeting. I would have expected the pastor to do it."

Marjie laughed. "I *did* expect that he would, and I'm not the least bit brave," she said. "Naive is more like it. Stupid may even be closer. The pastor really believed I was the right person to do it, and I didn't anticipate that very many people would come, so I thought I'd give it a try. But how did you know about my becoming a believer? I haven't said a word about that since you've been here."

Baby Robert had finished the bottle, and Doris was tucking the towel she had on her lap up over her blouse. Then she pushed her honey-colored hair aside, lifted the baby to her shoulder, and began to pat his back. "Over the past couple years, Benjamin has been writing us occasionally, and when he does, he gets right to the heart of what he thinks is important. He's given me a lot to think about. I love his letters, and I wish he'd write more often."

"I can hardly imagine Benjamin writing letters," Marjie said. "What does Jack think?"

Doris raised her dark eyebrows and shook her head. "He does read Benjamin's letters, but I know he doesn't understand most of what his father is writing about. Jack's not interested in spiritual matters, so there's always a section that he dismisses immediately as unimportant. But he does seem to like to know how things are going."

"I take it that you see something more in what Benjamin is saying," said Marjie.

"Am I a believer?" Doris asked with a pleasant smile. "Is that what you're fishing for?"

"Yes," answered Marjie, looking a bit sheepish. "And I'm not fishing very well today."

"You're fishing fine, and I like it when someone cares enough to ask me about my spiritual life," Doris replied. Robert had fallen asleep, and she laid him down on her lap. "It happened a little over five years ago, when my doctor finally gave up on our being able to have a baby. We both wanted a baby so badly, and when we moved to Seattle I found one of the best doctors in the country. But even with the finest medical help available, it wasn't to be."

"What did you do when you heard the news?" Marjie asked.

Doris tilted her head back and sighed. "Fortunately for me, one of Jack's business partners has a wife who is a Christian. When she heard the news, Gladys drove straight over and let me cry . . . and cry . . . and cry some more. Then she talked, and I listened. She'd tried before, and I hadn't been interested in her help. But she came on the right day, and I knew I couldn't handle the pain on my own anymore. God heard the cry of my heart, and then Gladys helped me find a good church. I still can't fathom that Jack and I are childless, but my faith has seen me through some pretty dark days."

"Oh, Martha, I'm so sorry," Marjie blurted. "I mean . . . about the doctor. . . ." Without thinking, she had leaned over and put a hand on her sister-in-law's arm. "I thought . . . I guess I thought maybe you and Jack had decided to not have children so you both could pull all of your energies into the business."

"No," Doris answered softly. "I would have quit my job the next day if I could have gotten pregnant. And now we don't need two incomes to pay the bills, but I keep working because I can't stand to be alone in that big empty house all day. I did try to quit being Jack's office manager so I could become the secretary of our church. But it was a volunteer position, and Jack's not keen on giving anything away for free."

"How did Jack respond to the doctor's evaluation?" Marjie asked.

Doris twisted her lips and chuckled softly. "This will probably sound bad," she said, "but what he did was go to work. And he asked me if I wanted to ride with him or if I would be coming in later with my car. That was it, as simple as that. It was like we could just stuff everything into a drawer and close it, and that's the end of it."

"He couldn't win, so he changed games," Marjie said to herself.

"What?" Doris asked.

"Never mind," Marjie replied. "I was just thinking out loud. Have you tried to adopt?"

"No," Doris said. "Jack's not interested. He doesn't even want to talk about it."

"Does he say why?" asked Marjie.

"Oh, he said he couldn't stand having somebody else's kids running around our house," said Doris, "but I don't think he meant it. I think he just decided that the whole ordeal had been too painful for both of us and had already interrupted too much of his life; he just wasn't going to bother with it anymore. He's got a lot of irons in the fire, and when he sees a good deal, he goes for it, but when something isn't working he's pretty quick to cut it off."

"And that's one of the things that attracted him to you, right?" Marjie continued.

"Very much so," Doris replied, glancing down at the baby in her lap and then back up to Marjie. "Jack is a constant success, and it's a lot more appealing to spend your life with a sure winner than with a possible loser. I just didn't bargain for the possibility that his business might become more attractive to him than I am."

"That's impossible," Marjie sputtered out before she could catch her words. "I mean, I've never gotten to know someone as beautiful as you are. Jack can't—"

"He can," Doris broke in, "and he does it all the time." Her eyes grew wistful and sad as she stroked little Robert's sleeping form. "For a time I wondered if he'd found another woman, but gradually I came to see that it was the business that was consuming him. To do what he wants to do, at least in the time frame he'd like, he has to devote just about everything he has to his work. I suppose that because we work together in the office and see each other all the time, he probably thinks that that's enough."

"But it's not," Marjie added.

Doris ran her fingers through her silky hair and laughed. "You know, Marjie," she said, "I've already said way more than I probably should. I'm assuming that what I say you'll keep between you and me."

"Of course."

"It's not that I live in total secrecy," Doris said. "But if Jack found out what I told you . . . well, I really think he might leave me. And there are times when I wonder if that would be so bad. I sometimes feel like all he needs me for is to parade in front of others as a symbol of what a success he is. He runs a big business, he drives a fancy car, he's got the wife that other men dream about, and he owns the house that other women drive by just to look at. He's got it all, and he's going to get more."

"So what keeps you by his side?" Marjie asked.

Doris glanced out the window and pursed her red lips. "My marriage vows, believe it or not," she replied. " 'For better, for worse,' you know. I've thought a lot about those words, and they're words I spoke to God as well as to Jack. And Jack is a good husband in his way. He's honest in his business practices, he's not a drunk, he doesn't beat me or ever treat me cruelly, and he's always looking for something new to give me."

She sighed, and the sigh seemed to rise from the depths of her soul. "I'm just not sure that he still loves me."

Chapter Twenty-nine

The Big Offer

"Go on! Get out of here, you stupid cow!" Jerry yelled as he released the last Holstein from her milking stanchion and gave her a kick on the back of the right hind leg. She loped down the aisle and out the barn door to join the rest of the herd that was heading for the pasture.

"I came out to see if you were coming in for breakfast," Marjie said, standing by the milk parlor door. "But you sound like you better stay out for a while. What happened to you?" she asked, noticing that Jerry was limping as he walked down the aisle to shut the barn door.

"Ethel the Kicker nailed me right on the kneecap," Jerry groused, latching the door shut and limping back down the aisle toward her. "I'm so tired from last night that I wasn't watching her close enough. Should've sold her the day I found out she kicked. I'm so sick of all this."

"Grumpy, grumpy, grumpy. What were you guys doing out till midnight?" Marjie asked. "Doesn't the bowling alley close at ten?"

"Yeah, it does, but the tavern doesn't,"

Jerry replied, sitting down on his milking stool and pulling off his boots. "Jack met a couple of his old friends from the lumberyard, and I didn't think I'd ever get him out of there. I should've rode home with Billy instead of standing there watching Jack pour down the beers. Good thing they're taking off tomorrow for Doris's folks' place up in Duluth. I just can't take these late nights. Are they up yet?"

"Yes, indeed," Marjie replied. "And brother Jack says he'd like to have a 'serious' talk with us when you're done with breakfast. Doris is going to watch the kids so we're not distracted."

"Cottonpicker!" Jerry grumped, leaning his back against the barn wall and groaning. "What can be that important?"

"I have no idea, but your breakfast is going to get cold if we stay here all day," Marjie said. "What did you guys talk about with Benjamin yesterday afternoon? Maybe it's got something to do with that."

Jerry shrugged his shoulders. "I doubt it, although that little talk got pretty intense for a while. Dad apologized to Jack about some specific things that I could tell he's been thinking about for a long time. And Jack had completely forgotten them. The two of them seemed to connect in a way that I can't remember them ever getting on with each other."

"So did Jack apologize for the way he used to beat on you?" Marjie asked.

"No," Jerry said, shaking his head. "That was just typical big-brother stuff, I think. Beside, unless somebody else brings up the past like Dad did, I don't think Jack's even conscious of what's behind him. I've never met anyone who's more focused on the future than Jack is."

"So maybe that's what he wants to talk about," Marjie commented as Jerry stood up and flexed his sore knee. "But somebody oughta tell him that there are certain things in the present he should cherish as much as he does his future—like his wife. Jerry, she is pure gold."

"Did she like the prayer meeting?" asked Jerry, draping an arm around Marjie as they emerged from the barn and walked slowly toward the house.

"She loved it," Marjie said. "She couldn't get over how many people come, and she wants to try to start something like it in her church. I wonder if Jack will try to stop her from doing that, too."

"Why should he?" Jerry asked.

"Good question," Marjie answered. "He apparently frowns on her giving too much time to her church. She wanted to quit work and volunteer her time as church secretary, but Jack wouldn't allow it. And they don't even need the money she's making."

"Maybe we could talk Jack into shipping her salary back here to the poor farm," Jerry said as they reached the sidewalk.

"Good luck," Marjie responded. "I'm pretty sure that's not in his program."

Jerry ate his breakfast slowly and quietly while Marjie did the dishes. Doris was playing with Martha in the living room when Jack came whistling up the sidewalk and stepped confidently into the house through the front door.

"Cup of coffee?" Marjie asked as Jack sat down at the dining room table across from Jerry. She was already pouring it before he could respond.

"I'd like that," Jack said, rubbing his eyes. "Those cows must have looked good this morning, eh?"

"After I finally got my eyes opened, they were just as beautiful as ever," Jerry said. He took a drink of his coffee, staring at his brother. "How's your head?"

"I feel great," Jack declared. "Slept like a log, and it was beautiful out walking this morning. You surprised me last night. When did you quit drinking, anyway? I thought you liked beer."

Jerry chuckled and had to think about it for a moment. "I guess it's been a couple years already. I was in Norfolk, Virginia, and it was not an evening that I'm fond of recalling."

"So you never take a drink," Jack went on, taking his cup of coffee from Marjie. "Is that part of what happened to you when you went over the side of the aircraft carrier?"

"My conversion?" Jerry asked.

"I guess that's what you call it," said Jack. "Is it?"

"No and yes," Jerry said. "I don't really consider drinking a beer a moral issue, and I still like the taste of it. But getting drunk like I did that night in Norfolk was a sin I don't want to ever compromise on again. Also, I'm doing some work with the youth in our church, and I feel like I'd be a poor example to the kids if they heard I was out drinking."

"Fair enough," said Jack, nodding his head. "I was a little worried that you might be starting a temperance movement."

"Like Grandma?" Jerry said and laughed. "No, I think those days are behind us."

"So what was it you wanted the powwow about, Jack?" Marjie asked, holding her own cup of coffee in her hands. "You want me to stay or not?"

"Oh, you should definitely stay," he replied, sitting forward in his chair. "What I have to say is for both of you. It's about the future—yours in particular."

Big surprise, Marjie thought, glancing over at Jerry. Then she looked back into Jack's strong, handsome face and said, "I knew it. You've decided to pay off the balance of what we owe on the farm so we can sell the cows and Jerry can work an eight-hour day instead of twelve to fourteen. This is wonderful!"

Jack burst out laughing and rubbed his clean-shaven chin. "Not quite, but something like that," he said. "I've got a job offer that I'm hoping you'll consider, and it could mean ten-hour days and a lot more money."

"Are you suggesting that I'm looking for a job?" Jerry asked.

"No, not at all," Jack said, raising his eyebrows and shaking his head. "But I do know what kind of income a farm this size brings in. Jerry, I'm prepared to offer you a position that will bring in four times as much money, plus a company vehicle. That's for the first year, and there'll be incentives for you if you do well. Want to hear more?"

Marjie could see Jerry's jaw tighten and a frown build across his forehead, but then he tried to nod nonchalantly. "Sure," he said, managing a smile. "You've got a big farm out there that you want me to run?"

"Nope. No farms for me," Jack replied, tapping his fingers on the table. "I tell you what, Jerry. You work hard and long, you're honest and fair, and I like what I see. You're doing a better job with the farm than Dad did, and he was a force to be reckoned with. I've got a building foreman, and he's very good, but when the building market in Seattle explodes, I'm going to need another key man. I think you could do the job."

"Oh come on, Jack!" Jerry sputtered. "I don't know the building trade. I can figure out how to put together a garage, but I'm no builder. What are you thinking?"

Jack laughed and held up one hand. "Just listen. I'm looking for a good young man who can become a foreman. I didn't say he had to be a foreman today. I figure we've got about two years; then we have to be ready to go."

"Why two years?" asked Marjie. "You figure the war will be over by then?"

"No," Jack said, shaking his head. "It won't be that long. Our navy just wiped out the most significant remainder of the Japanese fleet in the Pacific at Leyte Gulf, and MacArthur is going to clean the Japs out of the Philippines in nothing flat. I've got friends with connections that tell me we'll be bombing Japan from the Marianas within a month. And the Germans'll go down before the Japs; if Hitler had a brain he'd surrender today. So I figure it'll all be over by next year. But you still have to add in time for the soldiers to get home and settle down enough to where they start looking for a home to buy. That's why I figure that in two years I'll really be in business."

"Sounds like you should be a spokesman for the war department," said Marjie. "Maybe you could tell the kamikazes to just stop crashing their planes onto our warships."

"Doesn't that tell you it's over?" Jack asked. "They're so desperate they load their planes with bombs and offer themselves as a suicidal weapon. No, I'm not telling you it's over yet, but I am saying it's just a matter of time. The Germans and the Japs have had it. So what do you say? You want a job?"

"What about the farm?" asked Jerry.

"What about it?" Jack returned. "Knowing Dad, he probably sold it to you for a song. You sell it, take the profits, and put it into a nice house in Seattle that I sell you for a song. You play your cards right, and you could have a house paid off in no time. By then you can build the house of your dreams and put some money away into a college fund. The cost of college is going to go up, you know. How're you going to manage that if you stay here?"

"It doesn't mean anything to you that Grandpa homesteaded this farm?" Jerry asked. "Or that our father and mother spent their lives here?"

"Or that we're happy where we are?" Marjie added.

Jack smiled and leaned back in his chair. "Sure, it means something," he said. "I like it here, too. But America's going to change after the war, and small farms are not where the growth is going to be. After all that the soldiers have seen and done, do you think they're going to be content back in their little towns or on their little farms? And do you want to spend the rest of your life working so hard for so little? The door's wide open, Jerry. I'd really like to have you come on board. And Doris would love to have you close by; she's really taken to Marjie and the kids."

Marjie looked into Jerry's blue eyes and tried to read what he was thinking. Everything that Jack said made sense, and it did bother her to see Jerry working so hard for the small amount of milk money that was left over at the end of every month. If their old black Ford died, there was no money to replace it, let alone acquire a second vehicle like

Jack was offering them. And while there was much that she loved about growing up and living in the country, she knew that a large city offered many advantages for the children's future. The thought of living close to Doris was a pleasant prospect as well; over the past few days, Marjie had come to think of Jack's wife as a true sister.

Jerry smiled and ran a calloused forefinger along the edge of his coffee cup. Then he stared down at the old oak table, obviously weighing the offer. Marjie was going to suggest that they wait awhile and talk it over themselves, but then she saw the expression on Jerry's face change, and she knew he had made up his mind.

"Jack," he said finally, looking into his brother's face, "I really appreciate the offer, and I'm very pleased that you'd even consider me for such a job. You're absolutely right about everything you've said, and I want to do what's best for the future of my family. I'd like my kids to be able to go to college, and I'm sure that if they're going to have a good future, college needs to figure into that. Having some dollars in my wallet to spend would be nice, and there are plenty of times when I get tired of the work around here.

"But there are two missing pieces you haven't mentioned," he continued. "First, I think that I am a farmer, and I can't imagine ever being happy cooped up in a big city. If I had to do it, I'm sure I could. But I don't believe the money would make me happy, and I suspect that if I was miserable living in town, I would pass it along to Marjie and the kids. Then we could be one unhappy family.

"The other missing piece is one that might interest you, Jack," said Jerry. "A friend told Marjie the other day that a house and a home are not necessarily the same. I've been thinking about that ever since I heard it. For better or for worse, Marjie and I have made this house, these old farm buildings, this land—we've made it our home. It's ours, and I love this place. We're going to give our kids a decent place to grow up, and I hope we have enough money to survive. So . . . this may be the biggest mistake I ever make, but I am afraid I'm going to have to say thanks, but no thanks."

Jack rubbed his lips and took a deep breath. "You don't want to talk it over with Marjie? Maybe she's—"

"No discussion's needed," Marjie interrupted. "You've made an outstanding offer, and I think Doris is one of the most loving people I've ever met, so I'd love to be close. But God has made us a part of this community, and we're putting our roots down here."

"If I put more money on the table, that won't matter?" asked Jack.

Jerry shook his head no. "This isn't about money, Jack," he said. "It's about being a family. It's about the life we want together, and more money won't make that life happen. Another dear friend of ours told us that some things last forever, that we can invest ourselves into eternal things. And we feel like that's going to happen right here on this rocky old farm."

Jack smiled and tapped his front teeth with his thumbnail. "Well, little brother, I guess I have my answer. But I'm curious; who said that about a house and a home? Sounds like a good line for selling our houses."

"I said it, Jack." Doris stepped around the bathroom corner with Robert in her arms and Martha clinging to one leg. Marjie saw the tears glistening in the beautiful eyes. "And it's not about advertising or selling. It's about us, Jack. You and me. I'm glad we've got a lot of miles to drive because there's a lot I need to talk with you about."

Chapter Thirty

Betty Grable

"Looks like a couple more Christmas cards," Jerry called out. He peeked his head in through the farmhouse door while he stomped the snow off his boots on the outside steps. "And one Christmas delight," he declared, holding up a thick envelope for Marjie to see. "A letter from Margaret and Chester!"

"Wonderful!" Marjie cried, jumping out of her chair at the dining room table where she'd been supervising Martha's efforts in a Christmas coloring book Benjamin had bought for her.

"Daddy!" exclaimed the toddler as Marjie dashed away. Hopping down from her chair, she ran to Jerry and leaped into his arms while he held out the envelopes to Marjie. "You cold!" she cried.

Jerry laughed and put his little girl back down. "I am cold," he said to her, taking off his coat and stocking cap. "Brrrr. Cold from the snow. What's my little girl been doing?"

Martha twirled a stray curl around a pudgy finger, then pointed to the table. "Kitty."

"Kitty," Jerry repeated with a smile, then he pulled off his boots. "Where's the kitty?"

"Color kitty," Martha replied with a hint of

condescension, still pointing to the table.

"She's coloring a kitty," Marjie intervened, looking up from the first page of Margaret's letter. "You can go help her for a while. She snuck a crayon this morning and tried her artistry on the bathroom wall."

"Uh-oh," Jerry said, raising his eyebrows at Martha, who returned his look with a familiar smirk. "Did you do a no-no?"

Martha nodded her head emphatically, then turned and ran back to resume her coloring at the table.

"Did it come off?" Jerry asked, turning to Marjie.

"She's going to have a baby!" Marjie cried, looking up. "Margaret and Chester are going to have a baby! In May! She's three months along already."

"Wow," Jerry said with a weak smile, then he walked over to the table and sat down next to Martha. "Isn't that going to set them back in their missionary training?"

"I'm glad you sat down," Marjie said, shaking her head. "You looked a little faint from the joy and excitement about the big news. Take a deep breath, then exhale real slow."

"Well," Jerry muttered, "it *is* good news. They'll be the best parents in the world. It just sounds like bad timing to me. They're just getting their training started, and Margaret's got as many classes as Chester. What's she going to do?"

"I didn't get that far," Marjie said. "Let me keep reading, and you'd better try to calm down."

"What a beautiful kitty," Jerry said, glancing down at Martha's coloring just as she decided to target her red crayon on the oak table. "No!" he scolded, moving her chubby hand. "You color in the book. . . ."

Marjie was about to say something, but the ring of the telephone interrupted her. Reaching over to the phone on the wall, she picked up the receiver and spoke into the mouthpiece. "Hello. . . . Yeah, we're all fine, Ma. How about you and Benjamin? . . . Yeah, this winter's gone on a little too long already, if you ask me. . . . Paul? Really? What's he up to now? . . . No fooling? He's bringing her over here tonight? . . . Boy, I'm glad you called. The house needs a good cleaning if we're going to have company. . . . Well, I'd better get moving, then. Thanks for calling."

"Paul's bringing his girlfriend out to see us tonight?" Jerry asked, looking over at Marjie.

"Yeah. They're driving down from Minneapolis. Ma said her name is Betty," she said. "I assume she's that nurse we heard about after Paul got out of the hospital. He must be pretty serious if he wants us to meet her. I wonder what she's going to think of our house. Her father must be loaded if he owns the bakery where Paul works. She probably grew up in a mansion or something."

"We could always add on a couple more rooms today, if you can find that hammer you lost before it started snowing," Jerry teased.

"I'd just like to make as good of an impression as possible," said Marjie, pulling the broom and the dustpan from the closet and holding them out toward Jerry. "I'm glad that your schedule is so flexible. I need to decorate the Christmas tree, and I'll never get it done without your help on some of the cleaning."

"Sorry," Jerry replied, leaning back in his chair. "I've got calf pens that I have to clean out today or they'll be bumping up against the rafters. It's getting mighty deep out there."

"One more day won't hurt the calves a bit, but I can't get anything done with sweetie pie coloring the walls and your son about to wake up hungry," Marjie said. "You have to help. We've got a city slicker coming."

"I have to get—"

"I can make it worth your while," Marjie said, wrinkling her forehead and smirking.

"A little later . . ."

"You know, I just put fresh straw down in those pens the other day. I don't see any reason why that job can't wait a day," Jerry declared. "Where would you like me to start cleaning?"

"They're here," Jerry called out from the kitchen.

Marjie put down the tube of red lipstick and pressed her lips together one last time as she stared at her reflection in the mirror. *I even look like a farm girl,* she thought. "Is the coffee ready?" she called back as she blotted her lips, turned off the bathroom light, and stepped out into the hallway to the kitchen.

"Yes, and all's well, Marjie Belle," Jerry teased, turning around from where he'd been looking out the window. "The children are asleep, the house is as clean as a whistle, and you look like . . . a million bucks! They can stay in their car for all I care."

"I already said later, farm boy," Marjie returned. She stopped and kissed Jerry straight on the lips, then she gazed deep into his blue eyes. "That's my promise. You be nice now."

"Whatever you say," Jerry agreed, nodding toward the dining room picture window. "They're coming up the sidewalk."

Marjie glanced toward the window and caught a brief glimpse of the girl who was walking beside her brother Paul. "Long blond hair!" Marjie exclaimed. "Did you see that?"

"You'll see more if you go and let them in," Jerry said as a loud knock sounded on the front door.

"Okay, okay," Marjie replied, moving quickly to the door. Taking a deep breath, she smiled and opened the door. "Betty!" she gasped, standing in the doorway with her mouth open.

"Betty Hunter!" Jerry echoed, staring over Marjie's shoulder in disbelief.

"Correct as always," Paul replied, putting his good arm around Marjie's friend, then the two of them burst out laughing. "I believe you've met before."

"Paul!" Marjie cried. "What's going on?"

"It's sort of cold out here," replied Paul, still laughing. "Do you mind if we come in and warm up? I thought Ma called and told you I was bringing Betty over."

"She did, but—"

"Pardon our bad manners, but you caught us off guard, I'm afraid. Come in, come in," Jerry greeted them, pulling Marjie back out of the doorway so the two guests could make it past her. "We got our wires crossed, it seems."

Marjie still could not believe her eyes as Betty Hunter stepped into the farmhouse with a beautiful smile across her face. Her sweep of smooth blond hair was striking against her black coat, and her almond-shaped hazel eyes were dancing with delight as she looked into Marjie's stunned expression. Tall and slender, and wearing makeup for the first time that Marjie could remember, Betty unbuttoned her coat and handed it to Jerry. Marjie was glad that he at least had recovered enough to be a gracious host.

"Oh, I get it now," Paul said, nodding his head and doing his best to capture a serious look. "You were expecting my boss's daughter."

"No, no, no," Marjie countered. She eyeballed Paul hard and said, "We were expecting Betty Grable. But instead of a Hollywood star, you surprise us with our friend Betty Hunter. We, of course, had no idea that the two of you had ever met. So, Mr. Bakery Truck Dispatcher, I'm expecting you to sit down in my living room and explain this mystery to me. And if you try to pull the wool over my eyes one more time tonight, I will make both of you pay. And," she added with a twitch of her eyebrows, "you know that I can. . . ."

They all burst out laughing, and Marjie was surprised again when Betty reached over and took Paul's strong right hand.

"Marjie, this was all Paul's idea," Betty said, wiping some tears from the corner of her eye. "He made me do this. I told him he should warn you, but he wouldn't budge."

"It looks like . . . ah . . . you didn't fight too hard," Marjie said, nodding toward Betty's and Paul's comfortably clasped hands. "Now, I want the two of you to go and sit on the living room davenport while Jerry and I bring in some coffee. Then we're going to have ourselves a little chat, and you two better be shooting straight."

Paul and Betty laughed some more and headed for the living room while Jerry followed Marjie into the kitchen.

"Is this for real?" Marjie sputtered as she reached up and pulled four coffee cups from the cupboard. "Or is this a gigantic joke that Paul's pulling on me?"

"I have no idea," Jerry replied, lifting the coffeepot and pouring steaming brown liquid into the first cup. "How could he have even met her? Did you introduce her to Paul when he went to church with us last spring?"

"No," Marjie said. "That was the weekend Pastor Fitchen died, wasn't it? Then the funeral. I don't think he met her then."

"Well, they met somewhere, that's for sure," Jerry said as Marjie put saucers under the coffee cups and handed two of them to him. "And if this is a joke, they're doing a great job."

"Time to find out," Marjie said, taking two of the coffee cups and saucers and heading for the living room.

Paul and Betty were sitting close together on the davenport, and as Marjie handed Betty one of the cups of coffee, she couldn't hold back a chuckle when she saw that Betty had her right hand over Paul's damaged left hand.

"I apologize," Marjie said, shaking her head and sitting down in the big wooden rocking chair, "but this is just too big a shock for me. I take it that this is not a joke, because if it is, I will personally make sure that Paul Livingstone does not escape this house with his life intact."

They all broke out laughing, and after Jerry had handed Paul a cup of coffee, he said, "What she means is: how did you two meet? Also, she wants to know how in the world you pulled this off without her knowing anything about it."

Betty flashed a shy, secret smile at Paul, then she turned to Marjie. "I saw this handsome young man come to church with you late last spring, and I chickened out from coming up and introducing myself. When I found out he was your brother and that he was living in Minneapolis, I got his address from your mother and started to write him."

"And you never said a word to me," Marjie sputtered. She shot a glance at Paul. "You must have sworn her to secrecy."

"Sort of," Betty replied. "I really didn't want people to know about it. You know how people talk around here, and with me being a widow and all, they'd talk even more about me. Plus, I didn't have any idea whether Paul would be interested."

"But why Paul?" Marjie asked before she'd thought about what she was asking. "I mean . . . what caused you to . . . um—"

Betty broke out laughing and had to hold her saucer with both hands to keep the coffee from spilling. "He's tall, handsome, smart—"

"One-armed," Paul added, shrugging his shoulders.

"One's better than none, right?" Betty said with a smile. "Actually, do you really want to know why, other than the fact that he's absolutely gorgeous?"

"You're tormenting me again," Marjie replied, tapping her toe on the hard wooden floor. "Talk!"

"*You* did it," Betty declared. "It all started

with you."

"What?" Marjie asked.

"When I heard that your brother had been wounded and was coming home," Betty said, "it made me wonder if he was anything like you. I thought that if he was, he'd be someone I might be interested in. So I wrote him."

"And all this happened via letters with a guy who never wrote me once in three years?" Marjie asked, raising her eyebrows.

"No," Paul piped up, shaking his head. "She came up to Minneapolis a couple of times and stayed with her cousin. We've seen a lot of each other."

"My folks didn't even know about it," Betty said.

"And whatever happened to the boss's daughter, seeing as you brought it up, Paul?" Marjie asked with a smirk.

"Ancient history," Paul said, draping his strong right arm around Betty and grinning. "We went out several times, and she was really nice, but I think she dated me more out of pity than real interest. I became a nice conversation piece for her social club, but I never could have fit in there. And I wasn't interested in trying."

"So what do your parents think, Betty?" Jerry asked. "I take it that they know about Paul now."

"Oh yes," Betty replied. She glanced at Paul and smiled. "It's been pretty interesting at home. They think Paul's a fine young man, but they also think that because I lost Fred in battle I'm settling for a wounded replacement. They'd like me to wait until the war's over and see if I can find someone who's—"

"Not damaged goods," Paul interrupted. "That's what I hear fairly often behind my back at work. At least her folks are honest about it."

"Honest, my eye!" Marjie sputtered, her own worries and reservations already forgotten. "Your folks didn't feel you needed to grieve for Fred after the funeral either, did they?"

Betty shook her head no. "I had to come over and cry with you, as I'm sure you recall," she said. "You know, when Fred left for the war, the biggest mistake I made was moving home, thinking I'd help my folks with the work around the farm until he returned. I became their little girl again, and they feel like they need to decide everything for me."

"So they want you to break off your relationship with Paul," said Marjie, staring into Betty's clear hazel eyes. "What are you going to do?"

"We're going to do what we feel we should do," Betty replied as Paul reached into his pocket. "Would you like to see the ring?"

Chapter Thirty-one

Alleluia!

"Yes, this is a day we'll never forget!" Marjie exclaimed as she ended her telephone conversation and hung up the receiver. Then she picked Martha up off the floor and danced around the dining room table with her daughter giggling at the celebration. "Victory in Europe, sweetheart! May the eighth, nineteen forty-five. You may not understand it, but this is one of the greatest days of our lives."

"What's going on in there?" Jerry said from behind them, peeking in through the screen on the west window in the dining room. He'd just finished the morning chores. "Looks like you two are starting the celebration a little early."

"That's not possible," Marjie replied, spinning Martha around one more time. "We should dance all day."

Marjie danced to the front door with Martha, then stepped outside to meet Jerry on the sidewalk. Setting the little girl down on the concrete, Marjie grabbed Jerry, who lifted her off the ground and spun her around in circles, both of them screaming and laughing. Their dance of joy caught the attention of Blue, who came dashing out of the barn to see what was wrong. With a cry of joy, Martha ran over to meet her favorite friend, quickly grabbing an ear and climbing on Blue's back.

"It's over!" Marjie cried as Jerry finally set her back down on the ground. "Three and a half horrible years, and it's finally over. Our phone has been ringing off the hook. People are so excited."

"The cows don't seem all that excited," Jerry said, kissing Marjie and holding her tight. "I'm jumping up and down in the barn, and they just don't get it. But Charlie keeps looking over the door like he's asking me what's going on."

"Go see Charlie!" Martha exclaimed from her accustomed perch atop the long-suffering Blue. She pointed emphatically to the barn. "Go now!"

"Not now, sweetheart," Jerry answered her. "We've got some celebrating to do." He turned to Marjie. "So where are we going to go?"

"Sounds like there's a celebration going on wherever you want to go," Marjie replied, giving Jerry another squeeze. "Maybe we should go into Preston and see what's happening there, and then drive on up to Rochester. I'll bet it's going to be wild there today. And there's a celebration at the church tonight. We can't miss that."

"Boo!" Martha cried, grasping the dog's leg as he pulled away at the sound of an approaching car. With a quick leap the dog cleared the fence and raced down the driveway, barking as Benjamin and Sarah's car came rolling around the corner.

"I figured they'd be coming over, but they must be pretty wound up to be here so early," Marjie said as she and Jerry waved. Benjamin beeped as he went by, causing Martha to jump.

Benjamin and Sarah emerged quickly from the car and headed straight to the front gate.

"Hey!" Jerry called out, giving his father a hug. "We did it!"

"We sure did!" Benjamin exclaimed. "I started to wonder back in December with the Bulge. What a horrible winter in Europe!"

"But spring always comes, even though it's never soon enough," Marjie said, hugging her mother and then Benjamin. "I'll bet Paul and Teddy are whooping it up today."

"I'll bet they are, too," Sarah replied. "Paul drove down last night when he heard it on the radio, and he and Betty are up at the parsonage now talking to the new pastor."

"They've set a date?" Marjie asked, jumping up and down. "When?"

"Today," Sarah replied, mimicking Marjie by trying to jump at the same time.

"Today!" Marjie went stiff halfway through another leap. "Today?"

Sarah and Benjamin broke out laughing, and both of them were nodding. Benjamin scooped Martha up into his arms and cuddled her close.

"Paul thought this was the perfect day to celebrate what he nearly gave his life for," Sarah said. "It's a grand day for a wedding, don't you think?"

"Sure, but . . . how are we going to get stuff together in time for it?" Marjie asked, sitting down on the steps to the front door. "They're going to get married in the church?"

"No," Sarah replied with a smile. "If Pastor Holmes is willing to do it, and if you and Jerry will let them, they'd like to get married right down the hill—"

"Where we rode our horses that first day!" Marjie interrupted, suddenly remembering their winter conversation.

"But why there?" asked Jerry.

Marjie didn't answer. She just shook her head, catching her lower lip in her teeth. A light warm breeze tossed her long wavy brown hair into her face, and she didn't bother to push it back. A single tear escaped her brimming eyes.

Benjamin cleared his throat. "Betty said that's the spot where she started to live again, thanks to Marjie. She thinks it's the perfect place to marry your brother-in-law."

"Sounds good to me," Jerry said. "So who's coming? They finally talk Betty's folks into this?"

Sarah shook her head no. "We figure it'll just be the preacher and his wife. Betty's folks told her that if she was going to marry Paul, she'd have to do it without their approval. Now they say that he won't be able to support her, even though he's been a manager at the bakery for well over a year."

"It's all about appearances with them, and it always has been," Jerry said, crossing his arms. "If anybody ever bent over backward to try to win someone's approval, Paul certainly did. Just waiting this long to get married should have told the Hunters something about his character. It's just too bad for them. You'd have to search a long time to find a better man than Paul is."

"I got the only one better than Paul," Marjie said, finally pushing back her hair. "And we're going to throw together a wedding meal they won't forget. Come on, Ma. Let's see what we can do with what I've got. And I'm going to call Ruthie and see what she can do. How much time do you think we have?"

"Ruthie, those chickens are huge," Sarah said, clearing a spot on the kitchen counter. "Where'd you get them?"

"Roy Maples was butchering yesterday, and Billy stopped by and got them," Ruth said, looking down at the two fat, dressed birds she had carried in. "Billy figured that with all the celebrations, we should have some meat ready for a party. Looks like he had that right. I cleaned them up, so they're ready for the roaster."

"Good," Sarah said, pulling the lid off the metal roaster pan and tucking the two chickens inside. Lifting the roaster into the heated oven, she said, "By the time the wedding's over, these birds should be ready to go."

"Let's see," Marjie said, gazing around the kitchen. "Mashed potatoes, canned corn, roast chicken, pickles, Jell-O, almost-fresh buns. Not bad for—"

"Here they are," Ruth interrupted, turning to look out the dining room picture window as Paul's car rolled past, followed by the pastor's old Ford. "So the pastor's daughter is going to watch all of the children and keep an eye on the birds in the oven while we're down the hill?"

"Yep," Marjie said, noticing Sarah's raised eyebrows. "Harriet's fourteen, Ma. When I was fourteen, you—"

"I sent you to live in town in your own apartment so you could go to high school," Sarah broke in. "How many times have you used that line on me? You think I wasn't sweating bullets the whole time you were away? I still get nervous thinking about it."

"I could stay up here and take care of Robert if he wakes up," Ruth offered.

"No, everything will be fine," Marjie said, walking toward the front door. "Harriet's been babysitting for me a lot lately. Let's get out there and get this show on the road."

"You're stealing my lines now," Ruth said, following Marjie to the door and laughing.

"Having you live so close is rubbing off on me," Marjie replied, glancing back into Ruth's flashing dark eyes. "Next thing you know I'll be dashing away from you when you stop to talk in church. Give you a little taste of your own medicine."

Marjie stepped out of the farmhouse onto the front steps and took a deep breath of the warm spring breeze. *What a gorgeous day!* she thought, drinking in the bright sunshine as well. Tiny green leaves fluttered in the elm trees, and the grass that had been winter brown such a short time ago was greening nicely. Jerry, Billy, and Benjamin had been watching the children play in the front lawn and now stood waiting for the wedding party.

"Fine day for a wedding," Marjie called out as Paul and Betty emerged from their car, followed by Harriet Holmes. Paul grinned and waved, then he put his arm around Betty as they stepped through the front gate. Then the handshakes and the hugs began.

Paul wore his army dress uniform, which Marjie thought made him look taller and even more strikingly handsome. His strong, chiseled face was all smiles, his big brown eyes almost squinted shut. Betty's satin cream blouse above the knee-length navy skirt set off the soft highlights of her long blond hair, and her face, which Marjie recalled once thinking to be so plain, was full of sweetness and graciousness. *What a lovely couple!* she thought.

While the others were greeting the couple, Marjie took Harriet Holmes into the kitchen and gave her instructions on when to take the chickens out of the oven, as well as what to do if Robert woke up. Ruth had made some grape drink and peanut-butter crackers for Martha, Ellie, and Timmy, who were going to keep playing in the front yard.

Marjie was just finishing with Harriet when she heard the front screen door open and turned to see Betty and Paul coming into the farmhouse. Betty was wiping tears, and Paul's face almost looked tired from having smiled so long.

"I'll be out in a minute," Betty said, heading straight for the bathroom. "Marjie, you wait for me."

Marjie giggled as Betty dashed past her, then she felt Paul's long right arm wrap around her and squeeze her tight. "Congratulations, big brother," she whispered, turning her face into his strong shoulder and hugging him. "I am so happy for you."

"I am so happy for me, too," Paul replied with a deep laugh. "And it's mostly because of you that this is happening. Thank you a million times. I love you, Marjie."

"You're making me cry, you big goofy sergeant," Marjie said with a quaver in her voice. "Don't say another word or I'll bust all over the place. Then I won't have anything left for the wedding."

"Oh, you'll have plenty left, but I'll be nice and let you off for now," said Paul, still holding her tight. "I'm going down the hill with the others, and Betty wants you to walk with her in a few minutes. We'll be waiting for you, okay?"

"Sure," Marjie said softly. She reached up and pressed the tears from the corners of her eyes as Paul pulled away. "Get out of here before you get a good kick like you always deserved."

Paul laughed and said, "You wouldn't kick a cripple, would you?"

"Move it or lose it, bud," Marjie joked, faking a kick.

"I'll see you down there," Paul replied, turning and heading back out the door. Marjie stood at the dining room picture window and watched as he joined the small group that had begun the short walk down the farm lane toward the beautiful overlook where Marjie and Betty had talked so long ago.

The wedding party had disappeared down the lane when Marjie heard the rattle of the bathroom door.

"Betty, you look beautiful!" Marjie exclaimed as her friend stepped into the hallway. Her dark brown eyes were gleaming as she hugged Betty, but she did all she could to hold back the tears. "I am so delighted that you love Paul. Welcome to the family."

Marjie felt Betty shake and breathe heavily against Marjie's shoulder. "You have been more than a sister to me already," Betty whispered. "I owe you everything for today."

"You owe me nothing," Marjie spoke quietly. "Just love my brother and take good care of him. That's all I ask."

Betty took out a white handkerchief and dried her eyes. "I do love him, and I can hardly wait to take care of him." She straightened and started down the hallway. "And I think we'd better get moving so I don't start crying again. Would you walk with me? It'd mean a lot."

"I'd be honored," Marjie said, following Betty out toward the back door to avoid saying goodbye to the children. "I'm sorry that it's gone so poorly with your family," she said as they pushed open the farmhouse door and stepped out into the cheery sunlight. "Are you okay about that?"

"Yes, I am," Betty declared, shaking her head. "It's taken a long time for me to resolve, but now I'm ready to move on. For whatever reason, they can't handle the fact that Paul's shoulder and arm are crippled. We gave them time to work through it, and they didn't. So, with or without them, I'm going to do what I know I should do, and that's to marry the man I love."

Marjie could feel the strength in Betty's voice, and she marveled as she thought back to how fearful Betty had been when she first approached Marjie in the church to talk about her first husband's death.

"It's funny," Betty continued as they walked in the shadows of the large pine trees that ran along the edge of the farm lane. "My folks think Paul is damaged, but I keep thinking that I'm the damaged one. I mean, I've been married before, and I haven't been in such great shape since Fred died, so maybe . . ."

Marjie stopped dead in her tracks and looked straight into Betty's clear hazel eyes. "Don't ever think that, Betty," she urged her. "You loved someone dearly, and that person was torn from your life. You've been hurt, but hurt doesn't mean damaged. God gives us new starts and new life, and He calls it a new creation, however we may feel inside about it. Don't let the feelings overshadow what's true about you."

Betty closed her eyes and nodded her head. "I believe you, Lord," she whispered, opening her eyes and looking straight up into the blue sky. "I believe!" she called out, then she laughed. "Let's go."

Betty and Marjie quickened their pace and came to the end of the farm lane. Down the hill, under the two gnarly burr-oak trees, they could see where the others were waiting for them. Beyond and below them spread the farm fields in their beautiful green valley.

"What a sight!" said Marjie as they headed

down the gently sloping hillside. "I wish Margaret was here to fill the valley with her voice like she did when Benjamin and my mother got married. Do you remember that?"

"No, I didn't go," Betty said, taking Marjie's arm again. "I couldn't handle the thought of a wedding right then. But this is fine. Paul and I wanted something small and simple. And besides, we couldn't get Margaret from Scotland in time."

Marjie laughed at Betty, then the two of them waved to the small crowd.

As if the women's wave was their cue, Edward Holmes nodded to Benjamin, Billy, and Jerry, and the four men began to sing out in four-part harmony,

All creatures of our God and King,
Lift up your voice and with us sing,
Alleluia, Alleluia!

At first their song was quiet, but with every word their voices gained strength. Pastor Holmes sang in a ringing high tenor, and to Marjie's surprise, the other three men complemented him wonderfully, and their voices resonated through the green hills.

O praise Him, O praise Him!
Alleluia, Alleluia, Alleluia!

"Alleluia!" Marjie gasped, squeezing Betty's hand. And then the tears did begin to flow.

Chapter Thirty-two

A Boiling Brightness

"Thanks for dropping off the sugar, Ruthie," Marjie said, bending over to look in the car window at Ruth and Ellie and Timmy. "I'm going to need it when the family's all here. But you're sure you can't stay for a little while?"

"No, my dad's got a crew coming over to put up his silage," Ruth answered, leaning her head back and stretching her neck muscles. "And those men like to have their food on the table, even if the smell nearly does me in."

"Still got morning sickness, I take it?" asked Marjie wryly.

"Whatever you want to call it, I got it," said Ruth. "But it's not just the morning, that's for sure. You could have warned me about this."

"I did, and you know I did," Marjie protested. "It's September first, and you've got . . . about seven months to go, honey. If you're lucky, you'll stop feeling sick."

"And if I'm real lucky," Ruth continued,

"you'll help me deliver my baby in your barn for a reasonable fee. You said that before as well, and I'm still considering your offer."

"It's not that bad a deal," Marjie joked. "As long as you can keep the dog out of your face."

"No thanks," said Ruth. "So are Teddy and Lavonne staying here?"

"Yeah," Marjie answered. "And Paul and Betty are going to stay at Ma's. But they're all coming over here tonight, and I've got a lot of grub to get ready."

"Don't talk to me about cooking, please," Ruth said. "But I would like to hear what Teddy has to say."

"If he says anything at all," Marjie replied. "Last time they were here, he and Lavonne couldn't talk about anything they were doing."

"After Hiroshima and Nagasaki, what would be the point of secrecy?" asked Ruth. "Japan signs the treaty tomorrow, but the war ended two weeks ago. Tomorrow we dance in the streets again."

"I've been dancing plenty already," Marjie said. "But I think I can do it one more time. I hope that Teddy does clue us in, though. It's hard to believe the reports of what happened in Japan. I don't even like to think about it."

"Tens of thousands of people," Ruth

mused, "all killed instantly." She shook her head. "At least our men didn't have to invade Japan. After all the men we lost at Iwo Jima and Okinawa, can you imagine what they would have faced in Japan?"

"No," Marjie said. "But hopefully the killing is over now. And now we can all make a brand-new start."

Ted and Lavonne Livingstone arrived from New Mexico early in the afternoon, their eyes drooping from having driven most of the night. After some teasing from Marjie about why they had traded their motorcycle for an old Chrysler, they went upstairs to take a nap and slept nearly until mealtime. When they came down, Sarah and Benjamin and Paul and Betty had arrived and were waiting for them, and Jerry was changing clothes after finishing the evening chores.

Introductions were made as Betty met Ted and Lavonne for the first time. Then as they sat down to the meal, Benjamin commented on how delighted he was to have such a large gathering of family around the table in the old Macmillan dining room. That was followed by such an extraordinarily long prayer of thanksgiving that Marjie had all she could do to keep Robert quiet in his high chair. Fortunately for Marjie, Sarah plopped some peas on Martha's plate, and the little girl kept busy spinning them from one side to the other until the prayer was over.

Four years, Marjie thought as she carried in the platters and bowls of food that were still in the kitchen. *It's been more than four years since all of the Livingstones sat at a dinner table together, and so much has happened since then.* Four weddings. Two babies. Three young men leaving home for war, and older, wiser men had returned. Hearing the chatter around the table, especially seeing her two brothers joking with each other, she felt almost bowled over by a wave of joy.

"So, what are you going to do when they let you out, Teddy?" Paul asked. "I can always use a good driver at the bakery, if you're willing to buck the union."

"You think I'd work for you?" Ted burst out laughing. "No thanks, big brother. You see, there are two things I don't want to do when I take off this uniform. One is to farm—forgive me, Ma, but I don't have a farming bone in my body. The other thing is having a grumpy old sergeant like you bossing me around all day. You got enough licks in on me when we were little to last a lifetime. And now, when I'm finally old enough to take you on, you go and get yourself shot up so I can't beat on you."

Everyone burst out laughing, including Martha. "You're funny, Uncle Teddy," the three-year-old mumbled through a mouthful of mashed potatoes, making everyone laugh even harder.

"Don't encourage her," Marjie scolded when she had managed to straighten her own face. "She's bad enough as it is."

"I'll tell you what we are going to do, though," Ted said, glancing over at Lavonne, who winked one cobalt blue eye at him. "We're going to move back to this area and start a television and radio business. It's just a matter of figuring out which town is the best one to start our shop. There's big money ahead in televisions."

"You really think so?" Sarah asked as she cut the last piece of her pork chop in two. "From what I've seen, I couldn't give a hoot about it."

"Me neither," Marjie added, partly to egg Ted on. "I'd rather listen to the radio any day."

"I'm telling you," Ted declared, nodding confidently, "it's going to grow like you won't believe—even way out here in the country. With antennas, you're going to see a television coming to every farmhouse. If you got some money you'd like to invest, Lavonne and I are looking for partners to get us going. She's got the business head, and I've got the electronics know-how. All we need is the right place and some money."

"I thought maybe you'd go to college and become an atomic physicist or something," Paul said jokingly, but Ted's face went somber instead. Ted laid down his fork and took a drink of water.

"Me and Lavonne, we've seen enough in the past year to know that atomic energy is not what we want to be around," Ted said, shaking his head. "The sooner we can get out of Los Alamos and away from the radioactivity, the better. It scares me to death."

"You got that close to the atomic bomb?" asked Jerry.

"Close?" Ted sputtered. "Shoot. I was at the test site in the desert when the first one was detonated. You can't get much closer than that."

"Unless you deliver a component to the test site," Lavonne added, rubbing one of her elegant cheekbones. "That was a ride I won't forget for a long time."

"Are you serious?" Benjamin asked. "You actually saw an atomic bomb explode in the desert—the same kind they dropped on Japan?"

Both Lavonne and Ted nodded. Then Lavonne said, "On July twelfth, I was assigned to drive for a man named Philip Morrison, and I knew something was up when an armed escort joined us. Before the war, I knew that Morrison had been a physicist at the University of Illinois, and when I picked him up, he was carrying a special metal container with rubber stoppers all over it. I found out later that it was the plutonium core for the bomb that was stored in the vault at Los Alamos."

Lavonne took a sip of her coffee and continued. "As we headed out into the desert, the car behind me was full of armed guards, and there was another car in front. I drove my Plymouth up to eighty miles an hour to an old one-story ranch house out in the middle of nowhere. I didn't know what was going on, but I was sure glad to get out of there when I did. Four days later, Teddy was there when it blew."

"You can't imagine what I saw," Ted said and almost seemed to shudder. "It was five-thirty in the morning, and I was in this concrete bunker ten thousand yards north of the blast site. And then all of a sudden there was this fantastic flash of light—like a thousand suns, and this reddish yellow fireball shot up into the sky. They said it turned the night into day for more than a hundred miles. Anyway, I started to pray, thinking I'd just taken my last breath on this earth.

"And then the shock wave hit," Ted continued, making motions with his hands, "and there was this big roar—not a boom, but a roar that just kept getting louder, and it seemed to go on and on. I could hear the echoes bouncing off all those mountains. And then, just minutes after the bomb went off, I noticed a section of what I thought was gas had peeled off from the mushroom cloud and was coming straight at us.

"Robert Wilson was the physicist in charge of our position, and he immediately ordered us to hop in the trucks and evacuate. We tore out of there as fast as those trucks would go, and as we left, that cloud of what turned out to be radioactive debris was right on top of us. You talk about spooky, man. I don't ever want to see anything like that again."

"What would have happened if you had stayed at the bunker?" Sarah asked. She had pulled out her handkerchief and was nervously turning it over in her hand.

"I don't know—don't want to know," Ted replied, shaking his head. "Wilson heard that the cloud came down on a bunch of cattle and turned their hair white. I heard that another physicist found a totally paralyzed mule twenty-five miles from the site. There've been reports about cattle losing their hair and suffering severe skin blisters. Some of the stories sound pretty bizarre, but after what I saw, I believe every story I hear."

Lavonne ran her fingers through her short auburn hair and said, "Back at Los Alamos, the place went crazy with celebrating. Somebody started a snake dance that wound through the streets. People were hugging each other, and some of them started passing bottles of booze up and down the line. Teddy thought he was going to get mobbed when he got back from the test site. Like they were heroes or something."

"Not everybody thought it was so great, though," Teddy added. "I saw Robert Wilson later that night, and he said, 'It's a terrible thing that we made!' I'm afraid I think so, too. I mean, I know it shortened the war, and that's good, but that thing is dreadful beyond your worst nightmare. I wish I would've never seen it."

"How can one bomb possibly be so powerful?" Jerry asked. "How'd they do it?"

Ted's snort of laughter broke the tension around the dining room table. "I told you I was going into television and radio, not nuclear science. All I know is that they split some atoms somehow and produced an extremely powerful explosion. The scientists at the test site told us the blast from one bomb is like exploding ten to twenty thousand tons of TNT. And you can drop it from one bomber, like they did at Hiroshima and Nagasaki."

"Good night!" Benjamin gasped, shaking his head. "And all that was going down in New Mexico, and we never had a clue it was happening?"

"It was like a whole secret city down there at Los Alamos," Lavonne said, "something like twenty-five hundred scientists and technicians. I should know. I drove enough of them around. And then some of them had their families, and there were all kinds of other support personnel—plumbers, secretaries, schoolteachers, electricians, carpenters, guards, cooks. . . ."

"It really was a city!" exclaimed Jerry. "Twenty-five hundred plus is a lot bigger than any town in our county."

"I'd take any town in this county over where we live right now," Ted said. "The desert is a beautiful place to live, but I'd like to get as far away from that test site as possible. The day they say we can leave, we're gone."

"I know how you feel," Paul said, rubbing his damaged shoulder. "When we were fighting in Italy, there were days when I counted the minutes, hoping that somehow the fighting and the killing would suddenly end, but it just kept on, and on, and on. You'd see someone get wounded and think they were the lucky guy because they got to go home."

Ted nodded soberly. "Paul, I know I didn't see combat, so I can't really know what you faced. But what I saw in that desert—well, I believe I saw something of what it'll be like when the world finally comes to an end. It was enough to make a man believe in God . . . or in the devil . . . or in both."

For a moment, even the two children sat motionless, as if the silence that had gathered around the table had silenced them as well. Every eye was on Ted.

"And which was it for you, Teddy?" Marjie finally asked.

Ted turned toward Marjie, then toward Sarah, and then he smiled. "I believe in both—with all my heart."

Chapter Thirty-three

The Reunion

"Margaret!" cried Marjie, racing out the back door of the farmhouse followed by Ruth and Sarah. "Chester! Oh, look at little Laura!"

Jerry, Billy, and Benjamin came around from the front of the house and joined the long-awaited reunion with their beloved missionary family. It was a sea of hugs and kisses and brief attempts to actually say something. Martha and Ellie and Timmy and Robert trailed slowly behind, unsure of what all the raucous celebration was about and whether it warranted stopping their game of kickball.

"Laura Stanfeld!" Marjie said, taking the shy two-year-old from Margaret's arms and admiring her brunette curls and round blue eyes. "What a beautiful little girl you are! Just like your mother. Thank goodness you don't look like your father!"

The joyous group burst into laughter, and little Laura buried her head against Marjie's shoulder.

"Almost three and a half years, and you're still as mean as ever," Chester sputtered, hugging Marjie a second time. "Now you're going to leave a permanent mark upon my daughter. She'll think I'm ugly the rest of her life."

"Is that you, Martha?" Margaret asked, walking over to take the hand of the barefoot girl who was standing at the front of the pack of children.

The five-year-old farm girl with long wavy brown hair gave Margaret a smirk and the slightest of nods, then she said, "Me good mother says you're a bonny lass."

The whole group burst into fresh laughter as Margaret scooped Martha into her arms. "Ye're the bonny one!" she exclaimed. "I held you when you were a wee bairn, indeed. How could ye grow so tall?"

"Grandpa says I'll get big and strong if I eat my vegetables, but I hate them," Martha replied, drawing another wave of laughter.

"Marjie, she's got your mouth," Chester said. "May God help us all."

"And this must be Ellie," Margaret said, putting Martha down and holding out a hand to the tall nine-year-old. "And Master Tim, who I see is missin' both his front teeth. Your mother has written us about you. I am so delighted to meet ye at last."

"I'm Bobby!" the stocky three-year-old with short blond hair and a dirty face piped up. "And I'm strong!"

"We call him the Bull," Benjamin said when the laughter had subsided.

"Mommy says he's like Grandpa," Martha added, looking up at Marjie, who was shaking her head no.

"And where's little Daniel?" Margaret asked, turning toward Ruth.

"Sleeping, thank goodness," Ruth replied, shaking her head. "Laura looks like an angel, so you probably don't know how crabby a fourteen-month-old boy can be."

"Oh, I think I do," Margaret said, her delicate lips curving into a smile.

"Obviously she does," Sarah commented. "She lives with Chester."

Chester groaned. "Three generations of this. Do you see what happened to the human race when Adam fell?"

"I'd forgotten until you got out of the car," added Marjie. "But now I remember."

"You won't ever win with her," Benjamin said, "so just surrender, and get it over with quickly. Then she'll leave you alone."

"I surrender," said Chester, raising his hands. "And I'm willing to do some serious begging if you'll let me ride Charlie. You still have him, don't you?"

"What sort of begging?" asked Marjie.

"I'll get him saddled up," Jerry broke in. "See if you can stretch his legs a bit. Marjie's been sloughing off lately."

"Getting lazy is another way of saying it," said Sarah, raising her eyebrows.

"Thank you for evening the score a bit," Chester said, then followed Jerry toward the barn.

"Grandpa, will you and Uncle Billy keep playing ball with us?" Martha asked sweetly.

"Sure," Benjamin replied, putting a hand on his granddaughter's shoulder. "We got all day to talk with our friends. Billy and I are going to try to tire you kids out."

"You always tire out first, Grandpa," Martha replied.

"And he always rewards himself with a nap because of it," Sarah added.

Billy and Benjamin led the children back to the front lawn, where they had bases laid out for kickball, while the women went into the house for coffee and talk. Little Laura spotted Blue, who was lying on the front steps of the farmhouse, and to his dismay, she jumped down from Marjie's arms and made a beeline to play with him.

"Margaret, Chester's mom said you'll be here for two months before heading for Japan," Marjie said from the kitchen where she was pouring coffee. "Is that all? This is 1947, you realize."

"Aye, that's right," Margaret replied, sitting down at the dining room table with Ruth and glancing out the window where the children were playing. "We want to get there in September of this year."

"What's the rush?" asked Marjie. "It's only mid-June. Japan's new constitution just went into effect last month. We figured you'd wait awhile and let them get more things in place."

"No," Margaret replied as Marjie and Sarah rounded the counter with their cups of coffee. "We feel the less things are in place, the more we may be able to do. We would have liked to have gone last year, but our mission felt it was more important that Chester spend a year pastorin' so he has more practical experience."

"Do you think you're ready now?" Ruth asked.

Margaret took a sip of her coffee and smiled. "I'm sure no one's ever been ready to do what we're going to do," she said. "We've had two wonderful years in Bible college with a strong emphasis on missions. And for the past year Chester served a church that was without a minister. So we hope we have a good foundation, but I doubt we're ready."

"Are you afraid?" Sarah asked.

"Oh, surely," Margaret replied, looking at Sarah with her enormous blue eyes. "As afraid as I was when I thought about getting married." She cast her glance over toward Marjie and Ruth. "Do you remember that conversation around this very table, ladies?"

"The one you specifically promised me that you would never tell anyone about," Marjie said.

"That's the one," Margaret said, giggling. Then she grew serious. "It's the fear of doing something that ye feel strongly about, but ye know so little about it until ye do it. The Japanese have always been extremely difficult to reach with the gospel. And even now that the state religion has been abolished and the emperor has declared he is not divine, we expect the going to be very hard."

"Seems like you'll face a lot of hatred," Ruth said. "I mean, they've been humiliated as a nation, and there's been that incredible loss of life and the destruction of their cities, and now they're occupied by their enemies. Won't they resent your even being there?"

Margaret nodded. "Well over a million Japanese died during the war," she said. "Every major Japanese city was bombed heavily except for the city of Kyoto, which is where our mission director feels we should go. So yes, I expect they will resent us."

"So what will you do when you get there?" Marjie asked. "Work with a church?"

Margaret shook her head. "No. We hope eventually to start a church, but right now there are almost no believers in Japan. The first thing we have to do is to learn the language, which sounds like climbing a mountain. Written Japanese is considered one of the most difficult writing systems in the world."

"Well, this old farm looks better to me everyday," Marjie said. "I can't imagine how brave you are to attempt it."

"Obedient, perhaps, but not brave, Marjie," said Margaret. "You wrote me about how you started the prayer group because no one else seemed willing to do it, despite how unprepared ye felt. And, Ruthie, you and Billy adopted two lovely children into yer home, even though ye were newly married and hadn't planned on children so soon. And, Sarah, you faced losing yer farm when yer husband died and then again when that son o' yers decided t' leave. It looks heroic, and it is heroic, but it's more than that. You did what ye needed to do, what ye were called to do. You stepped out in faith, and then God took ye a step further. That's true, isn't it?"

"Like I said, the farm feels real good to me," Marjie responded, and the intensity that had gathered around the table dissolved into a laugh.

"Tell me about what happened to your prayer meeting after the war ended," Margaret asked.

Marjie laughed. "To tell you the truth, I tried real hard to kill it, but it just wouldn't die. The longer the war went on, the more people got involved with it, and pretty soon other churches were calling me and asking for help to set up something like it. Then the war ended, and I figured that the main reason for our getting together was over, so I tried to pull the plug. But most of the people felt like the meeting had become such an important part of their spiritual lives that they wanted to keep on going. So we did, and the crazy thing kept growing."

"Tell her about Jerry," Sarah said.

"Well, one day we're sitting here eating breakfast, and Jerry tells me he thinks the meeting has gotten too big," Marjie continued. "And furthermore, he thinks it would be better if there was one prayer meeting for the men and one for the women. At first I felt like that was a bad idea, but the more I thought about it, the more it seemed to have some advantages. So I figured that old Smarty Pants Jerry should follow through with his idea."

"So you asked him to take the men's group?" Margaret asked. "Oh, I can imagine how our shy and retirin' Jerry took to that idea."

"Well, he wasn't very happy at first," Marjie replied. "But I reminded him that he had thought I was the one to start the original group because it was my idea. So he agreed to try leading the men's group. And you know what? He's done wonderfully, and he loves it. Some weeks he's got more men coming than I have women. And we've even been going out together to speak in other churches that want to hear all of our dynamic secrets to successful prayer meetings. Now that's a shocker!"

"Oh, praise the Lord!" exclaimed Margaret, laughing and applauding. "What a wonderful change in our Jerry's life!"

"Lots of changes around here," Marjie said. "Besides being the best mother in the whole world, Ruthie's got the best Sunday school program going in our church's whole denomination. Billy has the young people's group wrapped around his finger. He's got them leading their own meetings and having a ball doing it. Grandpa Benjamin's become a pretty fair Bible teacher since taking Chester's place, but he's proven to be an even better head elder for the church. He and the man who took Pastor Fitchen's place have become very close."

"And what about the grand lady who offered that I could stay at her house even though she had never met me?" Margaret asked, turning to Sarah.

Sarah smiled and fingered her coffee cup. "I just make sure that the fine head elder is well fed and clothed. And I babysit for my grandkids when their famous parents are out doing the Lord's work."

"Right!" Ruth sputtered. "This is the lady who kept her own car when she got married so she could visit the sick and elderly and lonely folks without having to be escorted by her husband. It's not something that a lot of people see, but just get sick while you're in this neck of the woods, and I can tell you who's going to give you a call."

"And your three families have continued to support us the whole time we've been away," Margaret added. "Do ye know how much that has meant to us? We write and try to say a proper thank-you, but it sounds so hollow. In the difficult times—and it's not been easy with a little child—it was your letters and the money you sent that pushed us on. We do want ye to be proud of us, as we are of you. Oh, I have been so blessed to call ye my friends, and we missed ye so much."

Margaret covered her mouth and closed her eyes, but that could not stop the tears. One by one—Ruth first, then Sarah, and finally Marjie—they all joined hands around the old oak table. And they cried, and they laughed, and they cried some more. And then they thanked God, one by one, through their tears and their laughter, for the gift of friendship, and the gift of family, and the gift of salvation.

Epilogue

"Go deep! Go deep, Danny!" Bobby Macmillan yelled, cocking the worn football in his right hand and waving with his left arm as his best friend Daniel Wilson raced down the lawn. Then Bobby threw a tight spiral that soared for forty yards and then tucked itself neatly into Daniel's outstretched hands. "Touchdown!" Bobby cried, raising his hands in delight.

His mother stood watching behind the front screen door to the old white farmhouse. Her husband sat on the front steps in front of her, trying to cool down after having run too many pass patterns with Bobby and his friends.

"Nice throw," Jerry said. His strong, suntanned arms glistened as he leaned back on his thick hands. "You keep tossing hay bales all summer, and that arm of yours should be ready to pile up some yardage by fall."

"This arm is ready now," Bobby proclaimed, flexing his muscles as Daniel came hustling back and tossed the ball to him.

"Preston's star senior quarterback and his flashy wide receiver," Marjie said from behind the screen. "Why don't you boys sit in the shade for a while so you're not so sweaty when Laura gets here. First impressions are important, you know."

"Oh, who cares?" Bobby grumbled, running his fingers through his blond crewcut. At six feet two and a hundred and sixty-five pounds of muscle, he reminded her powerfully of Jerry when he was in his late teens, except Bobby had none of his father's shyness. "Why'd her folks ask Grandpa and Grandma to pick her up at the bus depot, anyway? Grandpa drives that '56 Ford of his so slow it's embarrassing."

"Somebody in Japan probably told Chester and Margaret about how wild a driver you are," Jerry teased. "What if she brings instructions that say she can't get in a car with you all year?"

"Shoot! I'm a great driver," Bobby said, glancing over at Daniel.

"Just a little fast," Daniel added, a mischievous smile lighting his long, dark face.

"Marjie, I thought they'd be here by now,"

Ruth said from the kitchen, taking off her apron and wiping the flour from her hands. "I sure wish Tim and Billy could've gotten off work."

"How does Tim like working for his dad, the banker?" Marjie asked, turning around and going into the dining room.

"He loves it," replied Ruth. She picked up her glass of water and joined Marjie at the old oak table. "For a kid who's only had one year of college, it's a great summer job. Ellie worked at the same job shortly before she got married, and she hated it. Guess it's the difference between kids."

"Like night and day, isn't it?" Marjie said. "I wish Martha was here, too, but she's got those summer classes at the university, and there's no way she can get out of them. I'm glad she got to see Laura last night, though."

"So Paul and Betty and Martha picked up Laura at the airport in Minneapolis last night, and she stayed over with them, and then they put her on the bus?" said Ruth. "I'll bet Laura and Martha had a ball together. Remember the times when Chester and Margaret were here on furlough? Martha and Laura were always like big sister and little sister—fights, hugs, and all. Those were some great times."

Marjie nodded her head and chuckled. "I

hope Laura likes living with us for this year, even with Martha at the U. We tried to fix Martha's room up special for her, but it's still a long way from Japan. Chester and Margaret want her to get used to living here in the States before she tries college, but it's really going to be different for her. I'm glad Bobby's going to be in most of her classes and that you'll be one of her teachers."

"Me too," Ruth said. "I hope she likes Senior Composition. I have a feeling it's not going to be Bobby's favorite class."

"No class is Bobby's favorite class," Marjie said with a mournful shake of her head. "Football, basketball, and baseball—that's the whole world. My only consolation is that now he can drive himself to town. I feel like I've spent half of my life sitting in a car waiting for him to get out of practices."

"Laura's going be the youngest senior in the class," said Ruth. "She must be a smart cookie."

"I'm sure she is," replied Marjie. "Just look at what her parents have done. Remember how concerned they were about learning the language? Now they're planting their second church and starting a training school. She—"

"Ma! Ma!" a voice called out from the living room.

"Dennis, you come in here if you want to

speak to me," Marjie called back.

Jerry and Marjie's ten-year-old stomped around the corner and groused, "I can't get the cartoons to come in. This dumb TV!"

"You've had enough cartoons for the day, anyway," Marjie ordered. "Head outside and ride your bike."

"That's boring."

"Go."

The skinny, brown-haired boy slunk out the front door and plopped down beside his father.

Marjie shrugged her shoulders at Ruth and said, "I get so sick of that television roaring away—and I need to get Teddy out here and see if he can get our antenna working better. One day you can see the picture fine, and the next day it's all snow."

"Teddy got mine hooked up right the other day," Ruth said. "Billy had tried everything you could think of, but he only made it worse. Didn't take Teddy any time at all to figure it out. He had his son Jerry working with him, too. They're quite a team."

"Yeah, that kid is—"

"They're here!" Jerry called out, jumping up from the front steps of the farmhouse and waving as Benjamin's shiny new car purred slowly down the driveway.

Marjie and Ruth raced to the front door

and stepped out onto the landing. Laura was sandwiched in the front seat between the two elderly, white-haired grandparents, but Marjie could barely see her with Sarah waving as the car went past with the windows up.

"She must be baking in there," Marjie said, joining Bobby and Daniel as they headed down the sidewalk to where Benjamin stopped the car. "Those two old birds like the car steamy warm."

Sarah pushed the car door open and slowly got out, and she was followed by a lovely sixteen-year-old with shimmering brunette curls. For just a second Marjie thought it was the Margaret Harris from Scotland she had met on a cold winter night shortly before Christmas in 1942. Laura Stanfeld was every bit as beautiful as her mother, with the same innocent charm radiating from her enormous blue eyes.

"Wow!" was all that Bobby could whisper over Daniel's shoulder, and Marjie nearly burst out laughing.

The petite teenager glanced their way and caught their starry-eyed stares. But the boys couldn't help themselves and stopped in their tracks, clearly embarrassed and flustered.

"First impressions, boys?" Marjie whispered as she went past them. "Laura, welcome!" she called out.